'Utterly convincing ... The fictions Kushner creates have the certainty of fact'
New York Review of Books

'*The Mars Room* is mysterious and irreducible. The writing is beautiful – from hard precision to lyrical imagery, with a flawless feel for when to soar and when to pull back'
Dana Spiotta

'Rachel Kushner's *The Mars Room* shows what happens when a smart writer gets truly serious. It is a necessary and compelling book, and this year's must-read'
Anne Enright

'Kushner insists that we face the reality of what is being done in our names; and the energy and imagination of her craft enthrals on every page'
Kwame Anthony Appiah, Man Booker Prize Chair

'Kushner is a young master. I honestly don't know how she is able to know so much and convey all of this in such a completely entertaining and mesmerizing way'
George Saunders

'The whole history of the novel is alive in Rachel Kushner's hands ... I look to her books to see what fiction can do now'
Ben Lerner

'Kushner is going to be one we turn to for our serious pleasures and for the insight and wisdom we'll be needing in hard times to come. She is a novelist of the very first order'
Robert Stone

RACHEL KUSHNER

Rachel Kushner's debut novel, *Telex from Cuba*, was a finalist for the 2008 National Book Award and a *New York Times* bestseller. Her follow-up novel, *The Flamethrowers*, was also a finalist for the National Book Award and received rave reviews on both sides of the Atlantic. *The Mars Room*, her third novel, was shortlisted for the 2018 Man Booker Prize and won the Prix Médicis Étranger. Her fiction has appeared in the *New Yorker*, *Harper's* and the *Paris Review*. She lives in Los Angeles.

RACHEL KUSHNER

The Mars Room

VINTAGE

1 3 5 7 9 10 8 6 4 2

Vintage
20 Vauxhall Bridge Road
London SW1V 2SA

Vintage is part of the Penguin Random House group of companies
whose addresses can be found at global.penguinrandomhouse.com

Penguin
Random House
UK

First published by Jonathan Cape in 2018
First published in Vintage in 2019

penguin.co.uk/vintage

A CIP catalogue record for this book is available from
the British Library

ISBN 9780099589969

Printed and bound in Great Britain by Clays Ltd, Elcograf S.p.A.

Penguin Random House is committed to a sustainable future for
our business, our readers and our planet. This book is made
from Forest Stewardship Council® certified paper.

MIX
Paper from
responsible sources
FSC® C018179

I feel the air of another planet.
Friendly faces that were turned toward me
but now are fading into darkness.

I

1

Chain Night happens once a week on Thursdays. Once a week the defining moment for sixty women takes place. For some of the sixty, that defining moment happens over and over. For them it is routine. For me it happened only once. I was woken at two a.m. and shackled and counted, Romy Leslie Hall, inmate W314159, and lined up with the others for an all-night ride up the valley.

As our bus exited the jail perimeter, I glued myself to the mesh-reinforced window to try to see the world. There wasn't much to look at. Underpasses and on-ramps, dark, deserted boulevards. No one was on the street. We were passing through a moment in the night so remote that traffic lights had ceased to go from green to red and merely blinked a constant yellow. Another car came alongside. It had no lights. It surged past the bus, a dark thing with demonic energy. There was a girl on my unit in county who got life for nothing but driving. She wasn't the shooter, she would tell anyone who'd listen. She wasn't the shooter. All she did was drive the car. That was it. They'd used license plate reader technology. They had it on video surveillance. What they had was an image of the car, at night, moving along a street, first with lights on, then with lights off. If the driver cuts the lights, that is premeditation. If the driver cuts the lights, it's murder.

They were moving us at that hour for a reason, for many reasons. If they could have shot us to the prison in a capsule they would have. Anything to shield the regular people from having to look at us, a crew of cuffed and chained women on a sheriff's department bus.

Some of the younger ones were whimpering and sniffling as we pulled onto the highway. There was a girl in a cage who looked about eight months pregnant, her belly so large they had to get an extra length of waist chain to shackle her hands to her sides. She hiccupped and shook, her face a mess of tears. They had her in the cage on account of her age, to protect her from the rest of us. She was fifteen.

A woman up ahead turned toward the crying girl in the cage and hissed like she was spraying ant killer. When that didn't work she yelled.

"Shut the hell up!"

"Dang," the person across from me said. I'm from San Francisco and a trans to me is nothing new, but this person truly looked like a man. Shoulders as broad as the aisle, and a jawline beard. I assumed she was from the daddy tank at county, where they put the butches. This was Conan, who later I got to know.

"Dang, I mean, it's a kid. Let her cry."

The woman told Conan to shut up and then they were arguing and the cops intervened.

Certain women in jail and prison make rules for everyone else, and the woman insisting on quiet was one of those. If you follow their rules, they make more rules. You have to fight people or you end up with nothing.

I had learned already not to cry. Two years earlier, when I was arrested, I cried uncontrollably. My life was over and I knew it was over. It was my first night in jail and I kept hoping the dreamlike state of my situation would break, that I would wake up from it. I kept on not waking up into anything different from

4

a piss-smelling mattress and slamming doors, shouting lunatics and alarms. The girl in the cell with me, who was not a lunatic, shook me roughly to get my attention. I looked up. She turned around and lifted her jail shirt to show me her low back tattoo, her tramp stamp. It said

Shut the Fuck Up

It worked on me. I stopped crying.

It was a gentle moment with my cellmate in county. She wanted to help me. It's not everyone who can shut the fuck up, and although I tried I was not my cellmate, who I later considered a kind of saint. Not for the tattoo but the loyalty to the mandate.

The cops had put me with another white woman on the bus. My seatmate had long limp and shiny brown hair and a big creepy smile like she was advertising for tooth whitener. Few in jail and prison have white teeth, and neither did she, but she had that grand and inappropriate grin. I didn't like it. It made her seem like she had undergone partial brain removal surgery. She offered her full name, Laura Lipp, and said she was being transferred from Chino up to Stanville, as if we each had nothing to hide. Since then, no one has ever introduced themselves to me by full name, or attempted to give any believable-seeming account of who they are on a first introduction, and no one would, and I don't, either.

"Lipp double *p* is my stepfather's name, which I took later," she said as if I'd inquired. As if such a thing could matter to me, then or ever.

"My father-father was a Culpepper. That's the Culpeppers of

5

Apple Valley, not Victorville. There's a Culpepper's shoe repair, see, in Victorville, but there's no relation."

No one is supposed to talk on the bus. This rule did not stop her.

"My family goes back three generations in Apple Valley. Which sounds like a wonderful place, doesn't it? You can practically smell the apple blossoms and hear the honeybees and it makes you think about fresh apple cider and warm apple pie. The autumn decorations they start putting up every July at Craft Cubby, bright leaves and plastic pumpkins: it is mostly the baking and preparing of meth that is traditional in Apple Valley. Not in my family. Don't want to give you the wrong impression. The Culpeppers are useful people. My father owned his own construction business. Not like the family I married into, who— Oh! Oh look! It's Magic Mountain!"

We were passing the white arcs of a roller coaster on the far side of the big multi-lane freeway.

When I'd moved to Los Angeles three years earlier, that amusement park had seemed like the gateway to my new life. It was the first big vision off the freeway hurtling south, bright and ugly and exciting, but that no longer mattered.

"There was a lady on my unit who stole children at Magic Mountain," Laura Lipp said, "she and her sicko husband."

She had a way of flipping her shiny sheet of hair without using her arms, as if the hair were attached to the rest of her by an electrical current.

"She told me how they did it. People trusted her and her husband because they were old. You know, sweet gentle elderly people, and a mother might have children running in three directions and go off to chase one and the old lady—I bunked with her at CIW and she told me the whole story—she would be sitting there knitting and offer to keep an eye on the child. As soon as the parent was out of sight, this child was escorted to a bathroom with a knife under his chin. This old lady and her husband had a system worked out. The kid was fitted with a wig, different clothes, and then that sneaky old couple muscled the poor thing out of the park."

"That's horrible," I said, and tried to lean away from her as best I could in my chains.

I have a child of my own, Jackson.

I love my son but it's hard for me to think about him. I try not to.

My mother named me after a German actress who told a bank robber on a television talk show that she liked him a lot.

Very much, the actress said, I like you very much.

Like the German actress, he was on the talk show to be interviewed. Interviewees did not generally cross talk, while sitting on the chairs to the left of the interviewer's desk. They moved outward as the show progressed.

You start *outward*, some prick had said to me once about silverware. It wasn't a thing I'd ever learned, or been taught. He was paying me for the date with him, and in this exchange he felt he didn't get his money's worth unless he found small ways to try to humiliate me over the course of the evening. Leaving his hotel room that night, I took a shopping bag that was by the door. He didn't notice, figured he was off-duty from the vigilance of demeaning me and could luxuriate in the hotel bed. The bag was from Saks Fifth Avenue and contained many other bags, all with presents for a woman, I assumed his wife. Dowdy and expensive clothes I would never wear. I carried the bag through the lobby and shoved it in a trash can on the way to my car, which I'd parked several blocks away, in a garage on Mission, because I didn't want this guy to know anything about me.

The outward chair of the TV show's set held a bank robber who was on the show to talk about his past, and the German movie actress was on next and she turned to the bank robber and told him that she liked him.

My mother named me after this actress, who spoke to the bank robber instead of to the host.

I think he enjoyed that I stole the shopping bag. He wanted to see me regularly after that. He was looking for the girlfriend experience and a lot of women I knew considered that the gold standard: these men would pay a year's worth of rent, up front; all you needed was one of them and you were set. I'd gone on the date because my old friend Eva had convinced me to. Sometimes what other people want is wantable, briefly, before dissolving in the face of your own wants. That night, while this square from Silicon Valley pretended we had a complicity like lovers, which meant treating me like trash, telling me I was pretty in a "common" sort of way, using his money to try to have power over me socially, like this was a relationship but since he was paying for it we would interact on his terms, and he could tell me what to say, how to walk, what to order, which fork to use, what to fake like I enjoyed—I realized that the girlfriend experience was not my thing. I would stick to hustling my income as a lap dancer at the Mars Room on Market Street. I didn't

8

care what was honest work, only what wasn't repulsive to me. I knew from lap dancing that grinding was easier than talking. Everyone is different when it comes to personal standards and what they can offer. I cannot pretend to be friends. I didn't want anyone getting to know me, although there were a couple of guys I gave crumbs to. Jimmy the Beard, the doorman, who required only that I pretend his sadistic sense of humor was normal. And Dart, the night manager, because we were both into classic cars and he was always saying he wanted to take me to Hot August Nights, in Reno. It was just banter, and he was just the night manager. Hot August Nights. It wasn't my kind of car event. I went to the Sonoma dirt track with Jimmy Darling, ate hot dogs and drank draft beer as sprint cars chipped mud against the chain link.

Some girls at the Mars Room wanted regulars and were always looking to cultivate them. I didn't, but I ended up with one anyway, Kurt Kennedy. Creep Kennedy.

I sometimes think San Francisco is cursed. I mostly think it's a sad suckville of a place. People say it's beautiful, but the beauty is only visible to newcomers, and invisible to those who had to grow up there. Like the glimpses of blue bay through the breezeways along the street that wraps around the back of Buena Vista Park. Later, from prison, I could see that view like I was ghost-walking around the city. House by house, I looked at all there was to see, pressed my face to the breezeway gates of the Victorians along the eastern ridge of Buena Vista Park, the blue of the water softened by the faintest residue of fog, a kiss of moisture, a glow. I did not admire those views when I was free. Growing up, that park was a place where we drank. Where older men cruised, and snuck off to mattresses hidden under bushes. Where boys I knew beat up those men who cruised, and threw one off a cliff after he'd bought them a case of beer.

On Tenth Avenue at Moraga, where I had lived with my mother when I was a kid, you could see Golden Gate Park, then the Presidio, the matte red points of the Golden Gate Bridge, and behind it the steep, green-crinkled folds of the Marin Headlands. I knew that for everyone else in the world the Golden Gate Bridge was considered something special, but to me and my friends it was nothing. We just wanted to get wasted. The city to us was clammy fingers of fog working their way into our clothes, always those clammy fingers, and big bluffs of wet mist hurling themselves down Judah Street while I waited by sandy streetcar tracks for the N, which ran once an hour late-night, waited and waited with mud caked on the hems of my jeans, mud from the puddles in the parking lot of Ocean Beach. Or mud from climbing Acid Mountain on acid, which was what Acid Mountain was for. The bad feeling of extra weight tugging me downward, from the mud caked on my jean hems. The bad feeling from doing cocaine with strangers in a motel in Colma, by the cemetery. The city was wet feet and soggy cigarettes at a rainy kegger in the Grove. The rain and beer and bloody fights on St. Patrick's Day. Being sick from Bacardi 151 and splitting my chin open on a concrete barrier in Minipark. Someone overdosing in a bedroom in the white people projects on the Great Highway. Someone holding a loaded gun to my head for no reason in Big Rec, where people play baseball in the park. It was night, and this psycho attached himself to us while we were sitting and drinking our forties, a situation so typical, even if it never happened again, that I don't recall how it resolved itself. San Francisco to me was the McGoldricks and the McKittricks and the Boyles and the O'Boils and the

Hicks and the Hickeys and their Erin go bragh tattoos, the fights they started and won.

Our bus moved into the right lane and began to slow. We were getting off at the Magic Mountain exit.

"They taking us on rides?" Conan asked. "That would be dope."

Magic Mountain was left, across the freeway. Right was a men's county correctional facility. Our bus turned right.

The world had split into good and bad, bound together. Amusement park and county jail.

"It's cool," Conan said. "Wasn't really up for it. Tickets hella expensive. Rather go back to the big O. Or–lan–do."

"Listen to this fool," someone said. "You ain't been to no Orlando."

"I dropped twenty G there," Conan said. "In three days. Brought my girl. Her kids. Jacuzzi suite. All–access pass. Alligator steaks. Orlando is dope. A lot doper than this bus, that's for sure."

"Thought they were taking you to Magic Mountain," the woman in front of Conan said. "Stupid motherfucker." She had a face full of tattoos.

"Dang, you got a lot of ink. Just looking at this group of us here I'm voting you Most Likely to Succeed."

She clucked and turned away.

What I eventually came to understand, about San Francisco, was that I was immersed in beauty and barred from seeing it. Still, I never could bring myself to leave, not until my regular customer Kurt Kennedy forced me to, but the curse of the city followed me.

In other ways she was a miserable person, this actress after whom I am named. Her son climbed a fence and cut a leg artery and died at fourteen, and then she drank continuously until dying herself at forty-three.

I'm twenty-nine. Fourteen years is forever, if that's what I have to live. In any case, it's more than twice that—thirty-seven years—before I will see a parole board, at which point, if they grant me it, I can start my second life sentence. I have two consecutive life sentences plus six years.

I don't plan on living a long life. Or a short life, necessarily. I have no plans at all. The thing is you keep existing whether you have a plan to do so or not, until you don't exist, and then your plans are meaningless.

But not having plans doesn't mean I don't have regrets.

If I had never worked at the Mars Room.

If I had never met Creep Kennedy.

If Creep Kennedy had not decided to stalk me.

But he did decide to, and then he did it relentlessly. If none of that had happened, I would not be on a bus heading for a life in a concrete slot.

We were at a stoplight past the off-ramp. Outside the window, a mattress leaned against a pepper tree. Even those two things, I told myself, must go together. No pepper trees, lacy branches and pink peppercorns, without dirty old mattresses leaned up against their puzzle-bark trunks. All good bound to bad, and made bad. All bad.

"I used to think those were mine every time," Laura Lipp said, peering out at the abandoned mattress. "I'd be driving around Los Angeles and see a mattress on the sidewalk and think, hey, somebody stole my box spring! I'd think, there's my bed . . .

there's my bed. Every time. Because honestly it looked *just like* mine. I'd go home and my bed would be where I left it, in the bedroom. I'd tear the covers and sheets off to check the mattress and be sure, see if it was still mine, and every time, it was. I always found it still there, at home, despite having just seen my exact mattress flopped out on the street. I have a feeling I am not the only one, and that this is something like a mass confusion. Fact is they cover all the mattresses with the same exact material, and quilt them the same way, and you can't help but think it's yours when you see it dumped at a freeway exit. Like what the hell did they drag my bed out here for!"

We passed a lit billboard: THREE SUITS $129. It was the name of a business. Three Suits $129.

"They'll hook you up in that place. Walk out looking like a baller," Conan said.

"Where they get this fool?" someone said. "Talking about cheap-ass suits."

Where did they get any of us. Only each of us knew and no one was telling. No one but Laura Lipp.

"You want to know what they did with the children?" Laura Lipp asked me. "That old lady and her sicko husband at Magic Mountain?"

"No," I said.

"You won't believe it," she continued. "It's inhuman. They—"

An announcement exploded through the bus PA. We were to remain seated. The bus was stopping to let off the three men caged separately near the front. Guns were pointed at them and at us while the transfer took place.

"Crazy mothers up here," Conan said. "I was in six months."

The woman in front of Conan got excited, as in mad. "You a dude for real? For real? Shit. Officer! Officer!"

"Settle down," Conan said. "I'm in the right place. I mean, the wrong place. Nothing right about it. But they fixed my file.

They were confused and put me with the caballeros downtown, at Men's Central. It was an honest oops."

There was laughing and snickering. "They put you in the men's joint? They thought you was an actual dude?"

"Not just county. I was at Wasco State Prison."

Disbelief rippled down the aisle. Conan did not challenge it. Later, I learned the details. Conan really was at a men's prison, at least in receiving. He truly did seem like a man, and that was how I thought of him from the moment I met him.

I regret the Mars Room, and Kennedy, but there are other things you might want me to regret or expect me to that I don't.

The years I spent getting high and reading library books I do not regret. It wasn't a bad life, even if I would probably never go back. I had an income from stripping and could afford to buy what I wanted, which was drugs, and if you have never tried heroin I have news for you: It makes you feel good about yourself, especially in the beginning. It makes you feel good about other people. You want to give the whole world a break, a time-out, a tender regard. There is nothing so soothing. My first dabble in it was morphine, a pill that someone else melted in a spoon and helped me inject, a guy named Bill and I hadn't thought much about him or what the drug would be like but the careful way he tied off my arm and found my vein, the way the needle went in, so thin and delicate, the whole experience of this random guy I never saw again shooting me up in an abandoned house was exactly what a young girl dreams love can be.

"This is a pins and needles high," he'd said. "It'll grab you by the back of the neck." It grabbed me by the back of the head with its firm clench, rubber tongs, then warmth spread down through me. I broke into the most relaxing sweat of my life. I fell in love. I don't miss those years. I'm just telling you.

Back on the highway, I turned from Laura Lipp as far as I could and closed my eyes. Five minutes into my attempt to sleep, she started whispering to me again.

"This whole situation is because I'm bipolar," she said. "In case you were wondering. You probably are. It's chromosomal."

Or maybe she said, "chromosomical." Because that was the kind of people I had to be around now. People who thought everything was a scientifical conspiracy. I didn't meet a single person in county who wasn't convinced that AIDS had been invented by the government to wipe out gays and addicts. It got difficult to argue with. In a sense it seemed true.

The woman who had been hissing and shushing everyone turned around as best she could in her restraints. She had a faded and blurry teardrop tattoo and pencil-drawn eyebrows. Her eyes glowed a grayish green like this was a zombie film and not a bus ride to a California state prison.

"She's a baby killer," she called to us, or maybe to me. She was talking about Laura Lipp.

A transport cop came down the aisle.

"Well if it ain't Fernandez," he said. "I hear one more word from you I'll put you in a cage."

Fernandez didn't look at him or respond. He returned to his seat.

Laura made a face, a slight smile, as if something mildly embarrassing but not worth acknowledging had just taken place, like someone had accidentally passed gas, definitely not her.

"Dang, you killed your child?" Conan said. "That is fucked-up. Hope I don't have to room with you."

"I'd guess you've got bigger problems than a roommate assignment," Laura Lipp said to Conan. "You look like the kind of person who spends a lot of time in jails and prisons."

"Why you say that? 'Cause I'm black? At least I fit in here. You look like a Manson chick. No offense. I got nothing to hide. Here's my file: counter-rehabilitatable. ODD. That's oppositional defiant disorder. I'm criminal-minded, narcissistic, recidivistical, and uncooperative. I'm also a prunaholic and horndog."

People had quieted into themselves, and eventually some fell asleep. Conan was snoring like a bulldozer.

"We have some real characters going up valley with us," Laura whispered to me. "And listen, I'm no Manson girl and I know what I'm talking about. I know the difference. We had Susan Atkins and Leslie Van Houten at CIW. They both had the scar in between their eyes. Susan put special cream on hers but nothing hid it. She was an uppity snob with an X carved in her forehead. Had fine things in her cell. Fancy perfumes. A touch lamp. I felt bad when one of the girls got a guard to pop Susan's cell and they took all her nice stuff. That's what I thought about when I heard she died. Missing part of her brain and paralyzed and they still wouldn't let her go home. When I heard about it, I thought of them popping her cell at CIW, taking her touch lamp and her lotions. Leslie Van Houten is more of what you'd call a convict. Some people think that's a term of respect. But not to me. It's nothing but groupthink. She'll die in prison just like Susan Atkins did. They aren't letting her out. Not until Folgers coffee isn't brewed anymore, and that's as good as never because what are people going to drink in the morning? One of the victims was an heiress of Folgers, see, and they don't want

Leslie out and they are individuals of high influence. As long as there is Folgers, Leslie will die in prison."

Her mother had an affair with Hitler. The mother of the German film star. The one after whom I'm named. Her mother had an affair with Hitler, but back then, from what I understand, who didn't?

"How come you don't speak German?" Jimmy Darling once asked me.

The idea of my mother teaching me German had never occurred to me. The idea of her teaching me anything was difficult to imagine.

"She was too depressed to bother." Some parents raise their children in silence. Silence, irritation, disapproval. How could I learn German from that? I'd have to learn it from phrases like "Did you take money from my wallet, you little shit?" Or "Don't wake me up when you come in."

Jimmy said he only knew one German word.

"Is it *angst*?"

"*Begierden*. It means lust, desire. Their word for desire is *beer garden*. Makes sense."

I tried to sleep, but the only position for sleeping that the restraints allowed was chin to chest. Aches pulsed up my arms from the handcuffs, which were attached to the belly chain around my middle, immobilizing my hands at my sides. The air-conditioning on the bus felt like it was set to fifty-five degrees. I was freezing and uncomfortable and this was only Ventura County. We had six hours to go. I started thinking about those kids forced into wigs in a bathroom stall at Magic Mountain, outfitted briskly with sunglasses and different clothes. They would end up unrecognizable not only in their new disguises, but in their new lives. They would be strangers, different children, ones who were tainted and ruined by their own kidnapping, long before they ever got used for whatever evil purpose was their new and abrupt destiny. I saw the kids in their wigs and the scattered crowd of amusement park–goers who would not know to help a lost and stolen child. I saw Jackson, as if he was being torn from me by an old woman knitting on a bench, and there was nothing I could do but watch the pictures of his little freckled face in my mind, pictures that floated and pulsed and would not fade or disperse.

Jackson is with my mother. It's the single grace in my life that he has her, even if I don't like her much myself. She is not a psycho-grandmother who knits on a bench. She's a gruff and chain-smoking German woman who gets by on marriage, divorce, and remarriage. She has a glacial manner with me, but she is loving enough to Jackson. We had a falling-out, years ago, but when I was arrested, she took Jackson. He was five then. He's seven now. During the two and a half years I was in county, as my case made its way through the courts, she brought him to see me as often as she could.

If there had been money for a private attorney, I would have hired one. My mother offered to mortgage her condominium, a studio apartment on the Embarcadero in San Francisco, but because she had already mortgaged it twice, she owed more than it was worth. The old famous stripper Carol Doda, whose neon nipples had blinked red above Broadway when I was a child, lived in my mother's building. I used to see her in the hallway, struggling with grocery bags and a yapping dog, when I went to visit my mother. She didn't look so good, but neither did my mother, who was unemployed and suffering from a painkiller addiction.

For a brief period there was some charitable possibility for my legal aid, a gentleman friend of my mother's, a man named Bob who drove a burgundy Jaguar, wore plaid suits, and drank premixed Manhattans. Bob, she said, was going to pay for a lawyer. But then Bob vanished; he literally disappeared. His body was later found under a log in the Russian River. My mother doesn't have good connections; her connections are often dubious. I was assigned a public defender. We were all hopeful things would go differently. They did not go differently. They went this way.

Our bus groaned along in the right lane with the tractor-trailers. We were passing Castaic, the last stop before the Grapevine. I'd once been in a bar in Castaic with Jimmy Darling, after I'd fled to Los Angeles to get away from Kurt Kennedy, whose victim I was at that time. Jimmy Darling had moved down to Valencia to teach at an art school. He sublet a place on a ranch not far from Castaic.

The things you aren't allowed to say: I am still Kurt Kennedy's victim, even though he's dead.

I knew this area, and the Grapevine, too, which was windy and empty and demanding, a test you passed to get to Northern California. In our closeness to the scumbly land beyond the meshed window, I longed for reality to twist itself like a bag and tear a hole from the twisting, rupture the bag and let me out, release me into that no-man's-land.

As if she could read my thoughts, Laura Lipp said, "I personally feel safer in here, with what all goes on out there. Sick, creepy, disturbing stuff, you can't make it up."

I looked out the window and saw nothing but nature's carpet of rocks and shrubs darting past in an endless bumpy scroll.

"A lot of truckers are serial killers, and they don't get caught. They're on the move, see. State to state. The jurisdictions don't talk, so nobody knows. All these trucks crossing America. Some of them with bound and gagged women in the back of the cab. They've got those curtains, for hiding the women. The murdered ones get dumped in rest stop dumpsters, part by part. That's how dumpsters got their name. People dump bodies. The bodies of women and girls."

We passed a rest area. What an earnest and beautiful concept that was. Anything I could imagine was beautiful compared to this bus and this woman sharing my seat. What I would have given to be sleeping behind the rest area vending machines, whose cold light glowed as we flew past. Every person who might incidentally pass through a rest stop was my soul mate, my ally, against Laura Lipp. But I had no one, and I was fastened to her.

"*I'm* alive," she said, "but that doesn't mean much. I had my heart cut out with a chain saw."

We were on a descent and passing a runaway ramp, dropping through the mouth of the Grapevine and into the valley. I knew that exact ramp. It was a steep, loose-gravel road that went nowhere, for vehicles with failed brakes. I would never see that runaway truck ramp again and I loved it, it was a good and wholesome truck ramp, I could see that only now, how good and wholesome and dear, fragile and dear, everything was.

"You know how they say it's a thing you don't have, that you offer to someone who doesn't want it?"

I gave her a hostile look.

"I'm talking about love," she said. "Like, let's say I go out there and pick up a small stone. I hold it up and say to someone, here, this stone is me. Take it. And they think, I don't want that stone. Or they say thanks, and put it in their pocket or maybe into a rock crusher, and they don't care that the stone is me, because it isn't actually me, I just *decided* it was me. I *let* myself get crushed. See what I mean?"

I said nothing but she kept going. She was going to talk all the way to Stanville.

"In prison at least you know what's going to happen. I mean, you don't *actually* know. It's unpredictable. But in a boring way. It's not like something tragic and awful can happen. I mean, sure it can. Of course it can. But you can't lose everything in prison, since that's already taken place."

The bartender in Castaic had flirted with Jimmy Darling the night we'd ended up there. It was one of the liabilities of dating him that I had to watch bimbos try to communicate a tacit message to Jimmy Darling of let's-lose-this-bitch when he and I were together.

He didn't lose me, though. Not until later, when I was in jail and called him, and I knew by the sound of his voice that it was over, but I defensively didn't care. I needed to focus on what was happening to me. He asked how I was with polite formality. I said, "You just collected charges from an inmate at a Los Angeles County correctional facility, how the fuck do you think I am?"

The era of me, the phase of me, really, had ended, for me and for him both. He wrote me once but his entire letter was about the fact that it was almost baseball season, and did not acknowledge that I was facing a life sentence.

You might have done the same thing in Jimmy Darling's shoes. Not written a letter about baseball, but cut ties with someone doomed. Any sensible person would give up on a me who was going to be sent away permanently, if they were just a boyfriend or lover, if it was meant to be something fun. It's not fun anymore if it involves prison. But maybe it was me who pushed him away.

Jimmy Darling grew up in Detroit. His father worked at General Motors. As a teenager Jimmy Darling worked at an auto glass company. He told me that the first time he smelled the adhesive that was used to glue auto glass in place, he realized he had dreamed of that very smell, the smell of that particular glue, and that it was his destiny to work replacing auto glass. By Jimmy's luck, he had multiple destinies. After dropping out of college, he began making films about the rust belt. His background was the gimmick, a shtick, he was Mr. Blue Collar Filmmaker. I teased him about it, but I also found his romantic attachment to Detroit touching. One of his films was his hand turning over every card in a General Motors deck that his father was given for his retirement after forty years on the assembly line. The company thanked his father for decades of loyalty and backbreaking labor with a pack of playing cards. "You know what's in the GM headquarters on Cadillac Place now," Jimmy Darling said. "A lottery disbursement office." Jimmy stood outside it all day, waiting to film a winner walking inside to collect. None arrived.

I met Jimmy Darling through one of his students, who I was sleeping with at the time. A kid named Ajax who was young and broke and lived south of Market in a geodesic dome on a warehouse roof. Ajax was a janitor at the Mars Room. People teased me about sleeping with the kid whose job was to empty trash cans filled with used condoms, but I was unbothered. Also his name is scouring powder, they kept saying, but he told me it was Greek. These women and their bogus standards, that you sell your ass but don't date janitors. Still, Ajax was young and annoying; he'd come over with gifts for me but they were useless eccentric gestures, like a broken vacuum cleaner off the street, and once he showed up tripping on acid and speaking in an Irish accent and when I told him to stop, he said he couldn't. One night he took me to an art school party and introduced me to Jimmy and that was it. I left the party with Jimmy, who was handsomer and didn't get on my nerves.

"How come you didn't go to college?" Jimmy Darling once asked me. He thought I was smart, but he had that educated person's naive way of presuming the reason some other people didn't go to college must be because they simply could not hack it.

"I was too depressed."

"That's what you said about why your mother didn't teach you German."

"Which doesn't make it less true. You think it's a surprise a girl who works at a strip club is clever? Every stripper I know is clever. Some are practically geniuses. Maybe you can go around with your little camera and ask each one why she didn't go to college."

When I was growing up, they all said I had potential. I was told that, by teachers and other adults. If it was true, I didn't do anything with it. I did manage not to end up like Eva, and that felt like an accomplishment, not to be hooking on Eddy and Jones at seven in the morning on a weekday. I quit drugs when I found out I was pregnant, but I don't consider it an achievement, it was more that I averted disaster. I worked at the Mars Room, giving lap dances. It's not even the best of the strip clubs in San

Francisco. There isn't any status in it unless you'd be impressed to know that the Mars Room is not a middling or mediocre strip club but definitely the worst and most notorious, the very seediest and most circuslike place there is. Maybe I had a taste for it the way Jimmy had a taste for me. It was something extreme, and in that, special and amusing, and some of the women really were geniuses.

I'm not saying I'm special or extreme, but Jimmy Darling had never been with a girl who pushed him out of her Impala while driving. We were going slow, five or ten miles an hour. After I did it the one time, because I was angry, he asked me to do it again, for kicks, but I refused. He had never known anyone who lived in a Tenderloin hotel, and was always a bit disoriented by the scene on the landing, the chaos and shouting, the fact that he had to pay to come upstairs. At a health food store he and I had run into a girl I knew who was spaced out and scratching herself. She asked Jimmy if he knew whether the juice she'd chosen was organic, and he acted like he'd never encountered that kind of contradiction, junkies who refuse non-organic juice. He was a little sheltered, like most people who come to the city from elsewhere. Normal, educated, had a job, felt there was a purpose to his existence and so forth, and he didn't understand about people who grew up in the city, the nihilism, the inability to go to college or join the straight world, get a regular job or believe in the future. I fit into some kind of narrative for him. Which isn't to say that Jimmy Darling was dipping down into a lower class bracket by hanging around with me. He wasn't. He was as common as I was, commoner, but he was the one slumming.

Did you ever notice that women can seem common while men never do? You won't ever hear anyone describe a man's appearance as common. The common man means the average man, a typical man, a decent hardworking person of modest dreams and resources. A common woman is a woman who looks cheap. A woman who looks cheap doesn't have to be respected, and so she has a certain value, a certain cheap value.

At the Mars Room, I did not have to show up on time, or smile, or obey any rules, or think of most men as anything other than losers to be exploited but who believed they were exploiting us, and so it was naturally quite hostile as an environment, even as it was coated in pretend submission—our own. The Mars Room was a place where you could do what you wanted; at least I had believed that. When I was dating Jackson's dad, I broke a bottle over his head and he punched me back, in the face, and I showed up five hours late to work with a black eye and wearing sunglasses and no one said anything. I had arrived there on several occasions so drunk I could barely walk. Some girls, as part of their routine, spent the first several hours of their shifts nodding off in the dressing room with a makeup compact in one hand. There was no problem with that. The management did not care. There were girls who worked the audience in the standard uniform of lace bra and panties but with ratty broken-down tennis shoes instead of high heels. If you'd showered you had a competitive edge at the Mars Room. If your tattoos weren't misspelled you were hot property. If you weren't five or six months pregnant, you were the it-girl in the club that night. Girls maced customers in the face and sent us all outside, hacking and choking. One dancer got mad at d'Artagnan, the night manager, and set the dressing room on fire. She was let go, it's true, but that was exceptional.

We had to fake nice-nice to the customers but that was really it, the only thing we had to do, and we didn't even have to do that. We did it to make money, so the incentive was easy enough. Jimmy the Beard and Dart, you had to stay off their shit lists. But that was easy, too. Flirt with them, and everything was fine. It was almost comical how weak their big egos were.

Jimmy the Beard, by the way, is not to be confused with Jimmy Darling. They have nothing in common except the name Jimmy. Jimmy the Beard was a bouncer at the Mars Room and Jimmy Darling was, for a while anyway, my boyfriend.

I said everything was fine but nothing was. The life was being sucked out of me. The problem was not moral. It was nothing to do with morality. These men dimmed my glow. Made me numb to touch, and angry. I gave, and got something in exchange, but it was never enough. I extracted from the wallets—which was how I thought of the men, as walking wallets—as much as I possibly could. The knowledge that it was not a fair exchange coated me in a certain film. Something brewed in me over the years I worked at the Mars Room, sitting on laps, deep into this flawed exchange. This thing in me brewed and foamed. And when I directed it—a decision that was never made; instead, instincts took over—that was it.

Although Jimmy the Beard and Jimmy Darling did have more in common than just a name. They had me in common. And then they didn't have me in common.

Now I can see that certain targets of my anger weren't the real targets. Like the man who wanted the girlfriend experience, the one who corrected my table manners: the reason I disliked him was that he reminded me of someone from the recesses of childhood, a man I'd asked for directions. I was eleven and had gone downtown to meet Eva, to see a midnight show at a punk rock club. It was late, and I was lost. Rain began to pour. Downtown San Francisco is deserted late at night, but there was an older gray-haired man locking a beautiful Mercedes and he asked me if I needed help. He looked like someone's father, a respectable businessman, dressed in a suit. I did need help. I told him where I was trying to go and he said it was too far to walk.

"I could give you money for a taxi."

"Really?" I asked hopefully. The rain was soaking me.

He said he'd be happy to help me and we should go to his hotel, and then he would. He would be happy to help me, but we should first go up to his room and have a drink.

The man in the Mercedes was no more a someone than the man who wanted the girlfriend experience and corrected my table manners. I didn't know the name of either. And in fact they both wanted the same thing.

Our bus hurtled along the downhill grade into the Central Valley.

"Lot of people talk shit about prison but you got to live your destiny every minute," Conan said. "Just live it. Last time I was up in the big house, I had parties like you wouldn't believe. You would not know it was prison. We had all kinds of liquor. Pills. Killer beats. Pole dancers."

"Hey!" Fernandez was shouting to the guards seated in the front.

"Hey, this lady next to me, you better check on her."

The transport cop who knew Fernandez turned around and told her to quiet down.

"But this lady—something's wrong with her!"

The large woman next to her was slumped over, her head on her chest. That was how everyone was sleeping.

You would not have gone. I understand that. You would not have gone up to his room. You would not have asked him for help. You would not have been wandering lost at midnight at age eleven. You would have been safe and dry and asleep, at home with your mother and your father who cared about you and had rules, curfews, expectations. Everything for you would have been different. But if you were me, you would have done what I did. You would have gone, hopeful and stupid, to get the money for the taxi.

Somewhere deep in the Central Valley, the sky still dark, I looked out the window and saw two massive black shadows looming up ahead. They looked like dark oily geysers fluming upward on the side of the highway. What terrible thing was spewing into the sky like that, filling it with soot? They were huge black clouds of smoke or poison.

I had read about a gas leak, about pounds of pollution issuing into the sky in Fresno or someplace. When gaseous quantities are measured in pounds you know there's trouble. Maybe this was some kind of environmental disaster, crude oil that had burst its underground pipe, or something too sinister for explanations, a fire burning black instead of orange.

As our sheriff's department bus approached the giant black geysers, I got a close-up glimpse.

They were the silhouettes of eucalyptus trees in the dark.

Not an emergency. Not the apocalypse. Just trees.

At daybreak, we were in thick fog. The entire Central Valley had drifted out to sea. Damp tufts blew across the highway. I could see nothing but smoke gray.

Laura Lipp had been waiting for me to wake up.

"Did you read about the woman they found murdered in her car? Guy came up to her with a knife or something, some kind of weapon, says take me to a bank machine. He gets in her car and he ends up killing her, bashes her head in for no reason. No reason at all. They didn't even *know* each other. City life has become so crude and dangerous, imagine, two in the afternoon. Sepulveda Boulevard. A few hours later, police found her. This guy had been released from jail that morning. Wandered around until he found someone to kill. I'm telling you, we are safer in custody. Won't catch me out there, nuh uh. No way. No."

We were surrounded by agriculture. I saw no human beings working in the fields. The fields were abandoned to machines and I was abandoned to Laura Lipp.

"If they hadn't let him out she'd be alive. For some people reality is just too thin. For some people the light shines right through, a certain kind of person, a crazy kind of person, a person with a mental illness and I know about that—like I said, I'm here because I have a bipolar disorder—and I'm glad they have this AC pumping because the heat triggers my condition. Brings it on real fast."

As the sun rose, the fog evaporated. Wind buffeted the big bushy oleanders on the highway divider, their peach-colored blossoms bending moodily, crazily, then restoring themselves, the wind then whipping their peach-colored heads around again.

The bus filled with cow stink, which seemed to wake up Conan. He yawned and looked out the window.

"The thing about cows is they're dressed *all in leather,*" he said. "Head to toe, nothing but leather. It's badass. I mean when you really think about it."

"Poor woman had a child," Laura Lipp said to me. "Kid's an orphan now."

There were eucalyptus trees on the side of the highway, trees that I had thought, in the dark of night, were black shadows of the apocalypse. Now they just seemed dusty and sad. In Southern California, the same exact leaves stay on the same trees for decades. Trees that don't lose their leaves do something else: they collect dust year after year, load up with dirt and car exhaust.

"I heard about this steak they got now at Outback. The cows are given beer," Conan said, as he watched the miserable-looking creatures huddled in the dirt, nothing but dirt, so that the animals, too, seemed like dirt, living dirt, organic breathing shitting dirt, no grass anywhere in sight. "Budweiser, to be exact. They force-feed it to the cows. Force-drink it. Makes the meat tender. But hey, are those cows old enough to drink? I want to try that steak. That's what I'm doing when I get out of this bitch: Outback."

A guard came down the aisle to make a routine check.

"You ever had a bloomin' onion?" Conan yelled at him. The guard kept walking. Conan yelled at his back, receding up the aisle. "They blow that sucker open, batter it, deep-fry it. Damn, it's good. You can't get that anywhere else. It's copywrit."

We passed a ranch house with a tire swing. A clump of

shaggy California fan palm, otherwise known as the rat palm, the unofficial mascot of the state. A sign in the yard, Elect Kritchley Fresno County DA. Elect Kritchley.

In the left lane, a road crew was working, one man holding a sign for everyone to slow and move right.

"I made your shirt, motherfucker!" Conan yelled at the glass. The man could not hear him. Only we could hear him. "London, quiet down," a cop said through the PA.

"We make those road crew vests at Wasco. You glue on the reflectors."

I began to see white airy things moving past the bus window. They were all over the freeway. They didn't rain down, but hovered and whirled. White and fluffy debris let loose from a cargo vehicle up ahead of us. I didn't know what kind of debris until we passed the source, a truck that held many rows of stacked metal cages. In the cages were turkeys, crammed so that they had to bow their long necks. The wind was pulling out their feathers, which flossed the highway in white flecks. This was November. They were Thanksgiving turkeys.

"You better check on this one!" Fernandez was yelling again about her seatmate, who was leaning over sideways.

"Hey!"

The woman was massive. She might have weighed three hundred pounds. She began to slide from the seat. She slid until she was folded over awkwardly on the bus aisle floor. There was a commotion, people whispering and tsking.

"That's what I call a snooze," Conan said. "Out cold. Wish I could do that. Hard for me to get comfortable on transport buses."

"Hey!" Fernandez called up to the front. "You got to come deal with this. This lady is having an issue."

One of the cops got up and moved toward the back. He stood over the woman who had slid to the floor. He yelled, "Ma'am!

31

Ma'am!" When that did not work, he jellied her shoulder with the toe of his military boot.

The cop yelled up to the front. "Nonresponsive."

They call themselves correctional officers. Real cops would not consider prison guards cops, but losers at the rock bottom of law enforcement.

The one at the front made a phone call.

The other was about to return to the front himself, but he stopped and faced Fernandez.

"I heard you got married, Fernandez."

"Get a life," she said.

"Let me ask you, Fernandez. Do they have special weddings, like they got special Olympics?"

Fernandez smiled. "If I ever have to marry a retard like you, sir, I guess I'll find out."

Conan let out a hoot of approval.

"Retards like me don't marry fat ugly prison hos, Fernandez."

He went up the aisle and took his seat. He seemed to have forgotten about the woman who was unconscious.

Laura Lipp went to sleep, which meant she would finally be quiet.

We rode in silence, with a human mound slumped on the floor of the bus, half underneath one of the seats.

2

The trouble with San Francisco was that I could never have a future in that city, only a past.

The city to me was the Sunset District, fog-banked, treeless, and bleak, with endless unvaried houses built on sand dunes that stretched forty-eight blocks to the beach, houses that were occupied by middle- and lower-middle-class Chinese Americans and working-class Irish Catholics.

Fly Lie, we'd say, ordering lunch in middle school. Fried rice, which came in a paper carton. Tasted delicious but was never enough, especially if you were stoned. We called them gooks. We didn't know that meant Vietnamese. The Chinese were our gooks. And the Laotians and Cambodians were FOBs, fresh off the boat. This was the 1980s and just think what these people went through, to arrive in the United States. But we didn't know and didn't know to care. They couldn't speak English and they smelled to us of their alien food.

The Sunset was San Francisco, proudly, and yet an alternate one to what you might know: it was not about rainbow flags or Beat poetry or steep crooked streets but fog and Irish bars and liquor stores all the way to the Great Highway, where a sea of broken glass glittered along the endless parking strip of Ocean Beach. It was us girls in the back of someone's primered Charger or Challenger riding those short, but long, forty-eight blocks to the beach, one boy shotgun with a stolen fire extinguisher, flocking people on street corners, randoms blasted white.

If you were visiting the city, or if you were a resident from the other, more admired parts of the city and you took a trip out to the beach, you might have seen, beyond the sea wall, our bonfires, which made the girls' hair smell of smoke. If you were there in early January, you would see bigger bonfires, ones built of discarded Christmas trees, so dry and flammable they exploded on the high pyres. After each explosion you might have heard us cheer. When I say us I mean us WPODs. We loved life more than the future. "White Punks on Dope" is just some song; we didn't even listen to it. The acronym was something else, not a gang but a grouping. An attitude, a way of dressing, living, being. Some changed our graffiti to White Powder on Donuts, and many of us were not even white, which becomes harder to explain, because the whole world of the Sunset WPODs was about white power, not powder, but these were the beliefs of not powerful kids who might end up passing through rehab centers and jails, unless they were the chosen few, the very few girls and boys, who, respectively, either enrolled in the Deloux School of Beauty, or got hired at John John Roofing on Ninth Avenue between Irving and Lincoln.

When I was little I saw a cover of an old magazine that showed the robes and feet of people who had drunk the Kool-Aid Jim Jones handed out in Guyana. My entire childhood I would think of that image and feel bad. I once told Jimmy Darling and he said it wasn't actually Kool-Aid. It was Hi-C.

What kind of person would want to clarify such a thing?

A smart-ass is who. A person who is safe from that image in a way I was not. I was not likely to join a cult. That was not the danger I felt in glimpsing the feet of the dead, the bucket from which they drank. It was the proven fact, in the photographed feet, that you could drink death and join it.

When I was five or six years old I saw a paperback cover in the supermarket that was a drawing of a woman and her nude body had two knives coming out of it, blood pooling around her. The cover of the book said, "Killed Twice." That was its title. I was away from my mother, who was shopping somewhere in the market. We were at Park and Shop on Irving and I felt I was not just a few aisles away but permanently sucked out to sea, to the engulfing world of *Killed Twice*. Coming home from the market, I was nauseous. I could not eat the dinner my mother prepared. She didn't really cook. It was probably Top Ramen she prepared for me, and then attended to whichever of the men she was dating at the time.

For years, whenever I thought of that image on the cover of *Killed Twice* I felt sick. Now I can see that what I experienced was normal. You learn when you're young that evil exists. You absorb the knowledge of it. When this happens for the first time, it does not go down easy. It goes down like a horse pill.

At age ten I fell under the spell of an older girl named Tyra. She had glassy eyes and olive skin and a husky, tough-girl voice. The night I met her I was in someone's car, driving around drinking Löwenbräu lights. Lowie lights, green bottles with a baby-blue label. We picked up Tyra on Noriega, at a house that was an informal foster home for girls. The man who ran it, Russ, forced himself on the girls at night, unpredictably but predictably. If you stayed there, sooner or later you were going to be visited at night by Russ, who was old, and muscular, and mean. The girls complained about being raped by him as if it were a form of strictness, or rent. They were willing to endure it because they didn't have other options. The rest of us did nothing about it because Russ bought us liquor and what were we to do, call the police? One of them was known for taking girls out to Point Lobos instead of to the police station on Taraval.

Tyra called shotgun in a menacing way and got in the front, put her feet on the dash. She was already buzzed, she told us, slurring her words in a way I found glamorous. She wore diamond earrings. They flashed from her little-girl ears as she drained a Lowie light and pitched her empty from the window of the car. Maybe Tyra's earrings were fakes. It didn't matter. Their effect was the same. For me she had the magic.

That year I'd had a chance to know a nice girl, with two parents, middle-class. She came to my house for a sleepover. The next week at school she told everyone that at my house we ate Hostess pies for dinner and threw the wrappers under the bed. I have no memory of that. I'm not saying it isn't true. My mom let me eat what I wanted for dinner. She was usually with whatever guy she was seeing, someone who didn't like children, so they'd be shut up in her bedroom with the door locked. We had an account at the corner market and I'd go down there and get goodies, chips, liters of soda, whatever I wanted. I didn't know to pretend to live some other way to make an impression on another kid. It made me sad what this girl said about me and about our house. I was sad even as I stuck a pin in her ass as she got off the 6 Parnassus after school. Stood by the back doors, and as she exited I jabbed her, right through her pants. Everyone did that. We stole the pins from home economics. It was normal, but it made tears roll down your face if someone did it to you.

That diamonds are supposedly forever was something Jimmy Darling joked about. Every mineral here on earth is forever, he said. But they make it seem like diamonds are especially forever, in order to sell them, and it works.

A few days later Tyra called me and we made a plan to go to Golden Gate Park on a Sunday, to the bridge, where people roller-skate and hang out. Tyra came to my house, since I lived a few blocks from the bridge.

She said, "I need to beat this bitch's face in."

I said okay and we went to the park.

The girl whose face Tyra had an appointment to beat in was already there, with two older brothers. They were not from the Sunset; later I learned they lived in the Haight. The brothers were adults, both mechanics at a garage on Cole Street. The girl, Tyra's opponent, was tall and delicate-looking with a shiny black pony-tail. She was wearing pink shorts and a shirt that said WHATEVER. Her lips were tinged with the bluish effect of opalescent gloss. Tyra was athletic and tough. Nobody wanted to fight her. She and this leggy girl with the ponytail took off their skates. They fought on the grass, in their socks. The socks softened nothing.

Tyra threw a fierce kick, but the other girl grabbed her foot, and Tyra lost her balance and was on the ground. The girl jumped on top, pinned Tyra's chest with her own knees, and began punching Tyra in the face, alternating fists, left right left, like she was kneading dough, punching it down to size. Punching it and punching it, dough that was a face. Her brothers shouted encouragement. They were rooting for her, but if she were losing, they would not have stepped in, I knew. They were there as believers in the honesty of a fight and the pride of fighting well. She punched and punched. Her arms seemed too skinny to carry any force on contact, fist to face, but eventually they produced their damage. It never occurred to me to jump in. I watched Tyra get pummeled.

When the girl felt she had sufficiently made her point, she let up. She stood, retightening her ponytail, and pulled her shorts

37

out of her ass crack. Tyra sat up, trying to wipe away her tears. I went to help her. Her hair was tangled. She was covered in dead grass clippings.

"I got a good lick in," she said. "Did you see how I kicked that bitch in the chest?"

Both of her eyes were swollen almost closed. Her cheeks had turned to hard shiny lumps. She had an open gash on her chin from the girl's ring. "I got a pretty good lick in," she repeated.

It was the best way to look at things, but the truth was she had been brutally beaten up, and by a prissy girl in a WHATEVER T-shirt, an unlikely winner who was not an unlikely winner, it became clear the moment the fight began. The winner was Eva.

I did not become friends with Eva that day, but later. Whenever that later was, a year maybe, the memory of her and her punches was undiminished. I knew something about her. Most girls talk a big game, and then they scratch and pull hair, or don't show up for the fight.

I suppose you could say I traded Tyra for Eva, like I traded Ajax for Jimmy Darling. But in both cases, the first was there to lead me to the second. Life allows for assessments, and reassessments. And anyhow, who wants to be stuck with a loser?

Eva was a professional. One of those girls who always had a lighter, bottle opener, graffiti markers, flask, amyl nitrate, Buck knife, even her own sensor remover—the device that department store clerks used to remove theft prevention clips from new clothes. She stole it. The rest of us ripped out the sensors forcibly before leaving the store with our stolen loot. A sensor in a dressing room was a giveaway, so we took them with us, crammed up under our armpits, which muffled the sensor, deadened it to the detection alarm. We were not kleptomaniacs. That's a term for rich people who steal by compulsion. We were finding innovative ways to acquire makeup and perfume and purses and clothes—all the normal things a girl would be expected to have and want, and which we could not afford.

All my clothes had holes in them from where the sensors had been attached. Eva removed them from her stolen clothes properly, with her magic device. Once, she walked right into I. Magnin, clipped the wires from a rabbit fur coat with wire cutters, put it on, and ran for it. The wires fit through the arms of the fur and leather jackets, with large hoops dangling from the ends of the sleeves like giant handcuffs.

Eva went through a tomboy phase and stopped wearing fur jackets. She dressed like one of the Sunset guys, Ben Davis pants with a janitorial key ring dangling from a belt loop. The more keys on the ring, the better. It didn't matter if they opened anything, except beer bottles. She wore a black Derby jacket, with the gold paisley padding on the inside, the trademark shoulder-to-shoulder seams. Like the boys, she completed that look with steel-toed boots—for kicking peoples' heads in should the need arise.

One night I encountered a group of guys sitting in the dark drinking 151 in Big Rec, older people I had never seen, from Crocker Amazon, which was something like enemy territory. They wanted to show me Polaroids of Eva. Is this your friend? In the photos, Eva was passed-out drunk and stripped of her tough-kid uniform, with a baseball bat between her naked thighs.

Eva fist-fought guys and won. She one-upped everyone with drugs and drink. These boys with their photos, they knew what it meant to have done that to Eva and they wanted me to see.

I never told her, and even thinking of what happened later, Eva a crack addict in the Tenderloin, the Polaroid photos with the bat was still the worst thing that anyone had done to her. She did plenty to herself, but that is different.

Some kids have a powerful drive to take drugs. They can't help it. Eva was like that. The first time she stole Valium from her mom, we each took one and went to West Portal. I don't feel anything, do you? she asked. No, not yet. Let's take another. I still don't feel anything, do you? A little. Let's take another. Are you high yet? I'm not sure. We took the whole bottle and woke up several hours later with our faces warm from the surface of a sit-down Ms. Pac-Man video game at Round Table Pizza. We both stumbled home and slept for three days.

Not long after, I was at the bus stop on Laguna Honda, across from Forest Hill Station. It was midnight and the buses were on their late-night schedule, once an hour. There was one other person waiting, a man who offered me a cigarette and light, and then asked if I knew where he could get any pills. He was probably young—in his twenties, but at the time I didn't think about his age. Anyone over eighteen seemed old to me. He knew how to talk to young girls, to flatter. I boasted that I could sell him some Valium. It was a lie. I was a twelve-year-old whose friend had lucked into her mother's temporary supply. Still, I said I could probably get him some. Can I buy them now? he asked. I said I had to call my friend. He wanted to give me his phone number so I could call him after I spoke with her. Neither of us had pen or paper, and I secretly doubted I could get more Valium, but I was trapped in my lie. He took off his shoe. They were old-men-type shoes, suit shoes, and he used the black heel to write the seven digits of his phone number on the rough stucco of the retaining wall next to the bus shelter. I watched as this man, sweat-soaked on that cold night, scratched out his number on the wall with the heel of his shoe, so that I could call him when I got what he needed, and I thought, what have I done.

I usually wasn't planning on getting wrecked until Eva knocked. One morning she arrived with two hits of something called Delcourt, which was acid and PCP mixed together. We each took one. That was in the summer after sixth grade, one more dull and foggy day with nothing to fill it, maybe play video games at Café Roma on Irving, get a piroshki, which was a donut stuffed with ground beef and American cheese, drink dirty socks ale called Mickey's in the park, talk to the clerk at the comic book store, who told me what blue balls was (I was probably blue-balling him by asking).

To make that day different, we dropped the acid/PCP mix and walked the streetcar tracks all the way to Ocean Beach. We stopped at 7-Eleven on Judah. I bought a Butterfinger and took a bite and the candy bar turned to sand in my mouth. I thought, I hate my life. Later, we sat in a van in someone's garage listening to Slayer, and Eva threw her head back and closed her eyes and I looked at her face and her long black hair in profile and was convinced the devil was in charge of the future, mine and Eva's, and that nothing could save us.

That was before people started going to Anton LaVey's house, where everyone worshipped Satan together as a group. It was in the Richmond, on the other side of Golden Gate Park. I never went there, but kids I knew did. You had to be from a conventional background to go full tilt into devil worship. My mother was an atheist and would have teased me if she thought I'd gone into religion, even a satanic one. The Norse, my future woodshop partner in Stanville, would have loved to get an invite to Anton LaVey's house. But she is in prison, and Anton LaVey's house is in the past. Anton LaVey is dead and his black house is gone, too, replaced by condominiums.

The house that interested me more belonged to a group

of people called the Scummerz. Eva took me there. It was on Masonic, near Haight. A typical rambling old Victorian building with the bubble glass bay windows that rattled as diesel buses passed by going down the hill. The 43, headed toward Sears on Geary, where we would lie down on the beds in the furniture department when we were tired. I didn't know anything about the Scummerz, who they really were or how long they had been in that large apartment. Inside, it had never stopped being 1969. Every room was painted with tennis balls. The balls were soaked in different-colored paints and then ricocheted around the rooms—walls, floor, ceiling, a spaghetti-strands riot of color that gave the place a sameness that was not at all calming. It was the scribbling of a brain in chaos projected up over the walls, a kind of ambient filth. Many non-family-related people lived at the Scummerz, all of whom were part of a family business selling purple microdot. A huge woman sat in the kitchen parceling the microdot with a butcher knife into glassine baggies. The microdot did not go to waste. She apportioned the bags, and if you were there to buy, you sat at the table and when she was ready she looked up at you and took your money and gave you your bag. The first time I went there, a shirtless boy with a sleepwalker's vacated look stood behind her at the stove boiling water for macaroni and cheese. He was thin and lithe with hair as blondly colorless as lice egg casings. He had a concave area in the center of his chest, a divot that made him even more ghostlike as he waited for his water to boil. The sound his dry noodles made sliding from their box gave me a bad feeling. He opened the cheese and powdered it into the pot. He ate from the spoon he used to stir the noodles. He was barefoot, and his pants needed a belt. He looked about ten years old.

Who were those people, the Scummerz, and where did they go? A lot of history is not known. A lot of worlds have existed that you can't look up online or in any book, even as you think you have the freedom to find things out that I cannot, since I don't have access to the internet. Google the Scummerz and you'll find nothing, no trace, but they existed.

And if someone did remember them, someone besides me, that person's account would make them less real, because my memory of them would have to be corrected by facts, which are never considerate of what makes an impression, what stays in the mind after all these years, the very real images that grip me from the erased past and won't let go.

The bar on the upper Haight where Eva's mother spent her time was called the Pall Mall. They let kids in the bar and people bought us Love Burgers, which were just hamburgers, except you could get curry on the bun if you wanted it and that part maybe was the love, a sauce that stained your hands a bright pollen yellow. Outside the bar, you gave what you weren't going to finish to Leatherman.

Remember Leatherman? A lot of people from the Haight would remember Leatherman if you asked them about him. Leatherman wore black leather pants, a leather shirt, a black leather hat. His bare feet were sooted black from the streets. He stood outside the Pall Mall, or wandered the park's eastern edge, along Stanyan, a shoreline he sifted. It was littered not with shells but trash from the McDonald's franchise across the street. Leatherman was rumored never to remove his leather clothes. He had not taken them off in decades. Once, as Eva's mother stood with us outside the Pall Mall, we watched Leatherman scrounge in a garbage can. Eva's mother said,

"You girls know what'll happen if he takes those clothes off, don't you?"

We shook our heads.

"He'll die."

She exhaled smoke and flicked her cigarette into the street in a way I later copied, off thumb and pointer finger, a tiny gesture that made me feel tough.

Leatherman picked up her cigarette butt and enjoyed the last few puffs that Eva's mom was rich enough to part with.

Leatherman was not to be confused with Liverman, but no one who knows about both would do that.

Liverman rode the 71 Noriega. I saw him only once and knew immediately that this was the infamous person I'd heard about. A hard plastic form that looked somewhat like meat, like liver, was melted or molded to his head. It was the permanence of the thing, affixed to him, part of him, that made him a brutal sight. A thick, shiny slab attached where hair might have been, or a scalp. Someone said he was a Korean War vet. A veteran of some trauma, which had resulted in the gluing of this object to the top of his head.

The Shuffler was another occasional sighting. That was on the other side of the park, near the Baskin-Robbins on Geary where I worked in high school. The Shuffler walked at a normal gait and then suddenly his legs stirred into quick action, like he was a machine designed to buff the sidewalk, buff it with shoe soles. He slid and shuffled all the way down the block, paused, then went back to regular walking. It could have been a kind of disorder, a nerve thing, but it seemed like destiny. He was the man who broke into a shuffle on Geary, and then broke out of one.

Worked is a bit strong. We served ice cream and didn't punch in all the sales on the register, took the stolen profits at the end of the night when we tallied our drawer. We hit the nitrous oxide tank that was used to fill whipped cream canisters. Mostly girls were employed there, and we let boys skateboard around inside the store, go behind the counter, help themselves to the nitrous tank, and scoop their own ice cream. We slopped water on the floor at the end of the night, to fulfill our duty to mop, after moving the clock forward, to close early. Place was run by kids, unsupervised, because the evening manager, a Scottish alcoholic named Helen, left early every day, after making the ice cream cakes, which was a specialized skill we did not possess.

The man in the bus shelter on Laguna Honda who wanted the Valium, it was his pushy optimism that alarmed me, the insistence of writing down his telephone number on a wall with the heel of his shoe. He needed his drugs and was ready to do business with a twelve-year-old girl. He needed to believe her, when it was plain she was probably lying.

Eva's mom was white. Her dad was Filipino. Her mom was a heroin addict. Her dad was strict. He worked for a security service that had him posted at the entrance of the gigantic old Lucky Lager brewery in Bayview, which had closed down. We went there once, to get money from him. He crumpled it up and threw it at Eva and went inside the gates. A decade later, I was with some guys who broke into that place. My friends stole a bunch of equipment. One of them later returned with a rented backhoe, to take machinery that was too heavy to lift. Eva's dad

45

was retired by then. Eva was on the streets. Her mother was dead of an overdose. The Pall Mall was closed. The Scummerz were gone. The Sunset was transformed. The grocery store on Irving was gourmet. A girl I was friends with in high school worked the meat counter. People who looked like frat boys crowded the streets, wearing college sweatshirts and sipping health drinks out of giant Styrofoam containers. They even moved the old post office, which felt like a grievous insult. Everything got converted by money and I started to miss these grim places that offered no happy memories, but I wanted them back. The bars with sticky floors and French tickler dispensers in the bathrooms, like the Golden Grommet, which we called the Golden Vomit, for the old Irish men who slept in its doorway, waiting for it to open at seven a.m. I missed the lonely, unreliable streetcars, which now ding-dinged every eight minutes and were full of people in expensive shoes with careful hair.

The little shelter where I used to wait for the 44 on Laguna Honda had been fixed up. Gone was its piss stink and the pinkish-beige color of the retaining wall and shelter, which had been the same drab tone as the Youth Guidance Center beyond the bus stop, on top of the hill. YGC was called something else now, meant to seem kinder, more caring. The wall where the man had written with the heel of his shoe was painted over.

But what if that wall would not have been painted over, if by some miracle the numbers the man scratched on rough stucco were still there, bleeding through time, numbers he wrote with the shoeblack from his heel? Who would answer that phone line? And where is that man now? Where is the boy who was stirring at the stove on Masonic, the young Scummer, where is Leatherman, and where is Eva? Where is everyone, and what has happened to them?

3

No orange clothing
No clothing in any shade of blue
No white clothing
No yellow clothing
No beige or khaki clothing
No green clothing
No red clothing
No purple clothing
No denim of any kind or color
No sweatpants or sweatshirts
No underwire or metal parts on brassieres
Ladies must wear brassieres
No sheer or "see-through" clothing
No "layering"
No exposed shoulders
No tank tops or "cap-sleeved" tops
No low-cut tops
No unnecessarily exposed body parts—no half shirts or "low-waisted" pants
No logos or prints
No "capri" pants
No shorts
No skirts or dresses above the knee

No pants that are actually "long shorts"

No shirts without collars

All shirts must be tucked in

No jewelry (one "tasteful" wedding band is acceptable and will be inventoried by corrections officers at check-in)

No piercings

No bobby pins or metal clips in hair

Hair must be tidy and pulled back

No shower sandals

No flip-flops

No sunglasses

No jackets

No "over-shirts"

No "hoodies" nor any clothing with a hood

No tight clothing

Clothing must not be excessively loose or "baggy"

Appearance, hair, and clothing must be professional and in good taste.

Those who arrive to a state facility in inappropriate attire will be turned away and their inmate visit canceled.

4

If his students could learn to think well, to enjoy reading books, some part of them would be uncaged. That was what Gordon Hauser told himself, and what he told them, too. But there were days, like when one woman walked into the prison classroom and slung boiling sugar water into the face of another woman, that he did not believe it. There were days when it seemed like the real meaning of this work he was doing was to destroy his own life by trying to teach people who wanted to burn each other's face off. The guards made everything more difficult, with their hatred of the women, and their hostility toward free-world staff like Gordon. The guards had been forced to undergo sensitivity training and were furious about it. "It's because you cunts cry and demand explanations," they said. "Everything with you bitches is why, why, why." They all reminisced about the better times when they had worked in men's facilities, where they watched high-blood-volume stabbings on closed-circuit monitors from the safety of the watch office, and dealt with prisoners who lived strictly by self-enforced convict codes. Female prisoners argued with guards and complained, and the guards seemed to find the way the women bickered with them, contested everything, more treacherous than having to subdue riots. No guard wanted to work in a women's prison. Gordon had not understood this until he got to NCWF, which he'd chosen because it was commutable from Oakland, and because working with women seemed to him less threatening than a prison classroom of men.

His first placement had been with juveniles in San Francisco. He did that for six months, but it was too depressing. Kids in cages telling him stories about their foster homes, about sexual abuse, all kinds of abuse. Most didn't have parents, but some did. Gordon saw them in the court's waiting area, before he passed through a sally port to get to his classroom: people with holes in their sweatpants, T-shirts advertising random logos, inadequate shoes, poor people with chaotic lives. Couldn't the juvenile judges see from looking at the guardians that the kids didn't stand any kind of fair chance? There were signs to pull up your pants, because to wear them low was disrespectful. Gordon had a student who was always getting in trouble for having his pants too low. A big white boy whose eyes were spaced tight together in the center of his face. "You *talk* like you're black," a black kid had said to the white boy with his tight-stamped eyes, "but you *look* like you're retarded." NO BARE FEET, a sign at the building entrance warned. As if someone would try to come into a detention center and court, a municipal building on a bleak and windy corner, not close to the beach, without shoes. Another sign, NO TANK TOPS. Under it, typically, an entire three-generation family, all in tank tops, flesh spilling. And what was it about shoulders? What was law enforcement's fear of shoulders?

"To be in this place you got to be butt ugly, toothless, and fat as pull-apart buns," the yard captain at NCWF had told Gordon his first week there. As the yard captain said it, there were beautiful women passing behind him, porters with mops and brooms pushing trash bins on wheels, some of them thin, and with all their teeth, young things smiling and winking at Gordon, as if the joke was on the yard captain, who was himself obese.

There was one woman who immediately commanded Gordon's secret attention. Her brooding, childlike face and large dark eyes moved him. That was what beauty was, he supposed, when someone's face stirred feelings. She was always reading, her eyes cast down toward pages. More typically, the good-looking ones were overly aware of their beauty. It was something to which they subjected others, a thing they hawked, bartered, and controlled. Hauser had never been up for that kind of charade, in prison or in his other life, the real one, which was becoming less real to him. This girl did not know to use her beauty to manipulate, didn't even know she was beautiful was Gordon's sense, and when he one day looked at her and kept looking at her, she glanced at him, and before she turned away, he saw fear or what he thought was fear.

He didn't know which unit she lived in. She'd been on yard crew, but they must have switched her because she wasn't out there anymore. A few times, he saw her in the law library, working like every other prisoner on her habeas petition. Once, in the chapel, praying with a little group. And once in receiving, waiting on a package, and he had felt irrational jealousy that she was being sent a package—by whom? A rival, probably a man. She was too pretty for the package not to be from a man. And if the package was instead from the girl's mother or sister, it meant she was not just Gordon's foundling but someone's beloved relative, and the connection he imagined she and he might have would be overshadowed by her loyalty to other real people, unknown to him, involved in her life.

NCWF stood for Northern California Women's Facility, but the guards called it No Cunt Worth Forty K, which made it sound like these guards all faced a dilemma between their job and easy action with prisoners. In that fantasy, the guard pulled a slot lever by punching his time card, and got either dollar signs in triplicate or cherries in a row. And if the guard pulled the lever and the cherries came up, it was for each man to have the strength of character, the good judgment, to resist.

"You got a lot of self-control, that's one thing I'll say about you," Gordon's father had said to him when he'd picked up young Gordon from the Martinez public library, which was bigger than their own tiny library in the town near the Carquinez Strait where Gordon grew up. His father was a metal fabricator and thought that anyone who could sit and look at little symbols on a page all day must be denying other impulses. But for Gordon, reading was his impulse. It made the world bigger. In high school he fell in love with Dostoevsky, literature that matched his gloomy doubt. Dostoevsky was no belief in anything but the greasy earthbound world where humans wandered, fought, corrupted, and killed. Then again, Dostoevsky was a Christian, and those who fought and wandered in his novels had lost their way while God had not. Dostoevsky was something vast—universe-sized—a universe that had order, but not fixed and artificial Greek order. It was a scattered realm of chaotic trials, and Gordon knew he was stepping into the territory of truth when he read it.

His father was dead now, and Gordon finally had the kind of job his father would have approved of—unionized, with bene-fits. Gordon had never intended to work in a prison. There had been layers of resignation, attempts to stay in graduate school, the passing of oral exams on his second try, the granting of the midway point—the master's degree in English literature. But the dissertation that he had planned to write on Thoreau—Thoreau's image of a spiritual molting season, of a new man,

52

the fateful concept of an American Adam, an idea Gordon was fond of because of its precipitous arrogance and who doesn't want to change his life? Be reborn unfettered and sinless? The whole pursuit had been a crushing source of stress. He and his advisor didn't get along. The more progress he made of the sort his advisor wanted, the less able he was to locate any passion for his own subject. He felt trapped into an impossible commitment. He had debt, and he was about to lose his teaching fellowship. He needed to work. He found an adjunct position at a local community college in Oakland. The job barely covered his living expenses and left him no time for his dissertation. Maybe that was its upside. He was free to not work on it. But the adjunct work was intermittent. Broke and somewhat desperate, he submitted an application for a teaching position posted by the California Department of Corrections. He interviewed. They wanted to hire him as a full-time teacher, and just like that his stress over money faded away. His friend Alex filed his dissertation on Melville and went on the job market as an Americanist, even as Alex slagged Americanists, said they were a bunch of cornballs. Alex got the welcome reception, the interviews, the job talks. People called Alex the wunderkind even though he was the same age as Gordon and their other peers. Alex looked about eighteen; that was why. Alex knew how to behave around powerful people, presented the right blend of irony and deference. There were people from the department who took him under their wing, coached him. People who had never quite warmed to Gordon. Gordon went out of his way to remain friends with Alex. He wasn't envious, he told himself.

Before he realized it, the days of teaching at NCWF were structured by whether he might get a glimpse of this girl he liked wondering about. She averted her eyes when Gordon looked at her. He pondered trying to talk to her.

When Gordon made the discovery that she worked in cosmetology training, the chanciness of his days ended. There was a salon in cosmetology where staff could get haircuts for twelve dollars. He signed up, and made sure to go when she was there. On the momentous day, he sat down, was draped, by her, right up close, in an apron. The touch of her fingers to his scalp riveted him to the barber chair, setting off a chain reaction in his nerves.

It could have been the case, in the barber chair that day, that he was hypersensitive to touch, since he had been alone for months. The corner of the comb, when the girl drew it along the part of his hair, sent a shower of tingles down his head and neck. He was a wiring diagram, lighting up. The touch of this girl's comb produced a feeling that was both terrific longing and something like longing fulfilled.

"You have nice hair," the girl said. He had utterly normal and unexceptional hair. Straight, and brown.

It was strange to Gordon how sometimes beauty was magnificent and other times it was nothing and did not move him. Her skin was bad, and the bad skin made her even prettier, it made her real. She wore the state-issue tennis shoes, "bubblegums," the girls called them, shoes that meant you were indigent, because if you had any hustle at all, you'd order brand-name sneakers from a mail-order catalogue. She didn't seem to notice or care that she had no adorning marks of catalogue supply privilege, of outside help. In Gordon Hauser's dream of her, the state-blue clothes seemed to him almost like hospital scrubs, a nurse's clothes, not prison-issue: the uniform of a person who takes care of others, and she did take care. She trimmed his hair, touched his head with her comb.

There was something else. She was a black girl, but she spoke, to Gordon, like a white girl. She lived in the honor dorm and carried a Bible everywhere she went. That he associated her Bible reading with bookishness, maybe it was a confusion, but maybe not.

Gordon started going weekly for haircuts. One day the corpulent pig of a yard captain passed by in his club car as Gordon was walking toward cosmetology.

"You're going over there pretty often, aren't you, Mr. Hauser? Didn't I just see you getting a haircut *last week*?"

The yard captain and the other officers, many of them too fat to walk, reminded Gordon of the obese twins in the *Guinness Book of World Records*, twins in cowboy hats who rode mopeds to get from the bedroom to the kitchen.

Gordon looked at the yard captain with mild contempt, and then beyond him, to the woman he was there to see, as she swept hair from the base of the last barber chair in the cosmetology school, the chair where he would sit, where she would soon be touching his head.

Too fat to walk, and most of them brought in lunch boxes the size of traveling luggage. They were containers with collapsible handles and wheels, too big to lift and carry. What business of the yard captain's was it how often Gordon paid twelve dollars to have his head touched by this girl? It was none of his business.

He said to the yard captain that he guessed his hair must grow fast. The yard captain seemed satisfied that he had given Gordon a sufficiently hard time, made him a little nervous.

The captain rode away in his club car, his huge ass like a sideways letter B in his military pants.

Even people like Gordon's father, who owned few books, had a copy of the *Guinness Book of World Records* in their home. The prison library had several copies. It was a bible for the bookless under God.

That Gordon equated the thinness of his beloved with knowledge because the fat corrections officers were stupid did not occur to him until much later. In fact, he never really felt that to be the truth. It was everything together that had resulted in his infatuation: his own snobbery, his alienation from the military culture of the place, a physical attraction to the girl. All of it built a feeling in him, a kind of hope centered on her, the promise of something, but not what actually happened.

There had been a girlfriend, Simone was her name, a teacher at the community college where he'd been an adjunct. She was nice-looking and plenty smart and didn't talk too much. Most people talked to fill silence and didn't know the damage they reaped. Simone spoke only when she had something to say, but he'd ended the relationship and there was sometimes no why. She'd liked him more than he wanted her to, maybe. He understood there were people who didn't want to be the wanter, but he could not make himself feel that way. As soon as a woman turned to Gordon with a look of need, he was halfway gone. He occasionally missed Simone, but every time, right after feeling a desire to see her again, he was always relieved not to have to deal with her. If she could just appear at certain exact moments—when he was horny, or needed someone to talk to—that would have worked out fine, but people were not like that. There were hours built in where you had to hear someone express feelings about something that didn't seem important, and you nodded and pretended that it was. You had to mask your own ambivalence and pretend to be in love one hundred percent of the time, and he'd rather swim in a lake of hellfire.

The girl acknowledged their familiarity as if she knew why he came so often to get his hair cut. But she gave him no indication of her feelings. Other women called him cutie, taunted him to flirt. This one did no such thing. She cut his hair and avoided his gaze. Answered his questions shyly, minimally. There was nothing in her body language that suggested they were flirting. This made the whole thing safe. It was limited to the feel of her comb on his scalp. Her quiet breath. The slow textured sound of scissors closing over wet hair. Her fingers brushing clippings from his shoulders.

Even despite his obsession with this girl, he sometimes wanted out of the prison job, but change was such an elusive thing. A man could say every day that he wanted to change his life, was going to change it, and every day the lament became merely a part of the life he was already living, so that the desire for change was in fact a kind of stasis that allowed the unchanged life to continue, because at least the man knew to disapprove of it, which reassured him not all was lost.

As he was putting papers in his book bag one night, she came to his empty classroom with a program pass. She was not a student in his class. She shut the door behind her. The room had a small observation window, but Gordon knew an officer would not walk past for another ten or fifteen minutes.

He would like to say that nothing happened. Especially because so little did, and he felt he was placed on the wrong end of justice. After she shut the door, she went close to him. Their lips touched. Yes, he kissed her and not only. His hand grazed the front of her shirt and then it grazed lightly between her legs, to see how she would respond, and the answer was in the correct manner, in the interested manner, and you might call that thinking, choosing, proceeding, but Gordon didn't. It was not thinking. They were pressed together, nothing serious, fully clothed, for a minute, maybe less, and then it was night count and she had to get back to her unit.

She filed a 602 inmate grievance, claiming that he groped

her. This beautiful woman had targeted him. She did it, he later understood, for some complicated reason that had to do with the woman's girlfriend, who was his student. It was his word against hers. The Investigative Services Unit contacted him, conducted interviews, and found nothing damning, but deemed him at risk of overfamiliarity. They advised he be reassigned to a different facility. They kicked him down the Central Valley like a can down a hallway. Transferred him to Stanville Women's Correctional Facility, where no one but no one wanted to work.

5

You may decide to link my fate to the night I found Kurt Kennedy waiting for me, but I link it to the trial, the judge, the prosecutor, my public defender.

This is what I remember of the day I met my lawyer: Being put in an elevator that smelled of human sweat ionizing on stainless steel. The electric gloom of full-blast panel lighting. Courtroom room tone. Slippers that said LA County on the side of each shoe.

When it was time, the bailiffs directed me down a hall. They walked and I shuffled in leg irons to the long glass box in department thirty where in-custody defendants see the judge. I was brought into the arraignment box, which had an opening at face level so defendants could speak to their lawyers. I had a full view of the courtroom. My mother was there. I was her daughter and her daughter was innocent. Her presence gave me childish hope. When she saw me she waved unhappily. A bailiff approached her and said something. No waving, probably.

Signs in the courtroom said No lounging. No gum chewing. No sleeping. No eating. No cell phones. No children under ten unless state-subpoenaed as witnesses. In every courtroom where I had to sit as my case wound through the system, I tried not to read them. You have to project unbearable remorse every second that anyone might glance your way, a juror or victim's relative, the judge. At every moment you have to look like you can't live with yourself after what you have done. You can't look bored or hungry or tired. You can only look relentlessly guilty, in order to seem possibly a little less guilty.

I scanned for whoever might be my lawyer among the lawyers in the well before the judge's bench.

My case was after the defendant next to me, a person the court was calling Johnson, Johnson versus the People. I was anxious to meet my attorney, but since he or she had not appeared I watched as this Johnson tried to communicate with his lawyer, an old man with gray hair that flowed down his back.

"My mom's a sheriff," Johnson said in labored speech. His face was wired so that he could barely open his mouth. He made throaty sounds like someone being gagged.

"Mr. Johnson, your mother is a sheriff?" The old lawyer spoke in a fake-amazed tone. "Which division?"

"Not mine. My girlfriend's. It's bail bonds."

"Your girlfriend works at a bail bonds business? Then perhaps she's not a sheriff, Mr. Johnson?"

"It's her ma that own it."

"Your mother-in-law owns a bail bonds business? What's it called?"

"Yolanda's."

"Located where, Mr. Johnson?"

"They have it all over."

"So she works at a branch of it?"

"She own it. I told you. YO-LAN-DA."

The prosecutor on Johnson's case appeared before the judge. He gleamed like something pressure-washed.

From that day forward, on every occasion that I was forced to spend in court, the prosecutors were consistently the most competent-looking people in the courtroom. They were handsome and slick and tidy and organized, with tailored clothes

and expensive leather briefcases. The public defenders, meanwhile, were recognizable on account of their bad posture, their
ill-fitting suits and scuffed shoes. The women wore their hair
in short, ugly, practical cuts. The men had various styles or
non-styles of long hair, and every one of them was guilty of
exceeding width limits on their ties. The buttons on their shirts
dangled, ready to fall off. The prosecutors all looked like rich,
well-rested Republicans, while the public defenders were overworked do-gooders who arrived out of breath, late to court,
dropping loose papers that already had the waffle marks of shoe
prints on them from having been dropped before. Me, Johnson,
everyone here with state counsel, I felt like we were screwed,
just absolutely screwed.

Johnson told the lawyer he needed his high blood pressure
medication. He was without his psych meds. He needed pain-
killers. He had chronic aches from a gunshot wound. He lifted
his jail shirt and showed the lawyer. I couldn't see his chest. The
lawyer reeled backward.

"My goodness, Mr. Johnson. It's amazing you're even alive.
And what's the matter with your mouth?"

The old lawyer was yelling, as if Johnson was hard of hearing,
while I looked on, tense and alert because I was next.

"It's wired. My jaw broke. I'm a good citizen. I got a daughter."

The lawyer asked when she was born.

"Nineteen eighty."

"Mr. Johnson, I believe that's when *you* were born."

The defendant, this Johnson, was twenty-one years old.
Gunshot wounds. High blood pressure. Chronic pain. He looked
forty-eight. I watched as the facts of his life were exposed like
pants pockets pulled inside out.

"Okay, okay," Johnson said. "They got me drugged. I'm
sorry. Wait—"

I watched as he lifted his leg and awkwardly rolled up his pants with his chained hands. The daughter's birthday was tattooed on his calf. He read the date slowly as if trying to decipher a historic plaque.

"The judge does not like residential burglaries, Mr. Johnson."

"Tell her I'm sorry," Johnson slurred through his wired jaw.

In his own element, I wanted to think Johnson might be perfectly at home, a man on top of his game, whatever his game was. Life. On top of your game meant handling life. Doing it right. Being someone who inspired respect. Someone loved by women and feared by enemies, and now torn away from what made him shine. Either way, Johnson was fully a human being even if he could not remember when his daughter was born.

After my own immersion in this new world of Johnson's, I knew why he had seemed so dim in the arraignment box: the assholes had given him an involuntary injection of liquid thorazine. When certain types of inmates were slated for court transport, an invol by corrections officers made their own job easier. Drooling and high on unpleasurable brain-dullers, these defendants did not present well before a judge, or before their own public defender, who talked to them like they were three-year-olds.

When his arraignment was over, the bailiffs put on their blue rubber gloves for handling Johnson. He struggled to walk in leg irons. When they brought him past, the bailiffs held him as far away from their bodies as possible. Take it slow, one told him. They leapt out of the way when Johnson tripped. He fell on his broken face right there in the tank. No one helped him. His jumpsuit was brown, which meant medical. A county wristband

62

indicated open wounds. He might spread bacterial infection, or something worse. Defiance. Depression. Dyslexia. HIV. Mental degradation. Rotten luck.

I was next but nothing was happening. The judge left the bench. I sat for maybe twenty minutes, a bailiff behind me, no lawyer calling my name, feeling my mother's sadness, unable to meet her gaze, because if I did, this would be even harder. I inspected the eagle on top of the courtroom flagpole. The eagle hovered on the wooden flagpole as if what it had caught was the American flag that was attached to the pole. I have seen enormous flags ripple, strung high on towering poles. Car dealerships have them. Sometimes McDonald's have them, huge flags that fly for commerce and announce "America." Here in this courtroom, the flags hung limp and still, collecting dust. A flag needs wind, I thought, just as the judge was announcing my name and case number, and then again, my name and case number.

I'd been told I would have my first contact with legal counsel at arraignment. I stood as the bailiff ordered me to, but no lawyer appeared.

Johnson's lawyer, with the flowing gray hair, limped up to me. What does *he* want, I wondered.

"Miss Hall? Romy Hall? I'm your public defender."

You can have sympathy for Johnson's lawyer, if you must, but I don't have to. He meant well. But he was an incompetent and overworked old man. Got me two life sentences and failed to make admissible the whole sordid history of Kurt Kennedy and his obsession with me.

Kennedy had fixated. He had made it his life's work to be outside my apartment building. To be in the garage where I parked my car. To lurk in the cramped aisles of my corner market. To follow me on foot and on his motorcycle. When I heard the motor of that cycle, which made a high-pitched whine, I flinched. He had a habit of calling me thirty times in a row. I changed my number. He got the new number. He came to the Mars Room, or he was already there. I asked Dart to eighty-six him and he refused. He's a good customer, Dart said. I was expendable. Men who spent money were not. Kennedy hunted me and didn't let up. But the prosecutor convinced the judge that the victim's behavior was irrelevant. It did not establish an imminent threat on the night in question, and so the jury never learned a thing about it, not a single detail. It was the judge who disallowed the evidence, but I blamed the lawyer. I blamed the lawyer because he was supposed to help me and I felt he did not.

"Why can't I testify and explain?" I asked him. "Because you'll get destroyed on cross-examination," he replied. "I can't let you do that to yourself. No competent lawyer would put you on the stand."

When I asked again, he fired questions at me. About the work I did to make a living. About my relationship to Kennedy and other customers. About the decision I made to pick up a heavy instrument. About the fact—the fact, he reiterated—that I struck a man sitting in a chair, a man who could not walk without two canes. I tried to answer his questions. He tore my answers apart and made them into questions, and I tried to answer those but struggled. When he asked another question, I screamed at him to stop.

"You will not take the stand," he said.

What those twelve people knew was that a young woman of dubious moral character—a stripper—had killed an upstanding citizen, a veteran of the Vietnam War who had sustained a job-related injury and was permanently disabled. Because there was a kid present, they tacked on a charge of child endangerment. Never mind that it was my child, and the person endangering him was Kurt Kennedy.

Johnson's lawyer had tried to convince me to take a plea. I refused. I knew how the system worked, at least vaguely. Most cases never went to trial because prosecutors scared defendants into taking pleas, and lawyers encouraged that route for their own reasons of not wanting to lose a case. My situation was different. It had circumstances. Anyone who was there and knew the history would have understood what happened, and why, although no one was, or did.

What I didn't realize, at the time, was that most people took pleas because they did not want to spend their life in prison.

I never thought of him as my own lawyer. He was always Johnson's, even as I never knew Johnson or thought about what happened to him; he was just another body jammed through the system, a Johnson of thousands. Still, I liked Johnson. His girlfriend's mother was a sheriff and to hell with anyone who questions that.

In court, Johnson's lawyer kept saying, "Strike that," after half his sentences, "Strike that." Maybe it was normal. I didn't know. But every time he said it, my heart sank.

The jury did not learn what Kurt had done to me, the tireless stalking, the waiting, the following, the calling, the calling again, the surprise appearances. None of it was to be spoken of in court. What the jury knew was that a tire iron was used (People's Exhibit #89). That the victim had been sitting in a patio chair when he received the first blow (People's Exhibit #74), and that he had been heard crying out for help (Witness #17, Clemencia Solar).

How many autopsies have you performed, the prosecutor asked the coroner, his first witness.

"More than five thousand, sir."

"How many with head trauma?"

"Hundreds, I'd estimate."

The coroner located and pointed out in photographs two fatal wounds. The declared cause of death was severe cranial cerebral trauma. The coroner noted that Mr. Kennedy seemed to have vomited up a large amount of blood on the defendant's porch.

"How many impacts did Mr. Kennedy's head receive?" the prosecutor asked.

"At least four. Possibly five."

"Would there have been a fair amount of pain for Mr. Kennedy, receiving these injuries?"

"Oh, yes."

"Are these other injuries on his arms and hands typical when someone is trying to defend himself?"

"Yes, that's correct."

"Isn't it true that a person in his mid-fifties will require less force to fracture the skull than someone much younger?" This was asked by Johnson's lawyer, on cross-examination.

"I suppose so, but—"

"Objection. Hypothetical."

"Sustained."

The prosecutor called one of my other neighbors as a witness. Clemence Solar would say anything to get attention, such as tell them she heard Kurt cry out for help. She was a liar. A witness for the defense, a guy named Coronado, lived one house over from Clemence. He and I had never had a conversation. He only spoke Spanish and I only speak English. I remembered seeing him out there working on cars. Once, a car that belonged to him leaked an entire tank of gasoline onto the street, and another neighbor yelled at him. He had told the police he'd seen Kurt Kennedy pull up on his motorcycle, park, and wait. He heard arguing and was sure that what happened was self-defense. That was the plan. Johnson's lawyer had interviewed him and the man was agreeable. He would provide testimony.

"Mr. Coronado has bench warrants in San Bernardino County," the prosecutor told the judge. "He's had a series of DUIs over the years, and has done mandatory treatment."

An interpreter translated for the witness, my witness, my neighbor, Mr. Coronado, who turned to the judge and spoke. The interpreter translated.

"Your Honor, I want to clear this up right now. I'm ready to clear it up. I will do whatever is necessary."

The judge and a court clerk consulted loudly about the man's warrant, and which court took walk-ins, or didn't.

"Sir, your legal troubles are in San Bernardino County. You'll have to take it up with them. It's Friday and they don't take walk-ins today. Go there on Monday morning."

The man spoke again, seeming not to have absorbed what the interpreter told him.

"Your Honor, I'm ready. I will pay the fees and serve the time. I want to clear this up right now. I'm ready, Your Honor. I want to clear this up."

That was our witness. A man who wanted to help me, but couldn't.

On the day of closing arguments, Johnson's lawyer seemed drunk. He shouted at the jury and stomped his foot. He addressed them in a scolding voice as if they, the jury, had done something wrong. The jury didn't want anything to do with him, or me. They completed a form and handed it to the judge. There are two boxes on the form. The foreman checked one.

6

Children must be supervised, quiet, and behaved at all times, or guardians will be asked to remove them from the visiting area

Inmates cannot handle vending machine cards

Vending machines do not accept cash. You must buy a prepaid card in Visitor Processing

Cards cost five dollars. Two dollars and fifty cents will be returned *if your card is in reusable condition*

Inmates can stand no closer than three feet from vending machines

One short hug is acceptable at the beginning of your visit, and one very brief hug at the end of the visit. No sustained bodily contact or the visit will be terminated

Holding hands is sustained contact and not tolerated

No high fives

No hands under the table during your visit. Visitors and inmates must keep hands where officers can see them at all times

No hands in pockets

No yelling

No raised voices

No arguments

No "horse play"

No loud laughing or boisterousness

Keep crying to a minimum

7

The road to Stanville prison is straight. It goes toward the mountains, which can be seen from the main yard on low-smog days. In winter their caps are dusted white. The snow is far away. It never falls on the valley floor where Stanville is. We see those caps of white through the baked layers of valley air. The snow is as remote to us as home.

Only people who should be on the road to Stanville are on that road. The morning of our arrival, no one was on it but us. The road was lined on both sides by almond orchards. I would not have known what was growing, or cared, except that Laura Lipp was awake and talking again, and she said what they package as almonds are not real almonds, but instead poisonous fruit seeds, did I know, and that one of her children had almost died from eating them.

"You ever split open a peach pit?" Laura Lipp said. "That's where they come from. They aren't actual almonds. They're the poisonous part of a peach. A neighbor once gave my kid some without asking me first and if it weren't for the paramedics she would have killed him."

"*You* killed him," a woman behind us said.

I felt a wave around me, people tsking in disgust.

White women in prison have two crimes, baby killer or drunk driving. Of course they have many more crimes, but those are the stereotypes, which help to impose an order among the women, the races.

"They don't know what happened," Laura Lipp said. "About him and what he did to me, what he did to us—to me and the baby. None of you has a right to judge me. You don't know anything. Just like I don't know anything about you."

She turned to me, as if I were the one person she could reason with.

"Do you know who Medea is?"

"No," I said. "You need to be quiet. I don't know you and I don't want to talk to you."

"You want me to be quiet, but I'll shut up when I'm finished and not before. I went to college, unlike the rest of you. Medea's husband abandoned her and that's what happened to me. He took everything from her, including her children. She had to put him in pain. So he could know *her* pain. It's written into history. It's real. You can't do that to a person without damage. He tore her life apart, and so she found a way to do the same to him. That's my only comfort. It's very very very small. It's so small I can't see it most of the time."

My eyes were closed. I was turned away. I was trapped with her but willing myself elsewhere. I pictured a woman on the landing of a hotel, picking up lint from ugly red carpeting to see if it was crack cocaine. Picking up a crumb, a match head, rug fluff. Inspecting the object between her fingers, smelling it, giving it a little taste, putting it down. Picking up another crumb, inspecting it the same way. She starts to cry, this woman, in her search, her endless search. It's as sad as anything I've seen. I kept seeing it, though I did not want to, while Laura Lipp talked on and on.

The woman searching the carpet was Eva, I realized. I block certain things out. Everyone does. It's healthy. But in trying to block the words coming from Laura Lipp I accidentally thought of something bad. Eva went in for coke, early on. Freebasing it, then shooting it, and, finally, crack was enough and it was the thing. Turned skinny, lost a tooth in a fight, had a limp from a car accident. But she was still Eva and I loved her.

When you see lights even higher than stadium lights, you are at prison.

They hustled us off the bus two at a time, yelling, Move it, Let's go. I was trying not to trip. Conan, in front of me, was unhindered. He had a walk that was unaffected by the chains. I don't know how he did it. He practically floated. He was dragging and smoothly syncopated. It was a walk that belonged on the streets of Compton, or in the parking lot of the Inglewood Forum, out at the Pomona car show, not in a line of shackled women headed into prison receiving.

The officers who greeted us were angry. Especially the women. It was a rude and aggressive welcome but it shut Laura Lipp up. The only person who got gentle treatment was the extra-large-sized lady who had slid off her bus seat. They let her lie quietly as we more able-bodied and conscious women were prodded down the aisle of the bus. The woman looked to be peacefully sleeping when I shuffled past her. The last passenger, she was moved off the vehicle in a stretcher, by medics who pronounced her dead and placed her on the floor of receiving with a tarp over her face.

The rest of us lined up for debugging and muumuus. The lieutenant was called Jones, a big Mack truck–shaped lady who was, I later came to understand, partly shaped like that on account of her stab-proof vest. The vests make the men look gym-pumped and the women look like packing crates.

We slathered ourselves with Lindane Lotion to kill lice and whatever else. It's a poison; twice before I'd used it for scabies I'd contracted at the Mars Room and both times I started menstruating within hours. They wanted the girl, the fifteen-year-old who looked eight months pregnant, to use it as well. I told her not to. We were next to each other in the showers. They forced her, and she cried while applying her Lindane. If she were officially declared pregnant, she could be excused from certain procedures, but that designation had to be on her bed card, and none of us had bed cards yet. She would have to wait like the rest of us until her scheduled medical exam, and then for the requisite paperwork from her pregnancy test, which she had to have, even if you could practically see the baby kicking. Eventually she would be issued a CDC PREGNANT designation, with state clothing that announced it in enormous block letters on the back of her shirt and her state-property rain jacket. She'd be allowed no extra food, no prenatal exams, no vitamins, no counseling. All she would get was a bottom bunk, and extra time to go prone when the alarm sounded on the yard. That's why the jacket said PREGNANT. It was like SWAT. It meant DON'T SHOOT (I'M SLOW).

Next was the strip search, which I was accustomed to from jail. The guards were yelling at us to spread wider, especially at women with thicker pubic hair. They shone their lights on us, as we bent over for them. Some of the girls were crying. Fernandez, who had yelled at the young pregnant girl to shut up when we first got on the bus, was yelling again at the girls who were crying about the strip search. The cops all knew her.

"Fernandez, back again," they kept saying, and she would either be friendly and joke or tell them to fuck off. The other girls seemed afraid of her.

They gave us one-size-fits-all polka-dot muumuus and three-sizes-fit-most canvas slippers. Even big and burly Conan with his jawline beard was forced to wear a muumuu. He threw his shoulders back to show the cops the muumuu was too small.

"I need pants and a shirt. I can't wear this. It ain't right, Sarge."

He kept raising his arms. "It's too tight in the shoulders."

Jones said, "What are you planning to do in it, ma'am, conduct an orchestra? Shut up and put your arms down."

The muumuus made me think of that expression lipstick on a pig. No woman should be compared to a pig nor made to wear the garment they gave us. And no Conan, either. The slippers were okay. They reminded me of winos, the shoes we wore growing up, which you could purchase at the army-navy place on Market Street. It was where I got my school gym uniforms as well. Later, I passed it as an adult, on my way to the Mars Room. Both were near the corner where the businessman getting in the Mercedes had promised money for a cab on a rainy night. San Francisco was like that, a city where the layers of my history all compressed together onto a single plane. Between the army-navy place and the Mars Room was Fascination, where Eva and I spent many hours as teenagers while Eva flirted with the cashier, before she was lost to the Tenderloin, north of Fascination, up in the boisterous and dirty hotels that formed the pearls on the chain of her bare life, barer even than mine.

The last time I saw Eva was at the wedding of another friend, a former prostitute who got clean, met another guy in recovery, and joined, with him, the Church of Christ. We all went to an alcohol-free wedding where people smiled like we were on Christian TV. They had done something to our friend. I could see it in her face. She sobbed at the altar. It was clear to me that there had been a reckoning. They'd broken her down, and now they were her moral overlords. She looked beautiful like an arrangement of plastic flowers in a funeral home. Another Sunset District girl at the wedding kept making references to her boyfriend and how he couldn't come with her because a guy in his club had died and there was a funeral for him that morning. His club. There was a big public funeral that day for a Hells Angel. She wanted to brag, but she wanted to seem like she was being discreet. She kept talking about what good money she made as a waitress on Pier 39. She said, as if she somehow knew what I did for a living, "I make my money *respectably*." Pier 39 is garbage.

Eva showed up halfway through the ceremony. Walked in with this greaseball. They looked like they'd been up for three days. Eva's face was coated in foundation that was a full shade too light for her skin. She kept her sunglasses on inside. Turned to me in her half-erasing makeup.

"Romy, what the fuck is going on here?"

It was the right question, was the thing.

The greaseball was probably her dealer. She said boyfriend but that distinction doesn't matter. The year before, Eva had been with a guy who was originally a john. He became a regular, and then he didn't want her seeing any other johns. He started funding her drug habit so she didn't have to work the streets. This guy was waiting outside the Mars Room one night to talk to me. He was looking for Eva. He was distressed. He said he'd spent eighty thousand dollars on her cocaine habit that year and now she was gone. What did he expect? I didn't question that he loved her, or at least that he knew he'd never get a woman like Eva, that gorgeous and free, without doling out the money, and without her being first and foremost an addict who needed something from him. "Get away from me," I said, and left him standing at the entrance to the theater.

76

Henry was his name, the john obsessed with Eva. He started appearing almost everywhere I went, hoping I was on my way to meet Eva and he could trap her. But I hadn't talked to Eva, didn't know where she was, and she wasn't the kind of person you can call on the phone. I had about ten numbers for her and none of them worked. Later, I forgot all about Henry and that episode, because soon I had my own stalker, Kurt Kennedy. Henry wasn't really my stalker, but Eva's. He only stalked or shadowed me in order to locate her. Eva disappeared to escape him. When I think of Henry or of Kurt, the tissue of my throat goes hard.

We were chained to a bench in a hall, waiting to be interviewed in a little concrete room about drug use, sexual history, mental health, and whether or not we had gang affiliations or enemies currently serving time at Stanville. After several hours of this, they gave us each a bedroll and a CDC Offender's Handbook, as well as a forty-page Guide to the CDC Offender's Handbook. Conan wondered out loud if we would also be getting a guide to the *guide* to the handbook.

"The failure to report a rule violation," Conan said in a nasal voice, "is also a rule violation. The failure to report a rule violation of a failure to report a rule violation is another rule violation."

Jones said, "Not even six hours in prison, London, and you just earned your first 115."

I figured she was being sarcastic, but she went over to the cop shop and started writing him up.

"London," someone said, "*London*."

Some of the girls laughed and snickered that Conan was getting written up. You'd think we would band together. Even our ragtag crew from the bus, with all sixty of us we could have subdued the two transport cops easily enough, hijacked that vehicle, and gone to Mexico. But there was no cooperation. Just people eager to see others fall under the hammer they suffered under themselves.

It had been like that in jail, too. When I first got to county I had lost my Styrofoam cup right away. It looked disposable but was the only cup I'd be issued. I didn't know, and the other women had not told me. They laughed as I dug a soda can out of the trash. I used it to drink water out of for the next eighteen months. Jail is the perfect incubator for a police-like attitude, but there are cops in every environment. Backstage at the Mars Room women would critique other women for not having fancy costumes, or a choreographed and skillful floor show. Who cares—the job is about making money, not wasting it on costumes—and yet there were women in the dressing room who wanted there to be a set of rules to stripping. They believed you had to put on a good show and buy expensive costumes because it was more dignified and professional, respectful of some standard they wanted to uphold. But most of us worked in that environment because we were the kind of people who did not believe in standards and would never try to uphold any. You don't have to believe in anything to work at the Mars Room. The Russian women, when they started dancing at the Mars Room, brought a new post-Soviet ruthlessness, a bracing lack of regard for costuming and glamour, for anything that wasn't directly tied to profit. Most did hand jobs in the audience, which cut the rest of our business way back.

The sleaziest types of men arrived at the club in thin and slippery track pants for maximum contact, but many were less experienced, or more gentlemanly. Some didn't even want a girl on their lap, but next to them, for talking. I found the track pants type preferable. There was almost no work involved. No smiling, no fake personality, no pretend complicity. They moved you around how they wanted and you didn't have to exert yourself, and for twenty dollars per song. But after the Russian women invaded our club, the men all started requesting actual hand jobs for twenty a song. The Russian women undercut the rest of us. They siphoned the money out of all the wallets.

We gathered in the common area of our new housing unit while we waited for bed assignments. It was a big cinder-block building with rows of cells on two tiers. Everything was either raw concrete or painted a shade of dirty pink. Women in the cells pressed their faces to the narrow glass window of each door to stare at us. One woman shouted through the door that we looked like a bunch of ugly-ass scrubs. Hey, scrub! Hey, stupid! Come wipe my ass. Lick my cunt while you're at it. She kept yelling until a guard hammered on her door with his baton.

Laura Lipp sat down next to me. I tried to move but Jones barked at me.

"You sit where I put you. This isn't musical chairs."

"Next to the baby killer," Fernandez said, not quietly.

"You two are like the Bobbsey Twins," Fernandez said.

Who are the Bobbsey Twins? No one seems to know. She meant we were alike, because white, and I was going to have to do something. Break away from Laura Lipp.

"How many of you are dyslexic?" Jones asked our group of sixty.

Every person raised their hand except me.

Jones did a head count and didn't notice my own had remained down. That was fine with me. As I came to understand, the Americans with Disabilities Act was often the only barrier left preventing them from treating us with unlimited abuse. Laura Lipp took this moment as a chance for further bonding.

"I'm not really dyslexic but they give you extra time for filling out forms this way. Do you like to read?"

I looked away. I tried to catch someone else's eye, but no one would look at me. "If you eventually make it to the honor dorm, the girls there share books, although most read trash."

Jones began by deciphering for us loudly the signs in the day room, since we were all dyslexic or presumed illiterate. The signs all began the same way.

Ladies, report to staff if you have a staph infection.

Ladies, no whining.

Ladies, out of bounds results in an automatic 115.

The warning shots sign was more blunt. NO WARNING SHOTS IN THIS AREA.

The clock on the wall had a red wedge from five minutes to the hour until five minutes past the hour. This was for the women who could not tell time. Jones explained the red wedge. All you need to know, she said, is that when the big hand is on red, room doors are on unlock.

Everything in prison is addressed to the woman for whom the red wedge is painted on the clock face, the imbecile. I've never met her. Plenty I have met in prison cannot read, and some cannot tell time, but that doesn't mean they are not shrewd and superior individuals who can outsmart any egghead. People in prison are clever as hell. The imbecile the rules and signs are meant to address is nowhere to be found.

Jones read the guide to the handbook, and then the handbook itself. There were rules about everything, appearance and thoughts and letters and language, food and attitude and scheduling, tools and implements and use. Many instructions on who not to touch (anyone) or where (nowhere), and certainly no fornication was allowed, as Jones emphasized, saying the word slowly like a horny preacher.

"What is fornication again," Conan asked; "it's just fucking, right?"

Women started dropping off to sleep; we'd been on an all-night ride and everyone was exhausted. Jones never looked up, didn't cease her mechanical reciting. I nodded off, too, but was woken by screams.

The pregnant girl was clutching her stomach and crying out. Jones glanced at her and licked her thumb and turned a page of the handbook, continuing to read. She had to read the whole eighty-page guide and the guide to the guide every week on Fridays when the new busload arrived, and so she knew it well, could speed-read it in order to take a longer break. The pregnant girl interrupted Jones's reading of the rules by going into labor.

I told you that women enjoy participating in the punishment of their fellow prisoners, but it's not always true. Some of us helped that day in receiving. Jones told everyone to stay seated and wait for medical. Fernandez ignored Jones's orders and went to help the girl, the same girl she'd been yelling at on the bus. So did I. It was my chance to break away from Laura Lipp. And I could not bear to watch this helpless kid suffer alone. She was screaming in agony. Fernandez and I each held a hand. Conan blocked Jones and the other receiving cops from getting near us. When they pepper-sprayed Conan, he only grew more irate. He shoved Jones to the ground. An alarm sounded. I kept on talking to the girl. I reminded her to breathe. She said "no" over and over, like she didn't want to have a baby, like she could prevent the future from merging into the now. Cops poured into our unit. Four of them tackled Conan.

You're going to be all right, I kept telling the girl. It wasn't true, since she was in prison, but I comforted her as best I could, until more cops streamed in and yanked me away from her and put me in restraints. They were not attending to the girl in labor; she was alone and crying out in pain.

Fernandez, like Conan, was courageous. They sprayed her and she didn't seem to notice. She kept resisting them until they Tasered her and put her in a cage.

I was put in a cage, too. The cages were not quite big enough and I had to keep my head low on my neck. I had become the turkey on the freeway. Conan was practically stuffed into the thing. Conan in a cage was even worse than Conan in a muumuu. He filled the cage, all glare and rippling muscle. We were all three going to administrative segregation.

My first day in prison, and I had already blown my parole board hearing, which was in thirty-seven years.

Medical had arrived but it was too late to move the girl; she was fully in labor. She had the baby in receiving. It let out a cry that echoed through the concrete room, a piercing shriek of existence.

A birth should be joyous. This was a lonely birth. The mother was in the hands of the state, and so was the baby, and they each only had that one tie, to bureaucracy. The correctional officers seemed to think it was funny to see a baby in receiving. There aren't supposed to be any babies. The baby was contraband.

Jones was shaking her head, as if a birth here in her unit

was one more example, further proof, of our inability to live in society. The medics put the girl on a stretcher. She asked to hold her baby but her request was ignored by the medics, one of whom held the little newborn away from his body like it was a sack of garbage that might leak.

Jackson was born at SF General, where they have to take you even without insurance. The nurse put him on my chest and he looked up at me, a wet wild creature who had crawled from a swamp, all eyes, eyes wide, and his cry was not hysterical, not a lament, but an earnest question: Are you here? Are you here for me?

I was crying, too, and I kept answering, I'm here, I'm right here. A nurse cleaned him up and put him in a clear plastic box and all night different nurses and orderlies came in and out, prodding and poking and bothering him. I was there, as I'd promised, but I was not his protector.

Jackson's dad was a doorman at the Crazy Horse, a club down the street from the Mars Room where I also worked on occasion. He went out with his friends the night his own son was born, instead of hanging out with me in the miserable recovery room, which I shared with another woman who also had no companion and watched television all night. Every time Jackson's dad came around to my apartment, in the days and weeks after Jackson was born, I yelled at him for being a dead-beat, which he was, so he stopped visiting. I didn't want him around, but when I heard he died of an overdose, I could not look at poor little Jackson without feeling rotten. He'd lost his loser dad. He had only one person to rely on. He bobbled his head on his neck, his big wet blue eyes gazing at me in myopic wonder, his hair a crown of fuzz standing at attention, and he did not know he was fatherless. He knew only that I was the one. I was the one.

I was living out in the avenues then. When Jackson was three months old, the owner sold my apartment building. New management cleared the tenants to raise the rent. The city was changing. Rents were high. It was either live with my mother, who never offered that, probably because we fought and she was tired of me, or move to the Tenderloin, where you could still get an affordable studio, if you could tolerate the atmosphere in those buildings. I moved to Taylor Street. Eva-land, as I thought of it. I went back to the Mars Room and paid my new neighbor to watch Jackson. My neighbor had a three-year-old and was in a similar situation. No money, raising her daughter alone. She watched Jackson a lot, especially after I started dating Jimmy Darling.

We three hovered in our turkey cages while Jones bullied the other prisoners into sitting down for the rest of their orientation. Everyone was agitated. People were crying. Jones told them to shut up and reminded them that they had made choices, that Sanchez, as she called the girl who'd had the baby, had made really poor choices, and should have thought about her baby's future before she broke the law.

Jones summoned porters, two gloomy white girls with corn-rowed hair and abraded skin, to clean up from the birth. It was impossible to know if they were sad about the situation at hand, or in a general and permanent sort of way.

The gloomy porters squirted state cleaners and blasted hoses. Soapy runoff filled the drains.

The baby's shriek stayed in my head as I sat in my cage, long after it and its mother were gone. They were in no hurry to deal with us. Incapacitated, in cages, we could be left to wait, to stare at the dirty pink walls while someone slowly, slowly filled out paperwork for our transfer from receiving to administrative segregation, which was even worse than regular prison.

Unfortunately for that baby, it was a girl.

8

On the job experience section of the form, the suspect wrote that she had experience as an employee. The intake officer explained that this would not be sufficient.

On the transcript of the suspect's interview with homicide detectives, when asked what kind of work he normally did, the suspect answered, "Recycling."

Quality Control, she wrote for type of work.

I'm an employee, he'd told them, but seemed unable to specify what kind.

Recycler.
Maintenance crew.

Retail.

Wholesale.

Flyer distribution.

Warehouse distribution.

Dollar Store.

Dollar Tree.

Distribution warehouse.

Walmart.

He said he handed out flyers.

He had written recycler.

They both worked with a crew that handed out flyers.

He delivered free newspapers, but not regularly.

He worked at a distribution warehouse.

She wrote quality control.

He said he worked part-time helping a friend who cleaned dollar stores after hours.

Cashier.

Unemployed.

Not currently employed.

QC, which she explained meant quality control.

Truck unloader.

Package handler.

He unpacked crates, he told them, at a distribution warehouse.

When asked what she did for a living, the suspect said she worked.

Recycling, he'd written.

He brought recycling to a redemption center, he explained.

Recycler.

Recycler.

Recycler.

Recycler.

Redemptions, he told them.

Redeemer was what she wrote.

The suspect said she had mostly made her living by collecting bottles and cans.

9

When you google the town of Stanville, faces pop up: mug shots. After the mug shots, an article that cites Stanville as having the highest percentage of minimum-wage workers in the state. Stanville's water is poisoned. The air there is bad. Most of the old businesses are boarded. There are dollar stores, gas stations that serve as liquor outlets, and coin op laundry. People without cars walk the main boulevard in the hottest part of the day, when it's 113 degrees outside. They amble along in the gutter of the road, scooting empty shopping carts, piercing the dead zone of late afternoon with the carts' loose metallic rattle. There are no sidewalks.

Stanville is synonymous with its prison. Like Corcoran is, and Chino, Delano and Chowchilla and Avenal, Susanville and San Quentin, scores of towns that house prisons and share a name, up and down the state.

Gordon Hauser found a place to rent sight unseen, a cabin up the mountain from Stanville proper, in the western Sierra foothills. The cabin was one room with a woodstove. It would be his Thoreau year, he wrote to his friend Alex, sending him the realty link.

Your Kaczynski year, Alex wrote back, after looking at the photos of the cabin.

True both lived in one-room huts, Gordon responded. *But I don't see much connection between them.*

Reverence of nature, self-reliance. K was even a reader of Walden, Alex wrote. *It's on the list of books from his cabin. Also R.W.B. Lewis, your idol.*

Aren't you kind of oversimplifying?

Yes. But also: both died virgins.

Kaczynski's not dead, Alex, Gordon wrote back.

You know what I mean.

But Thoreau was worried about trains, Gordon replied. *Ted K lived in the time of the atomic bomb. He lived through the technological destruction of the world.*

I confess that is of course a significant difference. Can't remove either from historical context. Plus, Thoreau would have made a deeply inadequate mail bomb. His inflammatory act of resistance was not getting a welcome mat for his place.

For goodbye beers at their bar on Shattuck Avenue, Alex gave Gordon, as a kind of joke, a Ted Kaczynski reader. Gordon had looked at the manifesto. Everyone had. The guy had briefly been a young professor at Berkeley.

They toasted Gordon's departure. "To my rustication," Gordon said.

"Isn't that when they boot you from Oxford?"

"They just send you down to the country for a while."

Gordon left downtown Oakland in the late afternoon, and drove east, and south. Tunneling through the dark and flat expanse of big agriculture along Highway 99, a burnt smell of synthetic fertilizer coming into the air vents, even on recirculate, he began to see an orange glow way off the freeway, a huge nimbus surrounded by darkness. A mysterious light source, as if there were a large factory out in the middle of the night-black fields. It was them, he knew: the women, three thousand of them. Just like at NCWF, it was a place where there could be no night because security was twenty-four hours a day, seven days a week.

He checked in at a Holiday Inn. He would meet the property manager in the morning, get the keys to his new place. He wanted to ask the girl behind the hotel desk if she knew anyone who worked at Stanville Prison. He did not ask. He asked if the tap water in town was okay to drink. "I'm not the type of person who drinks tap water?" the girl said, upward lilting. He asked if she could recommend a place to eat.

"Now, are you a fried shrimp lover?" Apparently that was also a type.

Gordon's mountain place had a poisoned water supply. Not from agriculture. There was naturally occurring uranium, so you had to bring in bottled water. He liked the cabin. It smelled of fresh-planed pine. It was logical in its compactness. Cozy, even. It was up on stilts, on a steep hill with few neighbors, and had an enormous view of the valley.

He was meant to report to his new job in a week. He spent his days unpacking his meager belongings and chopping wood. Went for walks. Nights, he fed logs to his stove and read.

Ted Kaczynski, Gordon learned, ate mostly rabbits. Squirrels, Ted reported, didn't seem to like bad weather. The Ted diaries were mostly concerned with how he lived and what he saw happening in the wilderness around him, and Gordon could see that comparing him to Thoreau was not as crude as he'd first suspected. But Ted would never write this: *Through our own recovered innocence we discern the innocence of our neighbors.*

Gordon's new neighbors were all white, Christian, and conservative. People who tinkered with trucks and dirt bikes and made assumptions of Gordon that he did nothing to dispel, because he knew those assumptions would work in his favor if he needed their help. It snowed up there. Roads closed, cutting off access to supplies. Trees fell and knocked down power lines. In summer and autumn, fires raged through. Gordon did not enjoy the grinding zing of dirt bikes' two-stroke motors, which echoed down the valley on weekends, but that was the country: not a pure and untrammeled world of native wildlife and songbird calls, but country people, who cleared the trees off their property with chain saws and paved, or laid Astroturf, cleared paths through the woods for motocross courses and snowmobiling. Gordon withheld judgments. These people knew much more than he did about how to live in the mountains. How to survive winter and forest fires and mud flows from spring rains. How to properly stack wood, as Gordon's neighbor from down the hill had patiently showed him, after his two cords of chunk wood were dumped in the driveway by a guy named Beaver who was missing most of his fingers. Gordon learned to split logs. Part one of his rustication.

The guy down the road who helped Gordon stack his wood had a wife or a girlfriend. Gordon had not met her, but he'd heard the two of them arguing. Voices echoed up the hills.

One night in those early days of his new life in the mountains, Gordon was woken by what he thought was a woman's scream from out in the deep dark. He fumbled for the lamp. He was sure it was the neighbor's wife. Their place was down the hill maybe three hundred yards. He heard another scream. A frightened shriek. This time, closer. It sounded like someone in trouble.

He went out on the deck in his underwear. There were no lights on at his neighbor's place. He stood for a long time but heard nothing more. He decided he could not take the chance.

He put on clothes and walked down his hill in the direction from which the sound had come. He stood on the road and tried to listen.

There was no moon and his eyes did not adjust. He could see almost nothing, just the vaguest outline where the tops of the tallest pines met the sky.

The way the stars flickered unevenly, from bright to dimmer to brighter, reminded him of car headlights. A car at night, moving along a tree-lined road, lights shining intermittently. But stars were wondrous, and headlights could be sinister. Stars were nature. Cars were unknown human intent.

Air sent the trees hissing and rushing, and he wondered if wind was what made stars flicker, a wind out there that was continuous with this wind here.

He heard it again, the woman's shriek, farther away now.

He called out. "Is anyone there? Are you okay?"

He stood in the cold and waited. He heard only wind.

He walked up the hill and got back into bed. Tried to sleep and could not.

10

Out walking in the bitter cold I spotted a porcupine in a tree and shot it. At first it seemed to be dead, but then I noticed that it was still breathing. Because of the thick hair and quills, I couldn't see where the brain area of its head was. I put my gun against what I guessed should be about right and fired. It was difficult to butcher because the skin didn't pull away from the flesh cleanly and I had to watch out for quills. It had many tapeworms inside its abdomen, so after cleaning it I washed my hands and my knife thoroughly in a strong solution of Lysol. Naturally I will cook the meat very well.

This morning I went wading in the snow for a couple of hours. When I got back I boiled the rest of my porcupine (heart, liver, kidneys, a few lumps of fat, and a large clot of blood taken from the chest). I ate the kidneys and part of the liver, which were delicious. I also ate part of the blood clot, which tasted good enough but had a dry texture that I didn't care for.

After first thaw, dynamite blast began booming all over the hills. Occasionally audible at my cabin. Exxon conducting seismic exploration for oil. Couple of helicopters flying over the hills, lowering a thing with dynamite on cables, make blast on ground. Instruments measure vibrations. In late spring I went and camped out, hoping to shoot up a helicopter in the area east of Crater Mountain. This proved harder than I thought, because a helicopter is always in motion. Only once had half a chance. Two quick shots, as copter crossed a space between trees. Both missed. When I got back to camp, I cried, partly from frustration at failing. But mostly from grief about what is happening to this countryside. It is so beautiful. But if they find oil, disaster.

11

"Okay, flush!" Sammy Fernandez was teaching me how to pass things through the toilet. You run a line on the riser, to send things up or down. Burritos. Twinkies. Cigarettes. Pruno in a shampoo bottle.

Sammy and I were sharing a cell in administrative segregation for the next ninety days, the punishment we both got for refusing officers' commands. We were in a six-by-eleven-foot room with a toilet and two concrete beds with plastic mattresses. We talked to each other, and took turns standing at the little window in our door to watch the hallway, otherwise known as Main Street, where, if you were lucky, you could see some other person on ad seg being hustled to the showers in handcuffs with two cops behind her, which is ad seg protocol. We were confined twenty-four hours a day, except for the two times a week that we each got taken down the hall for a shower, and once a week when we were given an hour of yard time in an outdoor cage.

Death row was underneath us, in the same building. The cops call them "grade A." They say it about fifty times a day and probably the prison administration thought it was bad for staff morale to say "death row" over and over.

On our plumbing riser, one floor down, was an old friend of Sammy's, Betty LaFrance. Betty LaFrance, like the other women on death row, had access to canteen and contraband. We had access to Betty, through the toilet and the air vent, and thank goodness, because Betty did not speak to just anyone, much less transmit burritos or bunk-distilled liquor. She and Sammy had been in county jail together years earlier, when Betty was fighting her case.

"Is that my Chicana child? Sammy?" she'd shouted to us through the air vent on the first night. Betty had her black babies and her Chicana children and Sammy was her favorite.

Betty had been a leg model for Hanes Her Way pantyhose. "Her legs are insured for millions. Her foot has that curve under it like a Barbie doll, but it's real." Sammy said Betty had stiletto heels in her cell on death row. She paid a cop hundreds to smuggle them in, just so she could put them on now and again and admire her own legs.

Hundreds. Millions. You can't believe anything people say. But what they say is all you have.

Leg model or not, Betty's pruno, like all pruno, looked and smelled like vomit. The garbagy smell of pruno is so distinct that when people are brewing, they disperse baby powder in the air of their cell to mask the scent.

"That's the best hooch at Stanville but you got to double-decant it, honey," Betty shouted to us up the air vent. "Don't forget to decant. It's got to breathe."

She made it the usual way, with juice boxes poured into a plastic bag and mixed with ketchup packets, as sugar. A sock stuffed with bread, the yeast, was placed in the bag for several days of fermentation.

Betty sent up a wineglass next, the plastic kind with a screw-on base.

"Where the hell did she get this glass?"

"The regular way," Sammy said. "The vault or canoe."

Women smuggled heroin, tobacco, and cell phones from

visiting inside their vaginas and rectums. Betty was smuggling plastic stemware.

Sammy and I passed the pruno back and forth, and she told me Betty had arranged her husband's murder to get his life insurance. You don't talk about people's crimes. But Betty was different. Death row was different. They were the big celebrities of Stanville, and celebrity gossip has a role.

The hit man who killed her husband was her lover, but while she was waiting for the money to come through, Betty worried he was turning on her, so she had her hit man killed by a dirty cop she met at a bar in Simi Valley. She was going to have the second hit man—the dirty cop who'd killed the first hit man—knocked off when they caught her. She was afraid he'd squeal, or threaten to, and blackmail her. They were in Las Vegas, partying on her life insurance money. She asked a security guard at the El Cortez casino if he would murder the cop for a payoff.

"Honey, it was NOT the El Cortez," Betty yelled up the vent. "It was Caesars Palace. And honestly, if you're going to tell my story and you don't know the difference between Caesars and the El Cortez, there is just so much else you can't know. The El Cortez is for off-duty limousine drivers and Filipinos. Got nothing against them. Should have hired one to get rid of Doc while I had the chance."

Doc was the dirty cop, Sammy said.

"He's tried to take a bounty on me about five times. You'd think a woman on death row could get some peace. Be left alone."

Among the evidence that led to Betty's conviction was a photo of her lying nude under a pile of money. The photo was taken by Doc, the dirty cop, just after she got her husband's life insurance payout. Betty loved money, Sammy said, and had slept with a pillow stuffed with bills in county jail. She asked Sammy to guard her pillow when she went to court. Sammy said she felt like a queen, to think that a high-class person like Betty LaFrance trusted her with her pillow full of money.

Betty and Doc had been arrested in Las Vegas. Sammy knew the stories but any new audience for Betty was worth a repeat. She told us through the vent about the Nevada jail where she was held before they extradited her back to California. She said the girls there—the gals there—all worked. Every female in the Las Vegas county jail had to count playing cards, put them in proper order to make decks for the casinos. They made her do it, she said, and her fingers got terribly chapped.

We were buzzing by then from the hooch.

"Did she ever show you that photo, of her with the money?" I wanted to see it.

She had not, but Sammy said Betty had a whole file on herself down there, all the articles that had appeared in the newspapers, her trial transcript, everything. Her case was a big deal, big news, Sammy said. Betty hiring multiple hit men, the cop implicated in a lot of other cases, major scandal with the LAPD. Sammy shouted down to Betty and asked if we could look at the photo. All I wanted in my drunken state, my full set of hopes and wishes, was to see this picture of the person whose voice I heard through the vent, a woman covered in money. But really I wanted to see anything besides the concrete walls of our tiny cell.

Betty refused to send the photo through the toilet. She was afraid it would get damaged. You can wrap things tightly enough in plastic that no water seeps in. We send ice cream sandwiches from canteen through the toilets, wrapped in Kotex as insulation, then plastic wrap. She was playing hard to get. Sammy asked McKinnley, the sergeant working ad seg that night, if he'd pass a book from Betty for her to read. Everyone called him Big Daddy. "I got to finish it, Big Daddy," Sammy said. "I read every chapter but the final one, last time I was back here." If he said yes, Betty could slip the photo into the pages.

"I can't do any passing, Fernandez. You get caught with property that ain't yours, they're gonna add time. You know that. I don't like to see my little girls suffer back here. Just follow the rules, Fernandez, and you'll be mainlined soon."

"Big Daddy," Sammy said, "I wish you'd been my father. My whole life could have gone different."

"Now, Fernandez," Sergeant McKinnley said, "I'm sure your own father did the best job he could."

We heard his boots moving down the hall.

"I never knew my father!" Sammy called after him, through the food flap. "My mother didn't know him, either! She's not even sure who he was!"

Betty heard us laughing and that was what did it. She was no longer the center of attention and agreed to flush up the photo.

After we got the thirty layers of plastic wrap unpeeled, Sammy unfolded a newspaper article that featured the incriminating image. I had pictured a classic nude with a bikini of hundred-dollar bills, the long tan legs insured for millions.

The image was of a woman lying on a bed stony as a corpse, with an enormous landslide of money crushing her, only her head emerging from the pile. She looked as if a gravel truck had backed up to the bed and slid its multi-ton load over her, entombing her in money.

We didn't either of us say a word. Sammy folded up the image, rewrapped it, and sent it down the pipes.

Our once weekly yard time was not a real yard, just the ad seg yard. A small concrete area wrapped in razor wire. But we got to see Conan out there, on his own adjacent razor-wire concrete patch. Conan did push-ups and talked to me about cars. It had started when Conan asked where I was from.

"Frisco, huh," he said, "where they were doing that extended-axle thing back in the nineties. Pokers. Man, you guys have something to answer to."

To say "Frisco" is as goofy and wrong as an extended axle, but Conan was right. It was as if one morning I'd woken to discover that every neighbor on my block had extended their axles, so that the wheels of the cars stuck out on both sides. Now it was a distant memory, something unfashionable. That was before I'd moved from the avenues downtown, when the city was invaded and I could no longer afford anything but a place in the Tenderloin. Extended axles were no less important than any other memory we made the subject of our talk: life as we had known it.

Conan and I reminisced about big rims, floater rims, spinners. Neon undercar kits. Holley carbs and Hemis. Popular trucks and SUVs. The Chevrolet Intruder. The Dodge Rendition.

The Intruder, Conan and I agreed, looked like something that was designed to be inserted in something else.

"There's a new Nissan coming out called The Cube," Conan said. "You can only get it in Japan. But who wants a square car? The Cube. Now there's an aerodynamic concept. Nissan makes these trucks you can hacksaw the catalytic converter off in three minutes. I can't walk past one without stealing the muffler. I should sue the manufacturer for forcing criminal behavior on me."

We laughed about the Smart car. Those looked to me like the cap on a furniture leg. A blunt vertical thing that scooted around.

"What did you drive?" Conan asked me.

"Sixty-three Impala," I said.

"Dang."

"Hell yeah," Sammy said. "That's my girl."

But the moment I said it, the fun cracked to pieces. I had no car anymore.

"You know what I hate is when people put open headers on

104

an Escalade," Conan said, as I tried to steer my thoughts back, to listen, to not care about anything. "Fuck Escalades. Something about them is plastic, cheap. I'd take an El Dorado, though. The seventies is the end of good American cars. We used to make trucks in this country. Now we make truck *nuts*."

"Those ugly things dangling over the road at eighty miles an hour? I didn't know they were called that."

The idea that men would want to display an artificial scrotum—the most fragile part of a man's body—on the back of their trucks, I said it made no sense and Conan agreed.

"Where is the pride in towing those from a bumper? If I was a dude, I'd tow a big-ass trailer with a Harley on it," Conan said. "Or I'd just ride a Harley."

"I heard you bragging to McKinnley that you *do* ride a Harley," I said.

"That's what I mean. If I was a dude I'd be like I am right now. 'Cept not locked up."

Sammy told us she'd owned a Trans Am at age fifteen. Her dealer and boyfriend Smokey had given it to her.

"I know a Smokey," Conan said.

I did, too. Not personally. The Smokey I knew of was Smokey Yunick, the NASCAR builder. Smokey Yunick was someone Jimmy Darling and I had bonded over. Smokey Yunick cheated in all of his NASCAR innovations but everyone else did, too. Also, when he was a young stock car racer, he raced with one arm out the window, resting on the sill. Smokey Yunick had swagger. But Smokey Yunick was dead. I was in prison. Jimmy was wherever. With some other woman, no doubt, and whoever the other woman was reminded me of what I was not. Was no longer.

Conan said, "It ain't Smokey from Bell Gardens you're talking about, is it?"

It was, Sammy said.

"Smokey was your *boyfriend*? I'm from Bell Gardens, and the Smokey I know is a she."

"I didn't know that when I met him," Sammy said. "This fine-ass guy wearing, what are they called, those little white shells around his neck, shows up and we're partying—he's got a bottle of PCP—and the next thing I know I'm in a motel in Whittier, and it's two days later."

"Puka shells," Sergeant McKinnley said over the PA. He was in the program office, behind one-way glass, listening to our conversation with long-range microphones.

"I wake up with no memory of how I got there. I'm covered in hickeys, and this person Smokey is sleeping next to me. We're both, like, we don't have our clothes on. I peek under the sheet and he was the same as me down there. I was shocked. We were together for two years after that."

Smokey could hot-wire any vehicle. "She would steal a car, we'd party in it, wipe off the prints, and dump it." Once they were in a fight and Sammy was trying to buy heroin at the hamburger stand in Compton. Smokey came revving up in this horribly loud cement truck, the mixer on the back revolving full tilt. Sammy yelled over the grinding noise for Smokey to shut it off. "I could not score with a cement mixer next to me, so I start walking away, to lose her and that noisy thing, and Smokey's driving it the speed of my walking. No dealer was going to sell to me, creating a scene like that. I'm yelling turn it off, the what's it called, the spinning thing, and she's going, 'I don't know how.' All she could do was put it in gear and drive it. We were yelling at each other and finally I got in so we could fight in private. We go driving around in this cement mixer, and we're starting to get along. I'm not mad anymore. The driver had left his lunch box on the seat. I opened it thinking I'd drink his juice and eat his sandwich, whatever he had in there, and inside the lunch box is the dude's wallet. Smokey and I got in a fight all over again. She had this crack idea that because she hot-wired the cement mixer, the wallet was hers. Nuh uh. Sorry. I took the cash and got out. Our relationship had a lot of drama to it like that. Different ideas on things."

When the prison went on lockdown we got no yard time. Sometimes this was from fog. Other times, staff shortages. My third week, it was because a minimum-security prisoner walked off the almond orchard. You have to have sixty days remaining on your sentence to get a job in the orchard, which is outside the prison. The girl who made that decision was blowing everything. Betty learned about it on her television and shouted the news through the pipe. The girl was picked up at her mother's house. She'd gone straight home. Sammy told me no one had ever successfully escaped from inside Stanville.

"A lifer named Angel Marie Janicki almost did. She got close. I mean this close."

She had clothes stashed on the yard, a mechanic's jumpsuit and baseball cap, to disguise herself as one of the contractors working on-site. Someone had gotten her a pair of wire cutters. On a day of milk-thick valley fog, she worked in a blind spot of the guard tower, along main yard. Cut a hole in the fence, passed through, took off walking. A guard leaving the prison saw a figure on the side of the road and was suspicious. The roads around the prison were not for human beings. They were for unmanned industrial agriculture and prison-bound vehicles. She was caught within minutes. Now Stanville had an electrified fence. Electrissified, as Sammy put it. "You'll frizzle-fry if you touch it."

"What about hiding in the lockbox of a work truck?" I asked.

"You don't think they check those? They search every vehicle."

107

"Underneath, then. Strap yourself to the undercarriage."

"They have mirrors on rollers. They check under every vehicle. Unless you've got a lover with a helicopter who can shoot out the guard towers and land on the yard, you're not getting out. Or maybe if you faked a serious medical emergency and got taken to the hospital in Stanville, and had an entire crew waiting there to bust you out with grenades and assault weapons *and* a helicopter, and they also had a new passport, cash, everything you'd need, ready and planned."

Week five on the ad seg concrete yard, Conan told us about being classified male.

"I was at a station somewhere in the valley, where they put me with the homies and I knew to let them make their mistake. You never correct, because their wrong might be your right. You wait, see how it's going to play, see if you are getting some angle from their fuck-up. After half a night there, they rode me downtown. There were so many people processing in when I got to IRC that if you weren't a K-10 they were practically waving you through. I had a lighter and they didn't even see it. Just flashed at my crack and said next. I got interviewed and they asked am I gay. I said yes: always be truthful when you can. They're asking me what clubs do you go to, what's upstairs, and I'm guessing, but answering correct. What's the bouncer's name, the cop goes. Rick, I say. Are you sure? he asks. Yeah, I say, but I had guessed wrong, and the cop says, Get the fuck out of here. Only real faggots get the gay dorm. No Zumba for you, buddy. The cops kept saying that to me. No Zumba for you. Like I got caught up so I could take a Zumba class in the LA Men's Central Jail. I don't even know what Zumba is. I was given the regular dark-blue counties instead of the baby-blue powder props, and put in general population. It turned out fine. I had a cool cellie, guy named Chester. I helped him scavenge a piece of ventilation grate from above the shower because I was the tallest person on that tier, and in exchange he had my back. Men's jail is better in a lot of ways. Better food. Good gym equipment. Great library. More phones, stronger water pressure—"

"You showered and no one noticed you weren't a guy?" I asked him.

"The men's joint was jumping off," Conan said. "People had to stay ready for fighting and riots. Everyone took showers in their boxers and work boots.

"Suge Knight was in when I was there. The guards said he had eighty thousand dollars on his prison books. That's a lot of cup of noodle. A lot of deodorant."

What did Chester want with the ventilation, I asked.

"He was making a spear," Conan said. "That was the new thing down there, a spear with an extender bar you make out of rolled Bibles."

What was he going to do with it? I asked.

"I don't know. It's not your job to wonder about other people's business. Man, you would not last one minute in a men's joint, asking fucked-up questions like that."

From Men's Central Jail, Conan was transferred to Wasco State Prison. At Wasco, going through work exchange stripout one day, they figured out he was biologically a woman. He was put back on the bus, reprocessed at women's county, and taken to Stanville.

One morning McKinnley yelled through the door that my GED prep session was that afternoon.

"When staff come back here after lunch I want no monkey business, Hall."

I had not signed up for the GED, which is the only continuing education offered at Stanville. I had graduated from high school. I was not a bad student when I made the effort. I thought of what Conan said. You don't correct. Their wrong might be your right.

That afternoon, I was taken from the cell. It felt like freedom to be chained and hustled down a hallway after weeks of confinement. I was placed in a birdcage in the ad seg program office and left to wait, listening to the stutter and clank from the sewing machines on death row.

"You study real good, Hall. You prove everybody wrong. Show the world you ain't all bad."

McKinnley clomped down the hall in his huge boots.

If I'd understood how much guards hated civilian staff, I might have been nicer to G. Hauser, which was the name on the ID pinned to the GED instructor's shirt. The guy sat down in a chair next to my birdcage with a stack of worksheets. He was about my age or a little older, with a non-ironic mustache and ugly running shoes.

"Let's start with something simple." He read the first question on the math worksheet. "Four plus three equals (a) eight, (b) seven, (c) none of the above."

"You've got to be fucking kidding me."

"Is that (a) eight, (b) seven, or (c) none of the above? It sometimes helps to use your fingers, if you need to count it out."

"It's seven," I said. "I think we can move to something more challenging."

He flipped pages. "All right, how about a word problem. If

there are five children and two mothers and one cousin going to the movies, how many tickets do they need? (a) seven, (b) eight, (c) none of the above."

"What movie are they going to?"

"That's the wonderful thing about math, it doesn't matter. You can count without knowing the details."

"It's hard for me to imagine these people without seeing who they are, and knowing what movie they're going to."

He nodded, like my response was reasonable, not at all a problem.

"Maybe we got a little ahead of ourselves. How about we make up a question," he said. "Or rather, we take the question, and simplify it."

This guy had the patience of a genuine idiot.

"There are three adults and five children: How many tickets do they need?"

There was no sarcasm in his voice. G. Hauser was so determined to work with whoever he thought I was that I could not play along.

"If the theater lets kids in free, how can I know how many tickets they need? And, depending on what kind of people they are, what theater this is—are they ghetto, or are they squares like you? Because maybe they let in one of the adults, like that cousin, through an emergency side door, after they pay for two tickets."

I saw the plush stained carpet of the multiplex out by the Oakland airport, the one where a cousin would push in through the emergency exit instead of pay. It's probably gone, like all the other theaters I used to know. The Strand on Market, where as kids Eva and I drank Ripple wine with grown-ups. The Serra, in Daly City, which showed *Rocky Horror*. The Surf, out by the beach, where I went with my mother when I was young for a movie starring the actress I'm named after. The movie kept

111

showing the same car accident in slowed segments. I guess I asked too many questions, because finally my mother yanked me from my seat and said we were leaving. I had ruined the film for her.

"They're squares," G. Hauser said. "Like me."

"The kids all have to have tickets?"

He nodded.

"The answer is eight."

"Excellent," he said.

"You just congratulated a twenty-nine-year-old woman for adding three plus five."

"I have to start somewhere."

"What makes you think I can't count?"

"There are women here with innumeracy. Who have trouble adding sums. I can give you a GED practice test, and if you're confident you'll pass, I'll schedule you to take it."

"I don't need a GED," I said. "I'm here because I was called out here."

"You might think you don't need a degree, but in the future, when you are facing your release, you'll be glad to have it."

"I'm not getting out," I said.

He went into a calm and semi-robotic spiel about people who don't have release dates and the numerous long-termer programs for which I'd be eligible with a GED. I didn't explain that I was a high school graduate. I said I'd think about it and was taken back to the cell.

Jimmy Darling used to do math with Jackson, for fun. It started with a lesson about the history of counting, at the picnic table on the ranch in Valencia. Jimmy drew a circle on a piece of paper. "This is a stable where the man keeps his animals," Jimmy said.

He drew three circles for the animals. "What kind of animals?" Jackson asked. I guess we both liked to know the irrelevant information. "Sheep, how about," Jimmy said. "The farmer has three sheep, and they each have names: Sally, Tim, and Joe. Every morning the farmer lets the sheep out to graze. In the evening, he herds them back into the pen. Since there are only three, he can easily go over the short list of their names and confirm that Sally, Tim, and Joe are all safely back in their enclosure for the night, where they won't be eaten by wolves.

"But let's say the farmer has ten sheep, instead of three. If he names each one, he has to remember ten names when they return. He has to recognize ten sheep. Each name goes with a specific sheep. If Sally is the pregnant sheep, then he can recognize her broad belly and check her name off when she returns from grazing. But let's say the farmer has thirty sheep. Too many to name, right? So he gets a basket of rocks, exactly enough so that he has one rock for each sheep. He takes a rock out of the basket for every animal that leaves the enclosure in the morning. As each one returns in the evening, he puts a rock in the basket. When all the rocks have been moved back into the basket, he knows that all of his sheep are safely home. The sheep don't need names anymore. The farmer just has to know how many there are." He explained to Jackson that numbers started with counting and counting started with names. It was like prison, from a name to a number. Except my number was more like a name than the rock that went with the animal, because the rock could go with any animal, and my number went only with me. Although we had count every day. Count was a total count for the number of people in prison, and not by inmate numbers. So we were both: animals that did not graze, and individuals who could not be confused.

When they escorted us out for the weekly yard time, we could see down into the caged area of death row. Sammy hollered from the catwalk.

"Candy Peña, I love you! Betty LaFrance, I love you!"

Candy looked up. Her face dimpled into a sad smile. They were down there on their sewing machines, sewing a seam onto burlap, then moving the fabric ninety degrees, another seam, turning the material again to run a third seam, before tossing the piece on a pile. I didn't see Betty, who often refused to work and lost her privileges.

They sewed sandbags on death row. Nothing else. They had six machines and they sewed sandbags for flood control. If you see a pile of sandbags along the side of a California road, they have been touched by the hands of our celebrities.

Payment is five cents an hour, minus fifty-five percent restitution, and the work is repetitive and lacks the satisfaction of making even a single finished thing. They are not completed. They still have to be filled.

Who completes the bag? My guess is men. Men fill it with sand, and close up the top.

Other times when we showered they were on the two phones down there on death row, or waiting for the phones. Talking to journalists and lawyers, Sammy explained. The women on death row worked the media and were always communicating with folks in the outside world. They knew all kinds of people on account of who they were. They led people on and suggested they might consent to interviews or visits, promises they did not plan to keep. They weren't interested in doing interviews. They were interested in having people to call, people who wanted something from them; it felt good to be pursued. It was a game to get attention. A game that was not a game because it was all they had.

We were not allowed mail or phone calls in ad seg. Still, I felt lucky compared to those women downstairs talking to the *Fresno Bee*. My mother would come to the prison with Jackson as soon as I was allowed a visit, after I was done with this ad seg term, and transferred—mainlined—to general population. She would put money on my books so that I could buy what I needed, coffee and toothpaste and stamps, in order to survive. Sammy kept telling me how important it was to have someone on the outside, but I didn't let her know I had support. Or that I had two life sentences plus a six-year enhancement. It was no one's business but mine. Like in the dressing room at the Mars Room, you don't give your real name. You don't offer information. You don't talk about yourself because there is nothing to be gained from it.

Sammy had been back in ad seg the night that Candy Peña received her execution papers. Candy had to choose which method she preferred, and sign the form. Sammy listened to Candy Peña cry as she read the paper that offered her gas or injection. "We turned out our lights to protest," Sammy said, "and everyone on ad seg refused their dinner tray. It creates a lot of paperwork for the staff. They have to fill out forms for every person who refuses her tray and turns out her security light. Candy was screaming over and over. Everyone on ad seg and death row was crying. Even the guards were crying. There was one handicapped lady who accepted her dinner tray, but I think she just didn't understand what was going on. Candy chose lethal injection."

Candy Peña had knifed a little girl. She was out of her mind on meth and PCP when it happened. She prayed daily, hourly, minute by minute, at the altar she'd made in her death row cell, to honor the little girl. She cried and signed the papers and Sammy was a human if sometimes a bully and she felt for Candy. You go to ad seg and you don't stop having feelings. You hear a woman cry and it's real. It's not a courtroom, where they ask all the pertinent and wrong questions, the niggling repeated demands for details, to sort contradiction and establish intent. The quiet of the cell is where the real question lingers in the mind of a woman. The one true question, impossible to answer. The why did you. The how. Not the practical how, the other one. How could you have done such a thing. How could you.

Sammy's crime was that she'd wet the bed. She told me all about it. I know I said you don't give out personal data in prison, but Sammy told me everything.

"When I was four we lived in a trailer and there was no electricity because my mother was an addict and had to spend whatever money she could get on dope. At night, I would pee in the bed to warm it up. I got a rash on my legs. A neighbor saw my legs and called CPS."

Child Protective Services took Sammy away. She was in and out of group homes and wound up in Youth Authority, where she learned to fight. "You get a lot of skills there you'll need for prison." By twelve she was out of YA, back with her mom and turning tricks to support her mother's habit. The men liked young company. Her first sugar daddy was a bail bondsman named Maldonado. She eventually got strung out herself, was arrested, took a narcotics number, a never-never number she called it, and had been in and out of prison ever since, on sales and trafficking charges. Her mother was long dead. Many people she'd been in YA with were here at Stanville. Her network was extensive. It was a lifetime of prison connections.

Sammy had paroled six months earlier. Her time out of prison had been brief. She was eager to mainline in order to reclaim her possessions. She had a television, a personal fan, a stinger to heat water. Her friend Reebok had her eye mask. "It's got little piggies on it," she said, "and I want it back." She'd given things away but on the condition that if she returned she'd be able to repossess. She knew her leaves from prison were just that, not departures but vacations.

But she had not expected to be back quite so soon. Sammy had been released to a new husband, a guy she met through the mail. It all started with a letter he wrote, but not to Sammy. He'd written the letter to another woman inside Stanville, and that woman treated the letter as currency, something to sell to another prisoner who wanted a pen pal. People were always looking for pen pals. Someone would surely pay to start an exchange with this guy. The letter had been read by so many women when it got to Sammy that its pages were tearing on the crease lines where it had been folded and refolded. The letter and its writer, Keath Something—I never caught the last name—had potential, and so the woman who had received his letter kept raising the price. When the letter got to Sammy, bidding for it had risen to over fifty dollars. The high bidder would get the envelope with Keath's return address. Sammy told me that as soon as she started to read it she knew the letter was worth more than fifty dollars, a lot more.

"His writing was like a third grader's," she said with a grave tone, as if to suggest that such a thing denoted immense value.

"Even his own name was misspelled," she said. "K-e-a-t-h? Who the fuck spells it that way?"

Keath had victim written all over him and his misspelled name.

The woman selling the letter had used a photo of a high school beauty queen on her prison pen pal page. People put up photos they found or traded, someone's daughter, someone's cousin, someone. Not themselves. It was crucial to have runners—people who sent you money inside. One way to get runners was to find men to write to you. Keath had written to what he thought was this high school beauty queen, but was merely a woman who had used that photo. She was an elderly prisoner who'd suffered throat cancer and had a mechanical larynx. She held a battery-operated box to her neck to negotiate a price with Sammy, who offered her CD player as payment. The woman handed over the envelope with Keath's address.

Sammy wrote to Keath and introduced herself, said she'd felt an instant connection when she'd read his letter. A courtship began. She was paroling in a few months and needed not your typical runner, but someone to go home to. An apartment, financial stability, and proof of gainful employment, or the parole board would never let her free. Sammy had an old boyfriend named Rodney who might set her up at his place in Compton, but Rodney hit her, she told me, and she was done with that. Keath started to seem like the answer.

Keath said he had been in the air force and flew planes and had a good military pension. When he came to the prison for the first time, he proposed to Sammy. He was a big, lumbering, and doughy white boy with a wandering eye. She said yes but could not bring herself to let him kiss her in the visiting room. Like the rest of us, she'd done all kinds of sex work, but she couldn't let this innocent dope plant one on her cheek. She told him she'd lost her privileges and could not hug or kiss. Keath believed it. "Oh, golly, I don't want to get you in trouble," he said, "why don't we just shake hands." She paroled. They married at a county courthouse not far from Stanville, in Hanford, a dusty farming town where Keath's father sold tractor equipment. His family had fixed up an apartment for them and made everything in it blue, because

118

Sammy had said it was her favorite color. Blue curtains, blue couch, blue microwavable bowls. She didn't have a favorite color. She was just saying things to Keath that she thought he wanted to hear. She'd said blue because it was what she was wearing that day in the visiting room, like every other prisoner in the visiting room.

There she was, a Mexican girl from Estrada Courts in East LA, living in a small town in the Central Valley with a corny white husband who, it turned out, had never flown planes, never been in the air force, and instead spent all day watching car racing on TV. He said he was going to Daytona, talked incessantly about Daytona. Once a month he filled out his SSI forms with his left hand, so the government would think he was slow, even slower than he already was. His big doughy small-town family didn't know anything about Sammy, and didn't ask where it was Keath had met her. He took her to a picnic down the I-5. It was a gathering for people who liked to pretend they were fighting the Civil War. There were log cabins where women in old-timey clothes were making biscuits. Keath wanted Sammy to join the other women. Sammy had never made anything but prison spreads. She could whip up a prison cheesecake from Sprite and nondairy creamers, or tamales from canteen Doritos that were soaked in water and hand-pulped to masa. She stood awkwardly, wishing she had worn long sleeves to hide her prison tattoos. "I love your tan," one of the white women told Sammy as she rolled out her white biscuit dough. The men were firing cannons. One blew into a bugle. Keath was a pretend captain in the pretend army and won a real sword that day. He had to get rid of it, Sammy explained while they were on the long drive back to Hanford. She was a level four on parole: no firearms, and no knives over ten inches long, or she would go right back to prison. "Aw, durnit." Keath blew air and flapped his lips like a child. Like a Keath Something who lives in a dream. Gets himself a sureña from Stanville, takes her to a picnic where white people admire her tan.

But after that, Keath never took her anywhere. He only left the house himself one evening a week, Sundays, when he worked as a volunteer security guard at the Red Cross. He made a big deal about it. Always took a briefcase with him, and said it held important documents that he needed to study for his next Daytona run. It wasn't really a briefcase. It was the emptied container for a backgammon set. Once, Sammy opened it. It was filled with candy bars.

Sammy had no money, no car, was trapped with a meat-headed half-wit in an apartment next to a feedlot. Keath spent his days swiveling left and right in a chair, like he was on the racetrack that was inside his TV. He wore a shiny Daytona race shirt that said PENZOIL over the shoulder. Sammy started asking him for money. He reluctantly gave her a few ones. She would walk to the dollar store, buy a quart of malt liquor, drink it while talking to the farmworkers who lived in the shacks behind the parking lot. One night she came home drunk. Keath was swerving in his chair as race cars jerked around the track on TV. Sammy could not take it anymore. She picked up a heavy glass ashtray and beaned him with it, then ran from the apartment.

She was a fugitive with no place to go. At a railroad crossing she heard a siren in the distance. She hid behind a switching box, waiting for the sound to fade, and then followed the train tracks. She got to the freeway and stood on the southbound shoulder until she found a ride.

Sammy knew skid row, had survived there on and off between prison stints, and that was where she went. It was a place where a person could disappear if she was careful. She managed to elude arrest for several months, but eventually got picked up in a sweep. Keath pressed charges, but they never went through a divorce proceeding, and as far as Sammy knew, she was still married to this idiot country boy living right close by.

On our weekly hour in the paved outdoor cage, I spotted the GED teacher through the razor wire. He was on a path going into the ad seg housing block. I yelled a hello. He called back through the barbed coils. "Have you given any more thought to whether you want to work toward the GED?"

I said I had not.

"Let the administration know if you want to take the test. The questions were easy for you, and that's a good indicator. Although I didn't give you a reading assessment."

I know how to read, I told him. And I graduated from high school.

He nodded. "I didn't realize."

"I could have gone to college. I got into UC Berkeley." I wasn't much of a liar before I got to prison. The instinct to lie to staff and guards is automatic. They fucked with us, we fucked with them.

"No kidding, really? That's where I went to school."

I gave him a story about how sad I was not to be able to enroll, because my father was ill and so I had to take care of him. "I really miss reading," I said. "I love to read books." Not a lie.

"I'd be happy to get you some reading material, if you'd like. And now that I know you're at a higher level, it won't be GED workbooks, I promise. What do you like to read?"

"*What do you like to read*," Sammy said, imitating him, after he'd walked away. "That guy looks like a serious vic. Could be

121

your own personal Keath." Sammy made a motion like reeling in fishing line. "Do it slow, do it right, and you're looking at Keath II."

I pretended to be interested in reeling in the GED instructor, but only because I felt sorry for Sammy, who had to look at everyone as a possible victim, when victim meant savior.

The turkeys I'd seen from the prison bus the morning after Chain Night, their feathers wind-plucked and swirling in the car lanes, had not been headed for Stanville.

Thanksgiving Day marked one month in ad seg. We had our holiday meal shoved through the flap. I looked at my tray. On it sat a large and meaty drumstick. Unusually large. I had never seen a drumstick so large.

"Every year here it's like this," Sammy said.

"What do you mean?"

"Oversized Thanksgiving meat. People say it's emu."

Emus are big, ugly, aggressive birds that rise to six feet when they stretch upward. The neighbor next door to the ranch where Jimmy Darling stayed had emus. They sometimes got onto the property and wandered around. They were like people, violent and unpredictable, with brains the size of walnuts.

After the disgusting meal, McKinnley let us on the caged concrete square, a special privilege on account of the holiday. It was freezing. The sky was the bleak white of old kitchen appliances. Wind blew dust into our eyes as we sat on the ground, waiting to watch staff or guards walk by on the other side of the razor wire. Such was the excitement we lived for. A nurse ran past. Then, two more. Conan yelled, "Save a life!" The way he yelled it made their mission less of an emergency. Made it funny. Life didn't matter much. It was something for

122

Conan to yell while watching the breasts of the nurses bounce up and down.

I was hungry. I had not eaten my emu. Sammy hadn't eaten hers, either.

"If I wasn't stuck in ad seg I could have sold that drumstick," Sammy said. "Black girls will add it to stuffing mix and canned corn. I saw a black chick smuggle a big bird leg from chow last year. Got a blistering burn on the inside of her thigh."

"Why you got to be so racist?" Conan said. "Black girls this. Black girls that. Just because we run this prison."

"We could have ran this place," Sammy said, meaning Latinas, "if most of us weren't high."

"Good idea, though, to trade up for a spare drumstick, mix it with corn and stuffing," Conan said. "Maybe squeeze in some nacho cheese, add pickled jalapeños. They weren't fucking around with that piece of meat. It was serious. That was no Mortimer portion."

Mortimer was supposedly a woman at Stanville who sued the prison. Because of her, they had to serve us exactly 1,400 calories a day, so that we could not sue them for our fatness like Mortimer did. The Mortimer portion is not enough food. But instead of blaming the prison, the staff tells us to blame Mortimer, who ruined things for the rest of us by filing a 602 inmate complaint that became a frivolous lawsuit. There were a lot of rules like that, with a prisoner's name attached to them. To get medication, you stood in an Armstrong box. The Armstrong box is a red square painted on the floor around the pill counter. It's for privacy. If you were not called to the window, if you were even just walking down the hall and your foot went over the red line of the box, you got a 115, thanks to a paranoid named Armstrong.

We hated the prisoners who ruined it for everybody else, but these people probably didn't exist. Sammy told me where 602s actually went: into a paper shredder in the assistant litigator's office. I doubted a prisoner could make history, get her name attached to a new rule, when it was impossible to even lodge a complaint in the first place.

People say holidays are depressing in prison. It's true. It's because you cannot help but think of the life you once had, or did not have. Holidays are an idea of how life should be.

My last free-world Thanksgiving I had squandered. I worked day shift at the Mars Room. Men don't holiday from their addictions. Holidays are busy, because the men need to escape from their real lives into their really real lives with us, their fantasies.

No one forced me to spend Thanksgiving at the Mars Room. I didn't need the money that badly, on that particular day. Why didn't I do something with Jackson? I'd given him to my neighbor to watch. She and some friends made a meal. The kids had fun. I sat with Kurt Kennedy in a dark theater. At that point I'd eased myself into the hustle of having a regular. I was by instinct against it, but it had presented itself as a novel certainty. He would be there on my shift. He would choose me automatically. I would not scan the room and circle, waiting for someone who had decided on his lunch hour, in his dark fiefdom, the Mars Room, that I was the one he felt like paying, for company.

They get what they need or see something better, someone else, and tell you to go away. With a regular, that moment doesn't come. I was someone's choice before I even got to the theater, before he got there. Kennedy's choice. He would hand me, over the course of a few hours, several hundred dollars. All he wanted was to pretend I was his girl.

You're my girl, right? The rough, dry skin of his hands on

my thighs. The gravelly voice. He did most of the talking. He'd been shot in the leg while doing his job, and that was why he limped. He said he was a detective or something, but later he said that wasn't really true and talked for a long time about his actual job and I wasn't listening and didn't care what he did, nor if he lied or told the truth. He was on disability and had too much free time. He wanted to take me out on his boat. I hate boats, I didn't say. Sure. That sounds like a lot of fun. You have no idea how much it costs to pay for a slip in that harbor. I sure don't. It's twenty thousand a year, he said, handing me another twenty. Uh-huh. Do you like to be spanked? I want to spank you. Passed me another twenty. Sometimes his bills were new, and had a crisp, smooth feel that made me want to check to be sure they were real. Money is money. The great neutralizer: that is work, and this is payment. I'd like to make your ass red. Oh god I mean bright fucking red. Slapping it lightly with his rough hand. The lightness of his slap: he was lost in thought. If you called that thought. There would not be any spanking sessions. There was no need. I was his virtual reality machine, as I pushed my ass into his clothed lap, to empty his wallet. When the wallet was empty either he would go to the bank machine in the lobby of the Mars Room and get more or he wouldn't, but if he didn't he would be back tomorrow.

A few days after Thanksgiving, Sergeant McKinnley said there was a message for me in the program office.

I walked, cuffed, with McKinnley and another cop behind me.

At the program office, I faced Lieutenant Jones.

"You have a deceased relation," Jones said.

"Relation?"

"Your mother is what it says."

There are three thousand women at Stanville. It happens all the time that you get the wrong information, you're HIV positive, when you're not. Or they give you someone else's mail. I was sure Jones had something wrong. Or that she was tormenting me because it was her role, to torment.

I said I didn't believe her.

"Gretchen Becker, it says here. Died in a car accident last Sunday, November thirtieth."

"No," I said. "No. That can't be right."

"She and a child were both admitted to San Francisco General Hospital," Jones mechanically read. "Child sustained non-life-threatening injuries."

"That's my son," I said. "He's only seven. He doesn't have anyone else. I need to get there."

"You need to *get there*? You have two indeterminate state commitments, Hall. You aren't going anywhere."

"That's my son. He's in the hospital, I—"

"Hall, if you'd wanted to be someone's mother, you should have thought of that before."

I lunged toward the paper in Jones's hands. I had to see it.

McKinnley grabbed me. I tried to get away from him. I needed to see the paper.

McKinnley pushed me to the floor. I was restrained gently by his large boot pressing on my shoulder, holding me down. I knew McKinnley didn't want to hurt me. I could feel it. But Jones was a lieutenant, his superior. His boot pressed into me. His boot said, Your mother is gone. My mother was gone. It was just me and this, this war.

"Let me see the paper," I said. "Please."

I was not calm, it's true. When I said please, I screamed it. Please. Please. Give it to me. Give me the fucking paper.

"I used to feel sorry for you bitches," Jones said. "But if you

126

want to be a parent, you don't end up in prison. Plain and simple. Plain *and* simple."

I tried to get up. More cops were on me. I bit a hand, I didn't know whose. They pushed my head into the floor. I wedged it sideways and spit. I spit at McKinnley, and got a baton in the back of the head. An alarm sounded. The noise of the alarm bleated in my ears, and all I could do was struggle. "That's my family! It's my son! It's my son!"

I tried to lift my head, bucked upward, thrashed my feet until they were pinned, until every part of me was pinned.

II

12

Doc had been an early corruptor, among detectives at the Rampart Division of the LAPD. He was capering, as he thought of it, long before they got their bad reputation. For that, Doc thought of himself as ahead of his time. The time he was serving was life without, on the Sensitive Needs block at New Folsom.

The Sensitive unit had built-in concrete stepped seating and a broad stage on which the day room dramas took place before a set of automated doors, all blue, each with a small monitor window. Doc's cell was eight by ten like everyone else's, and like everyone else, he shared it. You don't choose your roommate. And in Sensitive Needs at New Folsom, there is a one hundred percent likelihood your roommate is a child rapist, a snitch, or a transsexual, since that's who Sensitive Needs was built to house. A transsexual cellmate—Doc would be fine with that. He didn't mind men with titties. He'd had a few, not frontally or anything, mostly fondled and explored from behind; an experience that, like everything in life, made sense in its moment. The transsexuals on his unit played powder puff softball and Doc liked watching the games just as much as the next red-blooded male. They all liked it. Who wouldn't, if you were a straight guy stuck in the joint for life with a bunch of other men? Suddenly, you've got these creatures with big asses and actual, real boobies bouncing around under their knit cotton state-issue jerseys as they run bases and jump up and down, cutely helpless at the batter's plate, or run after, and never catch, a ball that came their way. They were fun and stupid and uncoordinated and smelled good, just like women, and like women, they had pea-brains and spoke in soft, squeaky voices.

He would have bunked with one no problem. Instead he got housed with an unsavory character who had raped his own daughter. The guy said she was a *step*daughter, when Doc demanded the new cellmate's paperwork, a custom that was mandatory on sensitive yards. Okay, we all have our stories. Doc talked openly about being raped himself, as a child, by his foster father. He didn't hassle his roommate. This is prison. No one is friends. You don't need to deal with their feelings. You make rules for the cell and stay out of each other's way. Doc's rules were mostly cleaning protocols. A lot of the guys on Sensitive Needs at New Folsom had cleaning protocols. The concrete in the common area gleamed like glass, it was so polished and repolished; it was just layers of clean and gleam and perfection. The smell of Cell Block 64 brand cleaning solution in Doc's unit was overpowering. It moved beyond an omnipresent scent to a totalizing sensation, smell as the means of breathing, thinking, being. Doc, a porter on the block, had access. He had his own personal supply of Cell Block 64. He might have used it as cologne but Doc had money on his books and used actual cologne and not Old Fucking Spice, either. Good cologne by an Italian name-brand designer he can never remember. But then he remembers: Cesare Paciotti. It always takes him a minute to retrieve that name. The Cell Block 64 was strictly for keeping dust and dirt off his personal stuff, meaning his contraband. Any property in your cell, if they do a raid or extraction, and you didn't buy it and have the records to prove it, you will lose. Anything in your cell not explicitly allowed by the CDC, the California Department of Corrections, is contraband. Excuse them, the California Department of Corrections and *Rehabilitation*, a word they added just this year. But there is no new programming. There is just this bullshit letter—*R*.

Doc lies on his bunk going through his files to find a good image. There's no pornography allowed. They don't have the internet, of course. The mind is where you stash your stroke material. Doc flips through the images he keeps in store. He steps by a wide margin over the memory of the last woman he had sex with, Betty LaFrance, who put him here. He focuses on the era before she hung him out to dry.

He sees himself cruising the streets in an unmarked car. If he can get into his old life, he can jump-start a good scenario.

There was that button-nosed cocktail waitress. The bar in Eagle Rock he liked to go to, place called Toppers.

Plainclothes cop walks into a bar.

He never could remember any follow-through on that joke.

Plainclothes cop walks into a bar. Nothing more. It didn't go anywhere.

There was the night the cocktail waitress at Toppers was so drunk and high she did not take offense when Doc slipped a two-dollar Canadian bill—worth less even than two American dollars—into the side of her panties. Ha ha ha. Why was a cocktail waitress wearing nothing but panties? It was part of the mystery of Toppers. It was the only mystery of Toppers. He cracked the mystery, brought her back to his unmarked car. Pulled down the panties and put his hand against her crotch. She had used hair remover or wax and felt like a child down there, which was unacceptable to Doc, who was a protector and defender of children. The sensation of her hairless pussy alarmed him and he'd had to pull his hand away; he'd forgotten that part when he selected this file from the mental Rolodex. He'd thrown a crumpled twenty-dollar bill at her and told her to get out of his car. Now his mind is creeping into the territory of bad men and innocent children and instead of conjuring some sexy striptease thing or a woman begging him to put his cock in her mouth, he is dreaming about painting the landscape with an Uzi. Painting the whole huge landscape of child molesters.

Uzis. There was that kid in tiny, Sweet Tart–pink shorts who nicked off her instructor in Las Vegas. Everyone watched the news story on their personal TV, tens of thousands of men all over the state doing life without parole, like Doc, lying back with cheap tinny headphones connected to their world-machine, hoping to get a glimpse of the moment this child in the candy-color shorts guns down a grown man with an Uzi. The news showed her engagement, then a pause, and the instructor gives an encouraging "All right!" Like, *Way to go, this kid's okay.* And then she goes back to blasting but the news cuts away before she clips him. They never show it, but everyone on Sensitive Needs keeps watching that segment, hoping they will. As if by watching the segment, each time it replays, they produce the possibility that the news footage might, just might, by some fluke of technology, some glitch of the universe, lead straight into where it is not supposed to go, the part where she fragments her instructor's brain to meat and shards.

Doc gently steers himself away from that. He can have anything he wants. It is important to remember this when you are flipping through your storehouse. But sometimes too many choices is a tyranny.

The tyranny of choice, that's not exactly what people think of as the number one problem in prison. And yet Doc cannot settle on an image right now. His roommate will be gone until the door pops on schedule and he'd like to use this time productively.

Back to when he was still a detective, cruising undetected,

up to his mischief on a balmy night. Doc had become a great connoisseur of the bars in Los Angeles where prostitution took place in a frank and natural manner. The Polished Knob on Wilshire in Koreatown, a medieval-themed restaurant with a dungeon in the basement. Bobby London on Beverly and Western, which catered only to Korean men and LAPD, and only LAPD as bribery, and only Doc of the LAPD, and technically it wasn't bribery it was blackmail.

Cop walks into a brothel.

He could never remember that one, either.

There was Las Brisas on a rangily barren stretch of Sunset Boulevard near Dodger Stadium, where cars went seventy miles an hour. You could have sex with the bartender in the stockroom of Las Brisas, and she was gentle and maternal-sensual. She smelled of beef tamales and Fabuloso, a floral-oily fragrance that was not unlike the smell of Cell Block 64, come to think of it. His visits to Las Brisas started out with tight embraces and groin-to-groin hugs with various ladies who hookered at that establishment, but the visits always finished in the stockroom with the bartender who smelled like Cell Block 64. She squirted it in her hand and oiled Doc and herself and then they did the slippery in-out standing up, Doc pinning her against a stack of cases of canned beer. Generous lady always acted happy, like Doc's orgasm was her pride, he was her big baby boy bringing her a dozen long-stemmed red roses by coming all over the insides of her thighs.

Doc takes a deep breath but quietly because the door has popped: it will remain unlocked for the next ten minutes, on automatic timer. His roommate returns, sits down on the bunk below.

Red roses. There were red roses going full bloom outside the gates of Old Folsom, where he had served time first. He saw them through the closed and secure prison bus window, flowers that were heavy and oversized, and he was sure he was smelling them, never mind the smell on the bus of bleach and body rank. He smelled those big lazy-headed roses. They were the scent of someone else's freedom. The free world of elderly women in cat-eye glasses and cardigan sweaters. Women with upright pianos they do not play and photos of grandchildren who do not visit. Deceased husbands with pre–civil rights buzz cuts. The big, creased, flabby ears of retirees. Men with names like Floyd. Or Lloyd. The dead husbands of these elderly women with their needlepointed freedom and their perfect gatepost roses. Women who shook their heads as if saying no all the time, a tic of old age, or medication. Women who were permanently disapproving, like the ones in his own family, who did not love him and had given him to foster care.

They didn't have Sensitive Needs back then, when he first arrived at Old Folsom. People had needs, sure, but there was no unit dedicated to protective custodizing a prison population of rats and cops. He didn't wander out much. He'd gotten a threatening letter that was obviously somehow from Betty LaFrance even though she could not write to him directly, a letter in psycho blocky print from one Fred Fudge announcing that inmates on his yard would soon know he was nothing but a dirty cop. That was her thing. Come fuck me, dirty cop. And he'd gone for it. He was naive. It was her big mouth that had gotten them busted, and he was sure she was still talking to whoever would listen. He lay in his cell and dreamed of escape. The walls of Old Folsom were giant granite molars extending down into the ground farther than they rose, built by earlier convicts whom Doc resented and envied: their labor locked him in, and also, they'd been given something to do, an actual project. The American River was the rear boundary of the prison, boiling rapids with a guard tower perched over them.

"Folsom Prison Blues" had been a popular song when Doc

was young. Doc was ambivalent on account of Vic, his foster dad, who loved it and was a sadist toward young Doc. Later, as a grown-up with a shotgun bolted to the floor of his squad car, a man with weapons and badges who could no longer be Vic's punching bag, Doc heard that song again. It was on the jukebox at Toppers, and the part about shooting a man in Reno just to watch him die was a truth Doc knew better than most, because he had quite sincerely shot people for that exact reason, although never in Reno.

Johnny Cash was a cokehead, which was another thing he and Doc had in common. The singer had the creases in his face, that gaunt strained look of exertion like you see on a track athlete clearing the hurdle but it's from freebasing all night.

Vic's only addiction had been beating and raping little Doc. He was otherwise an insurance adjuster who smoked exactly six cigarettes per day and occasionally had a glass of Lancers. Vic maniacally policed his yard to be sure Doc raked every last leaf.

As a child Doc had seen Johnny Cash on television performing the famous concert in the cafeteria at Old Folsom, the very cafeteria where Doc later ate his meals when he had the courage to go to chow without fear of being stabbed. There was a riot in the cafeteria the second month Doc was at Old Folsom. Someone didn't get a big enough slice of cake and two hundred sixty men exploded in rage. The guards rushed out of the cafeteria, outnumbered. Doc went under one of the spider tables and watched the floor as utensils, blood, and bits of food hit it. The metal meal trays were used as head-smashing instruments, practically made for that. The cops came back but on the perimeter, the narrow fenced outer lane, separated from the cafeteria by a shatterproof wall. They were suited up in riot gear. They threw a tear gas canister into the cafeteria. Someone, a prisoner, caught the tear gas canister and threw it back out. It started to spew, in that small lane populated by cops bulked up in riot gear, squeaking and pushing to get past one another and away from the gas that was choking them. The prisoners roared, even as the gas leaked over the wall back into the cafeteria and made them cry, too. Tear gas cry.

What Doc liked about the bartender at Las Brisas was a sense of radical acceptance she offered. Sometimes ejaculating all over someone is a way for that person to communicate to you that they take you completely and totally as you are.

And there was the old man who sat at the bar at Las Brisas, and winked at Doc as he exited the stockroom, and no he was not a pimp, he was just an old Mexican man with a baked sundial face who liked to sip his Tecate and wink at the men and his wink said, I'm happy to see what I see and know what I know.

Guy goes on a blind date. Doc had that one, the blind date joke.

Guy named Richard goes on a blind date with a woman named Linda. They set it up over the phone. This Linda says, "Meet me at the soda fountain." The guy Richard goes to the soda fountain and waits.

A young woman walks up to him. "Are you Richard?" she asks.

He says yes.

She looks him over. Says, "I'm *not* Linda."

Doc was once married to a girl from Bulgaria. A temporary arrangement was how he later thought of it. He could never really justify or understand why he'd married her. He would fuck her now, if he had the chance. He imagines lifting the Sears nightie he'd bought her long ago, and putting his dick into her and moving it around. Sex was so simple he didn't understand why people had hang-ups about it. He liked to screw. He never had a problem with it. The girl from Bulgaria was deathly quiet while they had sex, which had creeped him out a little. She didn't even breathe differently while he pounded into her, reaching his critical point, when he was going to explode and put his snow on her belly. Doc is thinking about that now, as his roommate shifts in his bunk below. He's not thinking about why she was quiet. That does not concern him in the slightest. He's recalling what it felt like to pound into her.

It's very sad how normal it becomes to masturbate in broad daylight with your cellmate right there in the bunk underneath you, Doc almost does not need to tell you.

Sometimes, in the middle of the night, Doc thinks he can hear the entire cell block whacking off. A low chorus of wet rhythms. Gross, you are probably thinking. Doc would like to remind you these are human beings. Blood rushes into their penises whether or not they are incarcerated, and when a human penis is engorged and there's no imminent possibility of sex, the male human will instinctively wrap his fist around his engorged member and pull on it in an up-and-down motion.

Which makes him think of that joke.

It's the only joke he can ever completely remember. All the jokes that come and go—horse walks into a bar. How many cholos does it take to—To what? He can't even remember the opening.

In all his years, only one joke ever lodged reliably in his mind.

Guy and his wife are having marital problems. They don't screw is the problem. So they go to a what do you call it, a sex therapist. The therapist says it sounds like they aren't good at communicating their needs. The man and his wife agree that it's embarrassing to talk about sex. The therapist suggests they build a language of physical cues, a way to let the other person know when they're in the mood. The wife says, "Okay, honey, how about this: if you're feeling frisky, pat me on the stomach twice. And if you're *not* in the mood," she tells him, "pat me on the stomach once." The husband says, "That sounds good, dear. One pat, I'm saying not tonight; two pats, let's get this party started. And here's the code for you: if you feel like fucking, rub my dick one time. If you're not in the mood, rub it one hundred times."

The guys at Rampart referred to the Bulgarian girl as Doc's mail-order bride, but no one from the outside ever understands about two people and why they get together. He was twenty-three years old, a rookie just out of the Police Academy. She asked him for directions on the street. He liked her dimples and how she could barely speak English. He gave her a ride where she was going and got her phone number. She was like an orphan in a huge unknown country. Doc adopted her, for a while, and she was good at cooking and cleaning. But she sulked a lot, and he realized quiet people can control you just as effectively as loud ones. They do it differently is all. He got tired of the sulking and crying and ended it.

He was divorced at age twenty-seven and planned never to marry again. He enjoyed women and had quite a few. Didn't love any of them. Had not loved the mail-order bride. Ten years after his divorce, he met Betty LaFrance and fell for her. Fell hard, for this woman who neither cooked nor cleaned and made a great deal of noise when he fucked her, although it might have been theater, and what was the difference? In what way would such a difference matter? The point was to get off.

In a twisted way he misses Betty, even if he would love to have her murdered. He's tried, but it seems impossible. She's on death row and there is no way to get at her because women are too stupid to commit inspired acts of prison violence. In a men's joint you can put a hit on anybody. People will do it for cup of noodle. They'll kill for payment in bars of Irish Fucking Spring (smells good, makes a good jerk lather). But the only women who can get to Betty are the other sad psychos on death row, who probably lie around whining and crying, while the men exhibit resourceful qualities like filing a locker hinge to a chest-immolating point, or embedding a razor in a toothbrush handle so they can tomahawk someone's face off.

Betty, though, was a can-do broad, unlike most broads. In a way it was why he'd liked her. If he needed to put out a hit, Betty would be the one female who might be capable of such a thing, but since she was the target it wasn't an option.

Betty used to nag him that his women issues were a mother issue. But what did Betty know about Doc's mother? Doc himself knew little, since he'd only lived with his mother until age five. He remembered asking her what she did for her job because she was always bringing him to strange men's homes and leaving him to sit on a couch by himself for what felt like small eternities. "Favors," she'd told him. "I do favors."

Betty had said she wanted his baby but it turned out her uterus was broken. Or maybe his cock was broken. He means it worked fine for fucking, but she didn't get pregnant even though he aimed his scrizzle inside her plenty of times for the sake of a possible Doc junior. (Normally, Doc would prefer to ejaculate on a body, or, ideally, a face.)

Horse walks into a bar.

Horse walks into a bar and the bartender says, "Why the long face?"

Rub it one hundred times. The hilarity of that joke never dimmed for Doc, even though sometimes you wanted to do the rubbing all on your lonesome. In prison there's little choice in whose hand beyond your own unless you want another man grabbing your cock. He once gave a hand job in here and if you're a not-gay man and you've never done it, whoa are you in for a surprise. Another man's erect cock to a straight guy feels like a root vegetable. Women are used to it and every guy knows the feel of his own hard cock, but with your own, you don't feel *it*, you make *it* feel. When Doc touched someone else's member, somewhat like his own, but not his own, it sent him into bio-feedback brain-scramble. He pulled his hand away and did not go through with the act. It was one of those powder puff softball trannies. She was a pretty Latin honey, and he wanted her to beg and whimper and throw her head back like an actual lady might. It would be something different in a place where there is almost no variation from day to day, but then the chick had a huge erection in her pants and he doesn't like to think about it, but sometimes he lets himself think about it, to remember not to do it again.

The only penis he touches is his own. He is touching it now. Most men whack off most days. Then you wipe away the tears, the evidence, and everyone knows, and no one knows, and the truth is, you actually cannot hear that kind of activity on a collective or choral scale in Doc's unit. The stroking and jerking are just something Doc assumes, which is how many kinds of knowledge function: you don't wait for the empirical evidence. In this case you don't want it, either. You know. You just know.

Betty had this way of challenging him to be a son of a bitch. She liked low-down dirty people and had a special thing for cops. She and Doc drank a lot, did a lot of cocaine. Betty liked to eat hers. He never had met anyone else who did that, ate cocaine; he himself preferred the efficiency of injecting it.

Coked up and in love, he had stupidly assured her he was the dirtiest of cops. It was how they related. It was pillow talk. Stupid words people say to each other in the sack, about various abuses of their power, shit they got away with, people they'd killed.

Betty, facing the death penalty, dredged forth everything Doc had ever told her. He was convicted for the killing of Betty's original contract killer, and for another contract killing he'd been involved in years earlier, of the manager of a gentleman's club. But there were two more people whom he'd wasted, although they had no proof on those, could not convict. One was a guy no one misses. The scumbag had just raped his own five-year-old son. A neighbor, fed up with the abuse, had called 911. Doc was the first officer to arrive on the scene, guy wasn't even done zipping up his pants. Kid crying, bleeding from his anus. Doc told the suspect to relax, and as soon as he put his hands down Doc started firing.

The joke about Linda and Richard was actually Doc's own. His story. But when he told it, people always thought he was kidding. He was in high school when that happened. It was a single experience but his whole adolescence, the life of Richard Lyn Richards, aka Doc, could be summarized in that moment of humiliation by a girl named Linda at the soda fountain on Magnolia Street in Burbank. You could fit his life story on the head of a pin. I'm not Linda.

Floyd and Lloyd were real people. Brothers who were married to Doc's two great-aunts. One of Doc's few recollections of those unfriendly old women and their brother-husbands was a joke he sometimes tried to tell. Floyd had a peach and took a bite. He turned to Lloyd and said, "This peach tastes like pussy. It's incredible." The juice rolled down Floyd's chin. He handed the peach to Lloyd, who took a bite himself, but spit it in the grass. "Tastes like shit," Lloyd said. Floyd told Lloyd he had to turn the peach around, that he'd bit the wrong side. Doc gets confused. The joke has to be told like a scene but it's not a real scene that he witnessed as a boy. Floyd and Lloyd, his uncles by marriage, never spoke to each other. They were men of zero words to anyone, ever. They were men who lay watching TV, making women and children feel skittish and in trouble for existing. Plus, another thing, and everyone knows this, it is not about Doc's tragic family, it is universal: peaches are delicious, truly delicious, and they do not, he repeats, *do not* taste like shit.

13

My cellie Romy got transferred but I didn't know where. Big Daddy refused to tell me. "Mind your own business, Fernandez," he kept saying.

I was alone now. Another lady on ad seg claimed they'd moved Romy to suicide watch. I didn't believe her. Ad seg is a big rumor mill of people locked away and shouting through their door. Big Daddy would not do me any favors. I couldn't even get any books to read. He was just, "No passing, Fernandez. Nuh uh." Probably he was trying to get promoted.

One year I read eight Danielle Steel novels in ad seg. She did a prison novel that is straight-up killer. Everybody was reading it. We tore the book into sections for passing under cell doors, and it was all people talked about. It blew through the prison like a forest fire. It never occurred to me it was odd women in prison would want to read about other women in prison. You want to read about a world you know, not just ones you don't know.

I had nothing to do, and no one to talk to. I was tired of Betty LaFrance shouting up the vent. I was eighteen years old when I met her, and she'd impressed the hell out of me. She was rich and called everyone "darling." Taught manners to women at the county jail. But that was decades ago and you get sick of people. I'll always love Betty because she's part of my history, and she's just too trippy and weird not to like. But sometimes you want her to quiet down.

She kept yelling up through the air vent about her latest plans. She said she was finally going to get back at the rat-faced cop. I told her to hush. But she can't. That's Betty. She started rambling about the Bible. When I was young and stupid, Betty had me convinced the Book of Daniel is really about aliens coming to Earth. She spooked the hell out of me. This time, her ramble was all about Judges. "Hey, Sammy. What's sweeter than honey and stronger than a lion?" She kept asking me that through the vent pipe. "Sweeter than honey, and stronger than a lion?"

I didn't know what she was talking about. She's better when it's just about money, or her legs that are insured for millions.

"The lion is killed by Samson," she said. "He opens the lion's body and there's a beehive inside. Bees make *honey*, see?" She said "honey" like it was the key to her riddle, and now I was supposed to understand everything. Like honey was some kind of code.

"There's honey in the carcass. Sweet honey," she said. "But you don't get it unless you kill the lion. First, you have to kill the lion. I put a hit on him. I got him cornered."

She started talking about the war, but I had tuned her out.

"Are you even aware we are at war?" she asked, after I'd stopped responding.

"I know about it," I said. But I didn't know much. In county lockup there's no news on the TV. Too dangerous or something. They give us reruns of *Friends*. Everyone in jail loves *Friends*. The characters are practically our bunkies.

"There are American soldiers over in Iraq," Betty shouted, "protecting *your* freedom."

"They can have my freedom," I yelled back. "It sucks."

When I was in county, someone on my tier heard from her family that we'd invaded Iraq. I went around asking people if they knew where that is, and not one lady knew. Even the educated people in jail didn't know. It's like these places don't exist until we bomb them.

Betty started bothering the guard downstairs. I could hear her through the vent, asking him to pray with her for the troops.

Talking to Romy got me thinking about the past. I dreamed one night about the Snooty Fox. I was walking along the balcony outside the rooms. It was daytime and I could hear the traffic on Figueroa. I kept passing rooms with the Do Not Disturb sign on the doorknob, the curtains closed. I came to a room with an open door. The room was vacant and clean and I went in and shut the door and lay down on the bedspread and fell asleep. I think prison makes you so tired that in the very best dreams you have, you're actually sleeping. That's what we dream about. Sleep. When I woke up, I felt like I had gotten much better rest than usual. After Big Daddy put my breakfast through the flap, I shouted to Conan on the end of the tier, told him about my dream. I said I feel like I got double sleep, since I was sleeping in my dream at the Snooty Fox.

Betty LaFrance shouted up the pipe, "The Snooty Fox? The Snooty Fox? How do I know that name? What is it?"

"It's a motel," I said.

"I think Doc used to go there," she said.

Typical Betty. Everything always has to be about her.

The Snooty Fox was my spot. The nicer rooms had a red velvety covering on the bed, and the bed was a massager. You put in coins and it comes to life underneath you. The showers had two nozzles, one in the usual place up high and another at the level of the privates. A john of mine, an old man who worked downtown at the courthouse, told me a famous president, Lyndon B. Johnson, had a shower like that, with a crotch nozzle. Lyndon B. Johnson, with a shower to wash his balls just like at the Snooty Fox.

The less fancy rooms were ten dollars an hour. I would negotiate with a john and tell him the room was twenty an hour, or thirty, and take that profit on top of what he paid me. But we were only in the room together for maybe twenty minutes. I had people coming in one after another, sometimes five customers in a single hour.

One night the Korean lady from the front office comes and bangs on the door while I was with a customer. She was yelling, "TOO MANY UNCLES! TOO MANY UNCLES!"

What's she saying? the guy asked me; he had no idea what was going on. I was laughing so hard.

Eventually I switched to the Hub Motel on Long Beach Boulevard in Compton, where they didn't bother with how many uncles I brought to the room. Long Beach Boulevard was where I met Rodney, right there in the Hub. Not the motel. The Hub was also Compton.

I was with Green Eyes and we'd both just done customers and wanted to buy a rock, but my dealer wasn't around. Green Eyes said she knew someone so we went to an apartment where this dealer lived. We walked in, and the dealer was Rodney. I thought he was the ugliest person I'd ever seen. He goes to Green Eyes, "Who's that?" pointing at me, and Green Eyes is like, that's Sammy. And he says to me in a blunt, gruff way, "You like fruit?"

I was looking at Green Eyes for a sign, like how am I meant to answer this, because we were trying to score and you can't anticipate about people until you've dealt with them a few times. I was hoping to get a signal from Green Eyes, like what do I answer? Do I like fruit? And Green Eyes whispers, "Say yes, stupid."

See, he was asking me a *personal* question. It caught me off guard. What did this guy care what I liked?

He says, "You want a orange or an apple?"

I told him I only like strawberries and watermelon, that those were my favorite fruits. We left with our rock, me and Green Eyes. Later I was sitting at the bus stop working and a car pulls up and I negotiate but the guy didn't have enough money, so I let him go. Another car pulls up all slow. The window goes down and it's Rodney. He says I could get hurt on the street and should be careful. I didn't have a customer, so I agreed to go with him to the store. He bought me some strawberries and we took them to his house. I stayed there all night, smoking rock, talking, eating the strawberries, and that was how it started. Now he has my name tattooed in twenty-six different places on his body.

Rodney was from Gonzales, Louisiana. He was in Angola from age seventeen to twenty-two. He wears a mustache to cover the scar they gave him with the switch they used for whipping the horses. He had to work planting okra. His feet are ruined from standing in water without rubber boots. When he got out of Angola they banned him from the state. He took the Louisiana with him out to Compton. He was country and superstitious. No cooking when you're on your menstrual. And his idea of clean was obsessive. It was a lot like how some people act in here, me included. I like it clean. It's a way to have some control, probably. I can laugh at it, though. It's funny that most of us were doing tricks to maintain a crack addiction, living in tents and shitting in buckets on skid row, but in here, as shot-callers, we make the other women shower three times a day and bleach the bathroom after they brush their teeth. We run the room like it's the army, with rules and inspections and yelling and abuse and I'm the one dishing it. I'll come down on you hard if there's a single drop of water in the sink basin.

Rodney used to beat me like a dog. I really did think that he did it because he loved me, that it was a form of care, like the strict side of care and love. And I was an addict. I was like every other lost girl with a dealer, girls crippled by dope, and these ballers controlling them with money and power.

Rodney had eccentricities. He was a strange person. He ate only bland foods: no salt, no pepper, no ketchup, no hot sauce. No drinking, no drugs, no rap music, no R and B. I mean nothing. He was into money. That was it. Cash. Nothing else.

In the morning I'd get up and drink a forty of Olde English. Rodney would drink a carton of milk, and that was how we each started our day. We dealt together; I worked the night shift. We had three security doors along our apartment hall, one, two, three, so no one would rob us. And we kept our stash and money and weapons in a lockbox that was in the floor, under the refrigerator, which had a panel you could lift up, to get to the lockbox. The guy who installed it was a smoker, so we paid him in rock like we paid everyone. Keep them all dirty, just like in here. I used to keep my whole room dirty, handing out free dope to my cellmates so that no one could rat on me.

Rodney was respected in Hub City but he wasn't a gang-banger. He had a card. A pass. He could deal and they let him be, as a loner and non-affiliate. Not everybody gets to walk solo like that, but Rodney was connected to influential bangers, had done a lot of favors for people and earned his status.

We dealt mostly from Rodney's apartment. We handled the sales ourselves. We never had kids on the street corner doing it, like how it goes now. The way they exploit these children. You find a kid with a clean record to sell for you. When he gets busted, he won't go to jail, since it's his first violation, but he's not useful anymore so you get a new kid. Go from kid to kid and they all get records. We dealt only in fives and tens, because the twenties were the bills that narcotics officers marked. I remember a girl came to the gate with ones and Rodney shoved her into the street and said never to try to buy from him again with her loose change.

Rodney and I had two Cadillacs. One was root beer brown and it had an airbrushed painting of me on the trunk hood, like I was the virgin of Guadalupe, and underneath it was written, "Let me tell you about the blues." I was often the only Latina in the room. I got to know a lot of black women. But I've always mixed well with all kinds of people; I'm not into hanging with one race. I can talk to anyone. Rodney would take me to the players clubs. The girls there are something to look at. They get their hair and nails done every day. If they wait a day on the hair, they sleep with their hands propped under their cheek, so their hair won't rub the pillow. You go to the club and everyone is buying bottles of Hennessy. They have strippers on the bar.

We liked to travel. We went to Vegas. San Francisco. We always dealt on our trips, and we carried weapons. We would go up to Sierra Madre, where there was an illegal shooting range, to practice. It's past the big rock up there. You have to go with the dudes who run it, on a dirt road, in their huge four-by-four. I remember it had a skull for a shifter knob. These crazy white people. They sell hot, clean guns up there. We bought SKSs from them, which came straight from Iran. The kick on those was amazing. I was a better shot than Rodney.

Sometimes we did not agree about how to do business. One morning there was a guy painting a building on the corner near our apartment. He was doing exterior work and started talking to Rodney and they exchanged information. Later the guy—a white dude—calls and says he wants to buy a large amount of cocaine but that he's stuck in Laguna Niguel and wants us to come down there. It was pretty clear to me that if he was all the way in Laguna Niguel and a serious buyer, he would have a connection there. Why did he need us? I thought it was an unnecessary risk to go there, but Rodney was stubborn about it because he felt this deal could expand his business. We went. It was a fancy area, just as Rodney had suspected. The houses had long driveways with a call box at the bottom. We get to the box and say who we are and this huge gate opens by itself, presto. We motor up to a house with a circular driveway, and the guy comes outside. He hands Rodney the money and Rodney gives him the dope. Next thing I know, these people came out of the trees. Twenty or thirty of them, all in black, with face masks. There was a gun to the side of my head. I had an unlit Camel cigarette in my mouth. It was trembling up and down; the cigarette was bobbling like crazy. I was not scared to be arrested. Fuck no. I'd been to prison twelve times already and considered it part of life. I thought this guy was about to shoot me in the head; that's why I was scared. They pulled Rodney out of the car and pepper-sprayed him. We each got eight years flat. The dude from Laguna Niguel was a rollover. He had set us up, in order to clear his own case. Showed up in court, pointing us both out for the prosecution. No shame.

Rodney never pursued vengeance on that, but he could have. What you do is hire a private investigator to find the rat. The PIs get a lot of their clients that way in Los Angeles. People think what they do is all about cheating spouses. No. Most of their business is from dealers and bangers who need to hunt someone down. Sometimes it's to transact a hit. The PIs, they know not to ask questions. They find the person and that's it, they step back because their job is done. Of course they are aware of what comes next. If it's not a straight hit, the rat gets picked up and taken to a torture garage to learn a lesson. The garages are in secret locations all over South LA. I've been to two. They hang you from the ceiling. That's not a place where you want to end up.

Rodney didn't need a torture garage to punish and control

me. Now it seems like he's old and I'm old and we don't bother with each other anymore.

After I ran away from Keath, I knew I'd get picked up. I didn't care. It's hard to live on the streets. In prison, you can be someone. Life has order if you know how to do time, and I know. I'm an expert. Living in a tent is a temporary thing. You do it until you go back to prison. That's just how it works.

What happened to me is I got tired. Being an addict is a constant hustle; it takes so much energy. When I was in county after they picked me up, I had to kick because I had no access. After I kicked, I just knew, like a light got turned on. I was going to stay clean. Life was going to be different this time around.

14

"Miss Hall, can you stop crying, Miss Hall?" If an inmate can't stop crying, they check a box on the suicide risk form. They weren't hoping to spare a life. They were trying to avoid paperwork and internal investigations.

They had taken me to a different part of the prison, the nursing facility, where no one could hear me scream, no one but the cop on duty. They were following protocols on a behavior sheet. I was alone in a strip cell, no clothes, and no sheets on the bed, on a ward where they put mental cases.

My mother had sat in the courtroom, unable to save me, but in a sense, she had saved me, by existing. Now there was no one for me, and no one for Jackson.

Those days on suicide watch, I understood how it was that someone might come to believe that the way to get back at these people would be to kill yourself. Being given only spoons and soft food, no forks or knives, forced the mind to wonder in what way a forbidden utensil might be useful. Being given no sheets or pillow summoned a question into the room, of how to asphyxiate yourself, with what, and tied to what. But I was not suicidal. I was thinking about Jackson, and what to do, now that we were orphaned.

Jackson was the grain of reality in the center of my thoughts. I could see his sweet open face, made even more open by the cowlick that gave him an old-fashioned, almost Brylcreemed hairstyle. He didn't brush his hair. It swooped naturally off his broad forehead. Jackson was handsome like his father had been. Unlike his father, he was always looking to find a way to be happy.

When we'd first moved to LA, Jackson heard the horn of the vegetable truck that parked on our street and went running outside to see what the commotion was. The man who drove the vegetable truck got out and opened the back. The old women lined up in their house smocks to buy groceries from the back of the truck. I felt like the truck was a Mexican thing, and Jackson and I would just go to Vons and shop the regular white-people way. But Jackson insisted we get in the line. We bought avocados, mangos, eggs, bread, and sausages the vendor had hanging from the ceiling of his truck, and the food was half what it cost at Vons. That was how we met all our neighbors.

Jackson believed in the world. I searched his face with my closed eyes. Felt the dewy touch of his hand in my hand. I heard his voice, felt the warmth of his body when he wrapped his arms around my waist.

I focused on the grain of Jackson, the sensation of him. Nothing they did could touch that grain. Only I could touch it, touch it and stay close.

There was no way to contact him. They wouldn't tell me anything. He needed me and there was nothing I could do. I lay in my tiny bare cell and tried to see Jackson, to visit with him.

Jackson wanted me to know things that he knew, to study what he studied, and so he tested me on columns when he learned about them in a Greek coloring book my mother gave him. If there were a bunch of designs at the top, I knew to guess, "Corinthian." He asked questions like I was someone he could rely on for the truth. "Is the heel this whole area of my foot, or just this part on the bottom?" He nodded when my answers corresponded to the world he was building in his mind, with correct names and definitions, with facts. Testing out his facts. "Mommy, that cat might not belong to anyone, because she doesn't have a collar." When a man came down Alvarado Street swinging a golf club, hitting telephone poles and then the side of the bus shelter, Jackson said the man had a problem inside his brain, that it was a sickness and he hoped the man got better.

Jones, who was my assigned intake counselor, came to check on me. Counselor doesn't mean someone who counsels. Your prison counselor determines your security classification and when and if you get mainlined to general population. Your counselor keeps tabs on you and reports to the parole board, if you are headed for parole. Counselors have enormous power over what happens to us, and they are always assholes.

I asked Jones if there was some way to find out if Jackson was okay. Was he in a hospital still? What were his injuries?

"There are privacy rules in hospitals, Hall," Jones said.

"Do you have children, Lieutenant Jones?"

"Only his legal guardian or a court-appointed advocate can verify that he's in a hospital," Jones said. "You are not his guardian, Hall."

"But who is his guardian? I need to find out the condition my son is in."

She was walking away from my cell. I adjusted my tone of voice, hoping to summon her back.

"Please, Lieutenant Jones. Please."

It was happening. I was pleading with a sadist in a little girl voice.

Jones stopped, pretended to react with decency.

"Ms. Hall, I know it's tough, but your situation is due one hundred percent to choices you made and actions you took. If you'd wanted to be a responsible parent, you would have made different choices."

"I know it," I said, tears landing on the floor of my cell. I was on the ground, on all fours, with my face to the food flap in my cell door, which was the only way to communicate with people in the hallway.

I tried to think of what Sammy might do. She wouldn't cry. It was hard not to. I vowed to quit.

I focused on getting out of the mental ward, and back to ad seg, and out of ad seg, and mainlined, so that I could try to make phone calls, find a lawyer, get information, do something.

I dreamed one night that I was in Jimmy Darling's bed, at the ranch in Valencia. Jackson was asleep on a cot. Jimmy had just had a bad dream, he said, in which the police took me away. He held on to me, glad it wasn't real. I was glad, too, but then I woke up, with caged white lights buzzing in the ceiling above me.

Jimmy didn't love me like that. When the police in real life took me away, he moved me to the past. I'd known it when I heard his voice over the county jail phone.

You can't remain on suicide watch forever, and you can't stay in ad seg forever. They need the cells for other people they want to put in ad seg. Three months after my mother died, and four months after Chain Night, I was put in general population, on C yard, in unit 510.

A unit is 260 women, on two floors with an open common area and a guard station—a cop shop—in the center. The rooms were big, much bigger than an ad seg cell, and crammed with bunk beds. Each room was designed for four women but had eight.

I was happy to learn I was in Conan's room and unhappy to learn it was also Laura Lipp's room.

She approached as I was fitting a sheet to my mattress.

"Hi there, I'm Laura Lipp and I'm from Apple Valley."

I kept making my bed.

"That's in the Mojave Desert. It's drier than any bone and there are no apples. Applebee's, though."

Laura Lipp didn't remember our eight-hour bus ride together. I didn't question it, wasn't going to insist on familiarity.

I was putting my few possessions, the photos of Jackson, into my small locker, when another roommate came in. "Nuh uh!" she yelled, looking at me. "No hillbilly bitches in this room. Get the fuck out." Her name was Teardrop. She was huge and would have destroyed me if I had to fight her, but Conan intervened on my behalf.

"She's cool. I cosign her." They went out to the hall to talk.

"Except I think the Applebee's closed," Laura went on like nothing had happened. "We've had a lot of changes. None of them for the better."

I pulled a Fernandez and told her to shut the hell up.

"The town's got history though," she said, carefully moving away, out of fist-swinging range, just in case. "It was a fine place and it's gone downhill. We used to be cowboy country. All the country and western people came because of Roy Rogers. He had a museum with a big display of all his fishing lures. He owned the Apple Valley Inn. My father took us there for Sunday dinners. It was a carefree time. There weren't problems like now. You know what people were worried about? Static cling. That was the big fear on TV and in people's hearts. Static cling."

Conan and Teardrop returned. "Don't leave nothing outside your locker!" Teardrop yelled at me, but in a slightly nicer tone, like she was resigned to letting me stay. "And nobody runs the fucking water, no tap and no flushing, until I get up in the morning."

Button Sanchez, who had the baby in receiving, was also in our room. The other three roommates were what Sammy

159

would call nondescrips. Women with short sentences, minding their own business and staying out of trouble.

How I was hillbilly and Laura wasn't, I didn't understand, until I figured out that Laura was paying Teardrop extorted rent money to stay in our room. As a baby killer, nobody wanted her, so it was possibly her only choice.

At dinner I saw Sammy in line at the chow hall and tried to talk to her. She looked at me and shook her head. A cop shined a light on me. "BUS YOUR TRAY," his voice boomed over a microphone. They give you ten minutes to eat their shitty food and you have to do it in silence. Mostly it's people who don't have money who go to chow. Teardrop only ever ate in our room, from her personal supply of canteen food, ramen bowls that she added water to and heated with a stinger.

That evening I put my name on the sign-up sheet and waited in line for the phones in the common area. People were shouting into the phones because others were shouting next to them. The signs on the cinder-block walls were the same as in receiving, that cursive plea: *Ladies, no whining. Ladies, report to staff if you are experiencing signs of norovirus.* Same dirty pink paint on the doors and railings, a color that was probably meant to relax us institutionalized knuckleheads. The line for the phones went fast because the people being called didn't pick up. I dialed my mother. My mother had an account with Global Tel Link, the company that monopolized jail and prison calls. You can't get through to a number that has no Global Tel Link account. I knew she was dead. Still, I had to try. I didn't get through. The public defenders all have Global Tel Link, so I called Johnson's lawyer but he didn't answer.

For the next several days I signed up for phone calls and waited in line and dialed the lawyer. After my eighth try I finally reached him. I begged him to help me get information about Jackson.

He said he would try, and to give him a week at least. When I finally got through to him again, he said he'd been attempting to figure out who Jackson's case manager was, but had been unable. This work, he said, was really for a dependency court lawyer.

Would the state provide one, I asked him, trying to control my tone, not sound angry and desperate.

"Oh, no," he said, and in the gap where I might have pressed him, as if he were obliged to help me, he lunged into that silence before I could and said he was extraordinarily busy with his assigned caseload, and I was not on it, and that he had to get off the phone.

As soon as I was eligible, I tried to get a prison job. That was Sammy's advice. Sammy wasn't in my unit but she was on C yard, which meant we could hang out in our free time. "White girls get all the best jobs," she said. "You can clerk, sit in air-conditioning and type letters, while us black and brown women pull used tampons from the septic tank screen for eight cents an hour. Take advantage."

It was true that the clerks were all white. I tried to clerk, too, but you had to have a clean disciplinary record, and you had to be liked by the cops.

Sammy, Conan, and I all got assigned to the woodshop, which was hiring at twenty-two cents an hour: good money. Conan bragged that with his wages he was going to invest in a tattoo rig, start a side business and do some art on himself. We were sitting in the common area, waiting for the Friday night movie to begin. They were delayed because the film that was scheduled had profanity. They had to swap it for *Driving Miss Daisy*, which they'd shown us the Friday before.

"What tattoo do you want?" Sammy asked Conan.

"A big-ass portrait of Saddam Hussein," Conan said. "Tacked

up right here." He bulged his bicep. "Just to piss off these dick-wads."

Two unit cops were trying to work the film projector.

"Support our troops!" Conan yelled.

"Shut the fuck up!" someone else yelled. The movie was starting.

Every one of my cellmates got jobs in the woodshop, except for Button Sanchez, who was too young to legally work. Her stomach was flat now. Her face showed no grief that I could see. Her baby was gone. She took classes and, after school, played with her pet rabbit, which she'd caught on main yard and trained. It had a little box under her lower bunk with shredded Kotex in it, as a litter thing. It knew where to poop. She took it to class with her, hidden in her state-issue brassiere. "I'm its mom," she said. She sewed little clothes for it. Made a leash. Snuck the bunny on main yard so it could see its cousins. It bit her sometimes, and so did the fleas and mites that lived on it. Teardrop told her to get rid of it. Every room of eight had a Teardrop. The strongest woman in the room made the rules. Teardrop threatened to roll up Button, put her and her mattress and rabbit in the hall. Button and Teardrop had a knock-down drag-out. Button was tiny and Teardrop was huge, but youngsters have a dirty advantage. They'll hit you over the head with a two-by-four if they get the chance. Button went all-out, fought Teardrop with a straightening iron. The rabbit got to stay.

"Fill up your schedule," Sammy said to me. She had known lots of women in my position. Dire as it was, it comforted me to know I wasn't alone. Others had found a way to survive it. I had been in Los Angeles county jail when the towers of the World Trade Center went down. That was right after I got arrested. We didn't have access to news, but people were getting the details from their families over the phone. Everyone was freaking out, except for one girl who said it comforted her to know she wasn't the only one whose life was wrecked. People got on her, but I knew what she meant.

"Were you guys close?" Sammy asked about my mother.

I said no.

Was she healthy?

No.

"You might've ended up needing a different guardian for the kid eventually. Things happen in the free world that you can't control."

I could take the money I'd earn working and buy stamps and start flooding state agencies with letters about Jackson, Sammy said. She would help me. The library had directories with agency addresses. "You have to start from where you're at," she said. It was her motto.

On our first day in woodshop, the prison industries supervisor told us we were going to get excellent on-the-job training skills, which would translate into employment upon our release.

"What about those of us who don't got a release date?" Teardrop asked.

"Normally you can't work in prison industries," he said. "Normally, we can't use you, because you don't need the training, since you're not getting out, and this is all about training people to work jobs. But we have a lot of orders to fill, so you've found yourself in a lucky position. You will learn to build furniture here and I can tell you ladies that a finish carpenter makes great money."

Conan was impressed with the shop. "Dang, we get to use real wood? Table saws? Miter boxes? At Wasco the woodshop isn't even real. The wood there is all compressed particleboard. You glue these pieces together. That's your only tool: glue. You can't even drive in a nail or that stuff will split and crumble. We weren't learning anything. I told the supervisor, You keep talking about finish carpentry and we don't make stuff that will teach us it. He goes, 'That's because you people are animals and if we give you tools you'll kill each other.' I ask him, What are we here to learn? And he says, 'You're here to learn how to work. To show up on time. To be workers.' As if that's a thing. We didn't learn shit at the Wasco woodshop. We huffed glue all day. Then they came up with this huff-free glue. No Huff, it was called, that was its name, No Huff Glue. You can't huff it. It doesn't do anything. No power tools, no learning curve, no drug high. It was better than the other prison industries, though. The outfit down the hall, those dudes were making safety goggles for prison industries. And next to that building, they made *boots* for prison industries."

I was assigned to a workbench.

"I'm one hundred percent Norse," my new bench partner said.

The Norse was six feet tall, with long blond hair divided into several braids. The tattooed head of a bald eagle emerged from the top of her woodshop coveralls. The eagle on her chest had an American flag in its beak. It looked mad, even madder than eagles usually look.

The supervisor put Laura Lipp next to me and the Norse.

"Can I be moved?" I asked.

"No," he said.

"Thank god," the Norse said. "Whites." She looked over at Conan, Teardrop, Reebok, the three black people I'd walked in with. "How do you feel about blacks?" she asked me and Laura Lipp.

Laura Lipp, eager for such rare acknowledgment, someone asking her a question, lunged to answer. "Oh, I try to be color-blind, but it's not always. I mean, some people have had to come further than others in order to—"

"Do you let them eat your pussy is what I need to find out."

Laura gasped. "Heavens no!"

"I run this bench and I need to know who is who," the Norse said.

"Well, since you bring that up, I agree about sexual relations, as my husband was Hispanic and that was a disaster, ruined my life, but you might be interested to hear that I fainted one evening and the girls who came to my aid were black, and—"

The Norse ignored Laura Lipp and moved toward me.

"Do you like Iron Maiden?" she asked. "That's what I play."

"We have a radio?"

"I'm the radio in this part of the shop."

That afternoon, the Norse hummed. "Run to the Hills" and "Iron Man" were on repeat. I was in high school all over again. But when she asked where I was from, nodded, and said, "Frisco, cool," I was reminded that I was very far from where I was from. I didn't ask her anything. I couldn't have been less interested in knowing details about her Nazi Lowrider brothers and boyfriends in San Bernardino or wherever. That's snobbery but there's a cultural difference. The Sunset District was not exactly classy but we were adjacent to the Haight-Ashbury, and by that proximity to weirder cultures, not straight dirtheads, even if there were among us people who became full-on white supremacists, like Dean Conte, the sad kid from my junior high who was relentlessly made fun of. Dean Conte had experimented with various solutions to being maladjusted. Nerd, new waver, skateboarder, peace punk, hard-core punk, eventually skinhead, and finally, neo-Nazi in a suit and tie. When he was a skinhead, Dean and his friends ruined the Haight Street Fair. By six p.m., when the fair was ending and loading trucks were packing up the stage and the vendors' tables, the air became ninety percent beer bottles, a forehead-height kill zone, thanks to the skinheads. Back when

Dean had still been a nerd, he invited a bunch of kids who cut school to his father's place on Hugo Street and we drank all his dad's liquor and set the curtains on fire. I forgot about that day until I saw him all grown up on television. He was on a talk show as a spokesman for white supremacy. One of the skinheads on the show threw a chair at the host and broke his nose. Dean became famous. I still saw the kid, though, in the man. I'm not justifying his ideas. It's just that he was someone I knew. He was in love with Eva and Eva was Filipino, but that had not deterred him. It's always like that. I knew a guy in high school who later went to prison and joined the Aryan Brotherhood. The guy who joined the Aryan Brotherhood had a black girlfriend and mixed kids. Things are more complicated than some can admit. People are stupider and less demonic than some can admit.

Before lunch, Laura Lipp drilled her own hand with the drill press and was sent to the infirmary. That was it for her in woodshop. The Norse said it was her punishment for marrying a beaner. The Norse had been in prison so long she didn't know that particular slur had gone out of style, was no longer used, and this made me unexpectedly sad for her.

I don't know if it was right or wrong, but Jimmy Darling and I had shared the habit of sometimes feeling sorry for bigots.

Like the lonely woman tending an empty bar, whom we met while driving around Valencia, where Jimmy taught. The challenge of finding anything notable in that strip mall hell was something we both enjoyed. One night we passed a trailer park in Santa Clarita with a shabby sign that said ADULT LIVING. Man, Jimmy said. The things you can look forward to. We speculated that maybe they had glass shower stalls in those trailers. Waterbeds. It was a place for adults. Adults only. We found a tavern on an abandoned county road that was itself almost abandoned. The bartender said she was in the process of buying the place, but didn't want a Mexican clientele.

"Mexicans'll stab you first thing, minute you turn around," she said. She asked us how we thought she might bring in more white people.

"Offer sandwiches," Jimmy said.

"Damn, that's a good idea."

She and Jimmy brainstormed about her deli. "Pickles," Jimmy said. "Potato chips." She didn't know he wasn't serious. He was and he wasn't serious.

On the wall above us in the woodshop were brochures with pictures of the furniture proudly manufactured by inmates at Stanville prison industries woodworking facility.

This is what we made:

Judges' benches. Jury box seating. Courtroom gates. Witness stands. Lecterns. Judges' gavels. Paneling for judges' quarters. Wooden courtroom cages for in-custody defendants. Wood frames for the state seal that goes in the judges' chambers, and judges' seats, which then went to upholstery, next door.

Not among the state merchandise we built, someone, some time, had crafted a child's desk, like you see in schools, with a hinge so the top can open, to store supplies inside. It had a small matching chair. The desk and chair were at the entrance to the woodshop. "That little desk makes me sad," Conan said. I trained myself not to look at it.

When thoughts moved in about my mother, dead, really and truly dead, I reminded myself that Jackson was not dead. She was, but he wasn't. I confined myself to this very small form of relief.

On weekends, Sammy and I went out to main yard. The sight of thousands all dressed alike is really striking the first time you see it.

People clustered, catching up and hanging out, playing basketball or handball. Girls brought out guitars and strummed for small audiences (no gathering in groups larger than five). Some huddled and did drugs. Others had love affairs in the port-a-potties, or out in the open, with lookouts—pinners—watching for cops.

It was summer, and the hot wind rippled our loose clothing, which ranged from the palest blue, to navy, to the granite-speckle of denim—our fake jeans. The denim is not fake. The jeans part is. They are pants sewn crudely of denim, with an elastic waistband and a single lopsided, too-small pocket, and they are not jeans as I think of the term.

Sammy and I walked the track. We passed the 213 girls, who all waved to her. Main yard has area codes, just like the state.

Signs everywhere said NO RUNNING EXCEPT ON TRACK. If you ran anywhere else they could shoot you.

"Who got her the wire cutters?"

"Who are you talking about?"

"Angel Marie Janicki."

"Man, was she fine," Sammy said. "She was the best-looking girl at Stanville."

"Where did she get the wire cutters?"

"Free-world staff. Some guy. He was under the influence. I'm telling you, she was beautiful."

Orders issued from the PA, clear and tight and loud.

"You by the bathrooms. I can see you smoking. Put that out right now."

"Lozano, you're out of bounds."

A truck circled the perimeter of the prison, on a dirt road between the electrified fence and the outer, final fence.

"Copley, you left your dentures by the handball courts."
Audible laughter from the other guards near the microphone.
"Copley, heh heh, come to the watch office to pick up your
teeth."

When it was hot, the guards mostly stayed in the air-
conditioned watch office and observed us through binoculars.
They did that when it was cold also. The yard is massive, and
they are lazy.

"Which blind spot did she use?"

"Behind the gym. That's why we have lockdowns now.
There's before Angel Marie Janicki and there's after."

"They can't see the fence behind the gym?"

"Not from Tower One. But they don't need to now. They
have the electric fence."

It took the perimeter truck at least ten minutes to circle the
grounds. Maybe eleven.

How the guards know whose dentures: the inmate number
is printed on the side, in the artificial gums.

We passed whale beach, just as the guards started breaking
up their sunbathing party.

"Whale beach, no slingshots. Whale beach I said no slingshots. Everybody up and dressed."

It's not nice to say whale beach but that's what it's called, an
area beyond the walking track where women grease up and fry.
Slingshots are homemade undershirts. You were not supposed
to bare flesh on main yard, but people did anyhow, slathered in
cook oil or the fake butter they used in central kitchen, a brand
called I Can't Believe It's Not Butter! or, as Conan called it, I
Can't Fucking Believe This Shit's Not Butter.

No one runs on the track, since this was women's prison
and we were not training to kill. No one except Conan, who
jogged past me and Sammy.

"I just slaughtered ten thousand gnats with my open mouth!"

He turned around, running backward, facing us.

"Try closing your mouth," Sammy said. "You won't have that problem."

A female cop hurried past. "No sitting on the tables!" she yelled. It was also illegal to sit under them, which was the only way to get shade on the yard. Only regulation sitting was allowed.

Conan regarded the cop angrily marching past. He nodded approval.

"Boy, was she a different lay."

At Stanville you can assume it's a lie if the person volunteers it. It's also a lie if the person says it in answer to a question. Conan's tales were as tall as Tower One and Tower Two, where armed Fudds tracked us and ate pork rinds.

"She says to me, don't just use your tongue, I want you to *hum* into me, like I'm a kazoo. That's what she said. *Like I'm a kazoo.*"

The landscaping crew was working along the edges of the track with spray bottles of Roundup. Their job was to keep the yard one seamless expanse of dirt. "We keep it real tidy," said Laura Lipp, who was now on yard crew. A top layer of bare dirt lifted and blew around, from valley gusts, as a new cop named Garcia came toward us.

All new staff are marks for prisoners and cops alike, but there was something particularly vulnerable about Garcia; he seemed lost out there on main yard, which is three yards, B, C, and D: three thousand women with six Fudds.

Fudd is short for Elmer Fudd. It was Conan who had started that.

"Hey, Fuddrucker," he called to Garcia, who halted, and looked to be trying to decide whether to pretend he had not heard Conan, or to deal with Conan as a problem.

"But what *is* Fuddruckers?" Conan said to no one in particular, his usual audience.

"The joke is that it almost makes you say fuck, right? But then what is a ruddfucker? They make this stuff up and we all pretend these places exist, like, in history. Like Fuddruckers is some kind of grand family tradition."

"My family has *always* gone there," Laura Lipp said in a corrective tone, as she sprayed with her Roundup bottle.

"We went to Hooters," Conan said.

"With your *family*?" Laura shook her head.

"My girl and her kids," Conan said. "They have a good children's menu. But hey, you ever notice the *o* in Hooters is the same *O* like in IHOP? I was a cook at IHOP. To make the pancakes, you add water to a mix. It's the International House of Just Add Water."

I had been a waitress at an IHOP right after I graduated high school. It was one of the many things Conan and I bonded over. I was waitress 43, and the cooks would call, Forty-three! Your order is up! Which, as I only saw later, had been preparing me for here.

To work at IHOP, you first go to Walmart or a place like it to get work shoes. Where you see, if you didn't already know, that most of the adult-sized shoes they sell are for working on construction sites or in hospitals, prisons, restaurants, and schools, and the children's shoes are starter versions of the same. Waitress shoes and medical assistant shoes and work boots. Cheap factory knockoffs for people whose choices are to work these crap jobs or crack up and go to a much lower grade of low-grade shoe, made by prison industries.

This new cop pulled Sammy aside and started asking her questions. He was treading a familiar road: I want to get to know you. That is how cops here do things, they all say the same thing in the same way: I want to get to know you.

There are cops and staff who want the girlfriend experience with a prisoner. Sammy already had a getting-to-know thing with the head of maintenance, a civilian who took her around in his truck, brought her staff cafeteria hamburgers, and in exchange they went to a drainage ditch where he rummaged in her state-issue jeans. She had a male nurse at the skilled nursing facility ("Sniff" is how we say it) who checked her breasts weekly, and gave her tobacco. Conan had female guards who might have been lesbians or straight girls who found Conan convincingly male.

"You remind me of someone," Garcia said to Sammy. "Back home in Philadelphia. Where you from?"

"Philadelphia, huh," Conan cut in. "You ever notice something about that Liberty Bell? It has a crack in it. And no one cares. They display it like they're proud and the thing is cracked."

Garcia turned from Sammy to Conan. It was obvious what he wanted to say: get away while I work on this chick.

"Are those regulation clothes you've got on, ma'am? Because I see boxer shorts, which are not allowed here. I could write you up for that."

I was exiting work exchange when I ran into the GED teacher, G. Hauser. I had gotten into a scuffle in work exchange, where they said I was setting off the metal detector and went through all my stuff. They even tore apart the bologna sandwich in the sack lunch they give us outside chow hall, to take to work. I had to strip out and endure a search in the little curtained area of work exchange, and I was boiling with anger as I left. But when I saw Hauser, something flipped in me, a switch. I called out a friendly hello. You don't decide to intentionally alter your tone of voice. It happens automatically. Needs are the gearbox of the voice. Needs shift approach, adjust tone to something higher, more sympathetic. It wasn't calculated, but everything had changed for me since I'd seen him last.

"Hey," I said, "I was wondering if I'd run into you."

I had forgotten all about him. I had not thought of him once.

"I'm on C yard," I said, "and I've been thinking about your offer to get me some reading material. That would be great."

He was excited, like I was doing him a favor by asking for one myself. We chatted and in his growing excitement, he said, "Why don't you take my class?"

"All they teach is GED prep here. Which is the education level of our guards."

"Yeah." He laughed quickly, covertly. "But since it's the only thing offered, I structure it around reading. We read and talk about books. Try it out. I'd love to have you join us." He told me how to sign up.

Sammy was right that having a job would keep me from falling apart. It did. It kept my mind off things. Instead, I concentrated, like everyone else, on what there was to be exploited.

Conan was crafting dildos in woodshop. He began working on them as soon as our shop supervisor commenced his marathon reading sessions at his desk. Every day the supervisor brought a novel to work, settled in, and read compulsively. The book covers featured lurid images with raised-letter titles, like *Killed Twice*. They were all water-damaged paperbacks you would find in a free box. The supervisor read at them for seven hours straight, day after day, while Conan used sanders and chamfering tools to taper his creations. He and Teardrop had a rivalry going over who could craft the better dildo. They both also had contacts at central kitchen for illicit sale of cucumbers. The unit kitchens get their cucumbers prequartered, to prevent nonintended and illegal use of provisions, i.e., as dildos. Prisoners who worked in central kitchen sold cucumbers uncut out the back door.

The Norse made wooden swastikas and pentagrams. My own innovation was the lunch meat. At meal breaks, I began toasting my bologna slice with the branding iron we used for all our products. It said CALPIA, California Prison Industry Authority, and I was in charge of it. I branded my lunch meat on both sides with the iron, and then my sandwich bread as well. The iron toasted the bread and the meat perfectly. I toasted other people's sandwiches in exchange for baggies of instant coffee. I learned to hide the coffee for strip-out, after work. This was how it was going to be. Hustling for every little thing.

On Saturdays they let us go to the library. All they had for us to check out were Bibles. King James or International Version was the complete range of reading choices. Sammy and I went weekly to research who I could send letters to, about Jackson. Exiting one afternoon, I ran into Hauser again. I would be starting his class soon.

There isn't anything to read here, I told him.

"I know. That's why I ordered you some books. They haven't arrived yet? I had to get them from Amazon, since we can't give you books directly."

I pictured Sammy's hands, reeling in the line, cultivating a victim. Slowly, she'd said, you've got to do it slowly.

"I haven't got them yet," I told him, but things took a while. They had to sort the mail for three thousand women.

I continued to call Johnson's lawyer because he was the only person I could contact, since he had Global Tel Link. He mostly avoided answering, but once, he picked up. He had news, he said. He was retiring, after thirty years as a public defender, and I would no longer be able to reach him at that office.

The way things were closing in on me: it was hard to accept that this was real life. No one but me cared about the fate of Jackson. I didn't know where he was. I had no way to talk to him. I was trapped in a prison in the Central Valley, under the baked expanse of sunny sky, gazing into the razor wire, counting how long it took the perimeter truck to circle our big enclosure. Picturing tough and beautiful Angel Marie Janicki getting herself through the fence.

I kept going over a scene, from when Jackson was five. It was autumn, and my mother came with us to Tilden Park, in the East Bay. There were trees above us that had turned a color I might have dyed my hair, a bright, rich magenta. There were trees with gold and scarlet leaves. You don't see a lot of that in California. My mother and Jackson and I sat and watched the wind shake these bright-painted trees. Jackson was enchanted.

"All that beauty and for nothing," my mother said. "They'll fall off tomorrow."

"But after they fall off," Jackson said, "the tree will grow new leaves, Grandma, and then those will turn colors, like these ones." It would keep happening over and over, Jackson said, through all the years. The leaves falling off meant new ones were coming. My mother looked at him like she wondered what planet he was from.

He was born an optimist, and he didn't get it from her, or from me. When Jackson was three, he asked me how the Earth formed. "How did it get here?" I said no one knew for sure but maybe there was an explosion and they called it the Big Bang. "But where did they put everyone while the explosion was happening?" In his mind there were always people. People taking care of other people.

The lawyer had given me the phone number of child welfare, which he said might tell me the name of Jackson's case manager, but I could only contact people with a Global Tel Link account. I wrote letters and tried not to go insane. I sent one to Eva's old address, and one to her at her father's address, but I had little faith that either would reach her. I called Jimmy Darling, but the call did not go through, since he didn't have Global Tel Link. I told myself if I ever got out, I'd blow up Global Tel Link.

I got a package. Like one of the lucky women who have family, outside help, I, Hall, got called to receiving and release to pick up my package. Hauser had gotten me three books: *My Ántonia*, *I Know Why the Caged Bird Sings*, and *To Kill a Mockingbird*.

"That's what he got you?" Sammy said, stifling a laugh. "Even I read those already." I felt sad and a little protective of the teacher for not knowing better. I planned on keeping them, even if I didn't especially want to read them. They were a link to the outside world. But a woman in my unit offered me shampoo and conditioner in exchange for all three. The state gives us indigents only a gritty powdered soap for body and hair. Being able to properly wash and condition my hair made me feel happy, at least for an evening, in a way I had not experienced since before I was arrested, three years earlier.

I had been in Hauser's class for a couple of weeks when he stopped me after and asked if I'd enjoyed the books.

"I enjoyed reading them," I said, "when I was fourteen years old."

I didn't plan on saying that. It certainly wasn't tactical for reeling in a Keath.

"God. I'm sorry. That's embarrassing."

"It's okay. You just don't know me."

He asked me what I wanted to read and I said I didn't know. I said I had a lot on my mind and it was hard to concentrate.

He got me more books. One, called *Pick-Up*, was about two drunks in San Francisco in the 1950s. I started reading it and could not stop. When I finished it, I read it again. Scenes came into view for me, even though the character in the book doesn't name many locations except Civic Center, and Powell and Market, where the cable car turns around, which fascinated Jackson as it did all toddlers. I would take him down there to watch the street musicians. Some of them were friends of Jimmy Darling's. Jimmy knew all sorts of people in a way I didn't, and the night would go differently if by chance he and I ran into someone and they invited us to a concert or a party or a screening of a film.

When I was a kid there was a large Woolworth's at Powell and Market, with a wig department in the center of the store. Eva and I would go in and pretend we were wig shopping. The old ladies who worked there helped us pin our hair up in special nets and fitted us with grand and curly hairdos. We laughed and played around in the mirrors, sneaked makeup and hair products into our purses, and took pictures in the photo booth that was inside the store. Sometimes we went to Zim's on Van Ness afterward, ordered a lot of food and left without paying. It was something different from dining and dashing at the more

177

familiar Zim's on Taraval. We felt sophisticated downtown. Sometimes we went into the museum, up Van Ness, to hide after booking from Zim's. There was a painting inside that Eva liked. It was called *The Girl with Green Eyes*. Among the kids we knew, you weren't supposed to be into going to museums, but Eva was into whatever she was into, this painted girl with a long neck that looked like it was squeezed into a napkin ring. She stared at us, and we stared back.

The whole long era of my childhood I had run around like a street urchin, no more rooted than the teenagers on the posters in the Greyhound station on Sixth Street. Tall figures in silhouette, like long shadows, and the words RUNAWAYS, CALL FOR HELP. A hotline number. My childhood was the era of the hotline. But we never called any, except as a prank, and I wasn't a runaway. I even had a mother. I might have gotten to know her, but I had not, not really. By the time I was sixteen, it was too late for me and my mother. When I went to prison, it seemed really and finally too late. But I was wrong. It was only too late when she died.

I told Hauser I read *Pick-Up*. He asked what I thought.

"That it was good and bad at the same time."

"I know what you mean. The end is a surprise, right? But it makes you want to reread the book, to see if there were earlier clues."

I told him I'd done that. And that it was good to read a book about San Francisco, that I was from there.

"Oh, me too," he said.

He didn't seem like it to me, and I said so.

"I mean, near there. I'm from just across the Bay, Contra Costa County." He named the town, but I hadn't heard of it.

"It's an armpit behind an oil refinery. It's not glamorous, like being from the city."

I said I hated San Francisco, that there was evil coming out of the ground there, but that I liked *Pick-Up* because it reminded me of things about the city that I missed.

He had gotten me two other books, Charles Bukowski's *Factotum* and *Jesus' Son* by Denis Johnson. I would read the others next, I told him.

"*Factotum* is one of the funniest books ever written."

I said I knew of the other book, the Jesus one, because I saw the movie. Which was good except the people in it were supposed to be living in the seventies. "The girl in it, she's got her midriff showing, and wears a leather jacket with a fur collar like San Francisco hipsters in the nineties."

"But those people you're describing—maybe you, I don't know—they're all borrowing from the seventies to begin with."

It was true. I told him how Jimmy Darling used to go to this bookstore in the Tenderloin to buy 1970s-era copies of *Playboy*, which they had in stacks on the floor in the back. An old man once tapped Jimmy on the shoulder and whispered, "Sonny, they have the new ones up here," nodding in the direction of the plastic-sleeved monthlies, *Busty* and *Barely Legal*, which were on display in the front of the store.

"And Jimmy is—"

"My fiancé. He teaches at the San Francisco Art Institute."

"Are you . . . still engaged?"

"He's dead," I said.

That night, after lights out, I thought about North Beach and tried to revisit places I went with Jimmy Darling, who lived and worked over there, and before Jimmy, when I was a kid and North

Beach was an exciting place to wander on a Friday night with your friends. We would hover around the outdoor tables at Enrico's and finish people's drinks when they got up to leave. I saw the lights along Broadway. Big Al's. The Condor Club and its vertical sign, Carol Doda's nipples glowing cherry red, Chinatown red. The Garden of Eden down the street, its pink and green neon bright against the fog.

Later they took the sign of Carol Doda down, but for me it remained. All those lights stayed on, in the world that had been, and that still existed in me, the one I contained.

There was a club on Columbus where feminist strippers made eleven feminist dollars an hour. It was very little for what they gave out, and took in, watching men masturbate in the little booths around the stage. Regal Show World was a regular peep show without the feminism. The Regal's strange and uncomely accountant moonlighted with us at the Mars Room and, as far as I knew, never found a single customer, but showed up, night after night, a big awkward lady in thick glasses and discount lingerie who den-mothered us in the dressing room with snacks, and compliments on our makeup and costumes. She handed out baby carrots and called them "crudités." She was especially fond of my friend Arrow, whom she regarded as her dressing room daughter.

Arrow had made it into the pages of *Barely Legal*. She was my age, early twenties, but she had a lazy eye that gave her an innocent look, or at least the innocent look of women who pose as girls in *Barely Legal*. Arrow and I both took shifts sometimes at the Crazy Horse, where I first encountered Jackson's dad. He was good-looking and funny, the only doorman the girls at the Crazy Horse let in the dressing room. He pretended to read articles from the local newspaper out loud as the girls put on makeup, but inventing *Weekly World News*–type headlines as he flipped pages: Woman Lifts Volkswagen Beetle to Save

Last Cigarette from Storm Drain; Man Who Lost Two Hundred Pounds on Chocolate Chip Cookie Diet Run Over by Milk Truck. Breaking News: Toledo, Ohio, Is a Figment of People's Imagination. Jackson's dad did not lack intelligence, he just wasn't smart about life, which is to say, about authority. But he was smart enough to escape. He climbed a fence at a San Mateo county jail and ran all the way to San Francisco. I had heard that story before I knew him. I pictured a guy running along the side of the highway, as if to get from San Mateo to San Francisco you'd have to go the way a car would travel, but without the shell of the car, the motor. Just a man, running and sweating in the breakdown lane. I'm sure that's not how he traveled, but it was what I saw. He was caught almost immediately.

Jimmy the Beard had worked as a doorman at various strip clubs around town since the 1960s. He told stories. There was one about a crazy movie director who was in love with a porn star named Magic Tom. Magic Tom performed at a gay hard-core theater where Jimmy the Beard worked the door. Magic Tom wasn't interested in the movie director. Used him, and then left him for someone else. The spurned, angry movie director got on a Greyhound bus and went all the way to Syracuse, New York, where Magic Tom was originally from. The movie director knocked on the door of Magic Tom's mother's house. In the story Jimmy the Beard tells, the mother opens the door, a prim and buttoned-up old woman in upstate New York. Says, "Yes, can I help you?" The filmmaker says, "No, ma'am, just thought you'd like to see something." He holds up a nude pictorial of Magic Tom and Magic Tom's identical twin brother in hard-core poses. They worked together doing porn. Jimmy the Beard was laughing so hard by this point he could barely spit out the story. "The guy shows this old lady in Syracuse, New York, a photograph of her two sons fucking each other." He thought that was the funniest story he'd ever heard. It starts to explain Jimmy the Beard's sense of humor. Thinking it was funny to blow my cover with Kurt Kennedy. After I left San Francisco for Los Angeles, Kurt Kennedy persisted until he found out where I was. Jimmy the Beard told him.

15

By the time Gordon Hauser was into his second year at Stanville, he would not have mistaken the shriek of an animal for the shriek of a woman. The cry he had heard on that early night in his cabin had been a mountain lion. Not a woman, and not in trouble.

When snow blanketed the ground his first winter, paw prints went up around his property, scooped divots that matched exactly in pattern and spread those in his field guide, according to which, the voice of the mountain lion had been variously described as sounding like the screaming, yelling, or moaning of a female human.

He never saw a mountain lion, only heard them. In the early morning, on his way down the mountain toward Stanville, he sometimes glimpsed gray foxes, their lustrous tails trailing after them, as he followed the curves of the winding road, passing huge drought-desiccated live oak, their jagged little leaves coated in dust, and banks of rust-red buckeye and smoke-green manzanita. The buckeye branches without leaves glinted bone-white in the sun. The grasses were the rich yellow of wet straw. He'd never seen such beautiful grasses.

On the straightaway toward the brown basin, the scenery changed to oil pipeline and derricks, whose axles wound and wound. After the derricks was a dusty orange grove, one farmhouse with two palm trees in front, where the road split. The two palms were a curious variety, thickly shaggy and luxurious like an Inuit's snow boots.

On the valley floor, the temperature was twenty degrees hotter and the air heavy with the smell of fertilizer. There were no more oranges, no oil derricks, just power lines and almond groves in huge geometric parcels all the way to the prison.

Like all California prisons, Stanville flew three flags: state, nation, and POW MIA. The POW flag had always seemed pathetic to Gordon, since it was for those left behind in Vietnam, a war the U.S. had lost and badly. Any prisoners not returned were probably long dead, and either way, no one was going back for them, but prison guards at every state facility muscled up a flag in their honor. When people were captured now, it was different. A lot of them were private contractors, and they got beheaded live on the internet. President Bush went on TV and said he was building hospitals and schools for the Iraqi people. Most of the cars in staff parking at Stanville had the yellow ribbon on the bumper.

The prison was complicated to navigate. It all looked the same to Gordon, one- and two-story detached cinder-block buildings in a vast expanse of dirt and concrete surrounded by shrouds of razor wire. He went through three electronic sally ports to get to his classroom, which was in a windowless trailer near the vocational workshops and central kitchen. From the kitchen pumped a constant smell of rancid grease, overpowered only by the drift of solvents from the auto body shop, where a row of trucks—guards' private vehicles—were lined up for super-discounted paint jobs by inmates.

Gordon had clearance to enter this part of the grounds, but the housing units and yards were off-limits to him, with the exception of one cell block on A yard, 504, where he could work with people from death row and administrative segregation.

Gordon had dreaded death row but found that it didn't quite conform to his nightmares about it. He'd imagined iron bars, a medieval vision of misery. It was automated and modern, each tiny cell with a white-painted steel door and small glass window. There were twelve women, one to a cell, and a cramped alley with tables and sewing machines surrounded by meshed cage. A guard unlocked an entrance in the cage and led Gordon in to meet with students one-on-one, while others knitted or made hook rugs at nearby tables. Betty LaFrance, who was not Gordon's student but always insisted on speaking to him, brought a radio from her cell and played elevator music as she crafted. The women made greeting cards by hand in emulation of a machine-printed corporate look: their best work resembled cards you could buy at Rite Aid, with blandly inspirational messages in a neutral script. The women were allowed to come and go from their cells, which smelled of Renuzit air freshener and were blanketed in homemade afghans, for privacy and probably to have some use for these afghans they churned on the oily axle of time.

They called him Deary and Pumpkin and Doll. Deary creeped him out. It was what the old pawnbroker Elsabeta calls Raskolnikov before he carries out his plan to murder her, or at least that was the English equivalent the translator had chosen. Deary.

Administrative segregation, on the floor above death row, had no common area, and there was no interaction among women except yelling. The women hollered from one cell to another, heckled guards, made noise to have something to do. Gordon waited in a small office as a student clink-jangled down the hall in her restraints and was put in a cage for the lesson with him. That was where he first met Romy Hall, who was in his class now. What he had noticed about her was that she looked him in the eye. Many of the women had this way of looking at his shoulder, or past him. Their eyes rolled every which direction to avoid his. Also she was attractive, despite the conditions. Wide-set greenish eyes. A mouth with a cupid's bow, was that what it was called, an upper lip that swoop-de-swooped. A pretty mouth that said: trust this face. And the face said: this is not what it seems. She spelled well, read with good comprehension. He wasn't looking for a good speller. He wasn't looking for anything, among the women in Stanville.

He'd seen her again in what the guards called a dog run—the outdoor cages where women in ad seg were placed for exercise. The walkway to 504 routed past a series of them, and his instinct was to avoid staring at the women trapped in these barren little enclosures. Hall had called to him in a casual way like a woman asking a man for a light, or if he knows what time the train stops here.

He liked having her in class. She did the reading in earnest. A lot of his students thought Gordon was stupid, spoke in codes and laughed at him, but this seemed fair enough. They had state commitments he could hardly understand—LWOP, which was life without parole, or multiple life sentences. Even a single life sentence was difficult for him to get his head around.

He passed out photocopied sections of books, *Julie of the Wolves*, Laura Ingalls Wilder, but he didn't tell the prisoners they were children's books, and it didn't matter if the women enjoyed them. He kept it simple, since many had only an elementary school education. They wrote in bubble letters like adolescent girls. Even London, who the others called Conan and looked like a man, wrote in bubble letters. London was clever, it was obvious. Never did the reading but made the others laugh, which was something.

"Is *bosom* plural?" London asked.

"Depends on whose, maybe," someone said.

"The bosom of Jones. Sounds like an adventure film. Lieutenant Jones and the Bosom of Doom."

Geronima Campos, an old Native American woman, painted in her sketchbook all through class time. Gordon wondered if maybe she could not read or write. One day after class he asked her what she painted. If she admits she cannot write, he decided, he could suggest she work with him independently.

Portraits, she told him. She opened her sketchbook to show him. Each page had an image and, under it, a name. She could write. But the images were not faces. They were wild streaks of color. "This is you," she said, and showed him a scribble of black lines with a staining splotch of blue.

When his class discussed a chapter of *The Red Pony* by John Steinbeck, the women talked about the mountains in the book and the ones they could see from main yard. They seemed afraid of the mountains, which surprised Gordon. He figured they'd regard the mountains as freedom, the one thing they could glimpse of the natural world. "You got to fight bears up there," Conan said. "At least in here it's just cubs. Cubs and scrubs. And I know I can *win*."

When they got to the third chapter, "The Promise," about Nellie the pregnant mare, one woman raised her hand and said when she'd delivered, her belly was heart-shaped, "in two parts," she said, "just like a horse, and even the doctor confirmed it, that horses have a heart-shaped womb."

They read from the chapter out loud. At the mention of pigs, a student interjected that her cousin wrote her from lockup in Arizona that they had a gas chamber where they put a pig one Sunday a month, to test the machine.

Gordon tried to steer the discussion back to the book. What was the promise that Billy Buck made?

The girl whose cousin had written her about the pigs gassed on Sundays said that when the pig "went up the pipe," a smell settled down over the yard. "Smelt like peach blossoms," she said. "That's what my cousin told me."

Romy Hall raised her hand. She said Billy Buck promised the boy, Jody, a healthy foal. Earlier, Billy Buck had promised to look after the red pony and the pony had died. This new vow was Billy Buck's chance to be a man of his word, by delivering the foal safely.

Did he keep it, Gordon asked.

She said that was the trick of the story. Technically yes, but in order to deliver the foal, he had to kill the mare. He killed the mare to save its breach foal. He smashed its skull with a hammer and that was a bullshit way to keep a promise. The mare could have had other foals that weren't breach, but she had to die because some cowboy was hung up on himself as a man of his word.

"It's okay to *make* a promise," London said to Gordon, as if summarizing for the teacher how life actually worked, "but it's not always a good idea to *keep* one."

One evening, as class ended, Romy Hall hovered. Gordon started collecting papers from an awkward position, on the far side of his own desk, in order to create more distance between them.

She told him many things about herself in the span of about five minutes. She spoke them in a controlled voice. It seemed to Gordon she had been saving it up. He kept stepping back, to be farther from her, and she kept stepping toward him, and he was not going to be manipulated. One woman had tried to bribe him into smuggling cell phones for her, another tobacco. Staff and guards alike were involved in these schemes. Gordon wanted no part.

She was a lifer, she told him, and the mother of a young boy. She apologized for troubling him. Said she woke up depressed. Could feel the fog in her cell, even without a window, and said the dampness of it reminded her of home.

She wanted him to call a telephone number to find out where her kid was. She had it all written down and this was exactly the kind of thing he'd been backing away from, as she moved toward him. Just because he had bought her books or found her pretty, just because he thought about her sometimes, that didn't mean he was looking for family dramas.

The assistance he gave on his own, and against the rules, had all started with Candy Peña on death row. Candy had cried like a child because she had no more wool and no money and so she couldn't help the babies. The others on death row were knitting baby blankets that would go to a Christian charity in Stanville.

He knew he could bring in wool. They almost never looked in his bag. He was eating breakfast at Baressi's when he made the decision. The place soothed him, with its framed pictures of stock cars, victories from the local track. One side was a diner and the other a bar with a piano in the corner. On Saturday nights, a woman played it.

You could not get dental work done in Stanville. There was no shoe repair. You could not buy a decent cook pot, not even one up to Gordon's low standards, but there were three hobby and crafting stores. He went to one. Bought four colors of yarn. Candy had said wool, although the craft store sold no yarn that was made of wool, not even partially, but maybe wool no longer meant wool, but instead, fluffy knittables. The next day he gave what he'd bought to Candy. She melted in gratitude, which made him feel obscene. Not because it was against the rules, but because it had been almost no trouble and yet she cried and said no one had ever done anything so nice for her, not once in her life.

The only remedy seemed to be to do favors for others, so that he wasn't Candy's saint, to neutralize the act of giving by giving more.

Betty LaFrance asked Gordon if he would mail a letter for her, to an old lover, she explained, who was in a California state prison himself. Prisoners were not allowed to contact other prisoners without express approval from the Department of Corrections, this Gordon knew to be true, but he figured Betty probably imagined this romance she told him about. She'd been yelling to get the guards' attention the first time Gordon met her. "Officer!" she'd called. "Please tell the parking lot attendant to reserve a spot for my hairdresser!" She snubbed the other women on death row, told Gordon they were not of her caliber. Once, she asked Gordon if he'd ever flown business class on Singapore Airlines. When he said no, she seemed to pity him. She was a deluded woman sentenced to die. He felt for her. He sent the letter.

He bought seeds for a student in his class who gardened. She had brought Gordon fresh mint as a present, and when Gordon asked her where she got it, she said it rode into the prison on old lumber, four-by-twelves they were using for construction. She'd replanted it, watered it. She told him she watched the sky and waited for birds to excrete seeds, and germinated them secretly in wet paper towels. Rules were such that no plants were supposed to grow. But the captain on D yard, where she lived, let her have her plants. She was a lifer. Gordon gave her a seed packet of California poppies. She put her hands to her face to hide her tears. "This is a God shot," she said. "Thank you for this God shot." Which started the cycle over again, the discomfort, their outsized gratitude. The packet of seeds had cost him eighty-nine cents.

And so he had been sending books to Romy Hall. You go on Amazon. Click a button. What was twenty bucks to him, if spending it meant several weeks of freedom of thought for someone in prison? But looking into her personal life in the outside world, calling a number on her behalf: that was different. It was honest-to-god meddling, not just in her life but in his own, too.

He put the paper she had given him on his coffee table. A phone number and the name of her child. He did not call, and to his relief, or his mixed relief, she did not ask him about it. They chatted, but about insignificant things. She thinks I won't help her, that I don't care. But he wanted her to know that he did care, and that it was not nothing to him that she had asked him that favor.

He sat on his couch, picked up the scrap with the number, and put it back down. Instead of calling it, he went online and figured out how to order a new paint set for Geronima from a catalogue supplier. Something easy, that required no deep deliberating.

Geronima brought the new paint set to class and worked diligently for several weeks before approaching Gordon.

"I'd like to show you what I've been working on. Portraits, but the kind you probably prefer."

"That I prefer?"

"Well, most people prefer." She showed him. They were skillful illustrations, immediately recognizable. Herself. London. Gordon. Romy. Everyone in class. They had the economy of caricatures. She turned the page to an unfamiliar face staring from the paper, the cheeks streaked in tears. "That's Lily, who lives on my unit and reminds me of my younger sister. I don't have a picture of my sister, so I asked her to pose."

16

In spring I began hearing disagreeable noises and machinery, sometimes surprisingly loud, depending upon meteorological conditions.
Thawing winter meant otherwise pleasant excursions were ruined
for me by the moaning and howling of these iron monsters, audible
for miles over the hills. Made up my mind to get revenge. But it was
difficult to determine just where the noise was coming from. Had to
wait for summer anyway because my traps could have easily been
fouled with snow. But later in spring, the noise stopped. I began
hearing it again in summer. I followed the noise, to learn it came
from a logging operation at Willow Creek drainage. Logging off one
of my favorite wild spots. Pushing trees over with bulldozers instead
of cutting with saws. I watched from a high rock where I wasn't
visible. After they'd finished for the day, the whole surface of the
ground was stripped right off. I came down to the worksite after
they'd gone. A five-gallon can of oil was sitting on the machine they
used to pick up logs and load them on trucks. I poured oil over the
machine's engine and set fire to it. I spent a pleasant night sleeping
on top of the mountain, and came home leisurely in the morning.
I felt so good having done this, though a mite uneasy over the risk
of being suspected.

17

Doc had been to Las Brisas the night he got the call about the burglary of a pawnshop on Beverly in Filipinotown. The pawnshop's silent alarm was going off. Doc decided to pull up with no lights or sirens, in case the scene was still active.

The suspect, he sees, is still there. The guy's car, a beat-up Chevy Caprice, will not start. He keeps turning the key. The starter whines but won't catch.

Doc sneaks up on him, aims his service revolver at the guy's head, and asks him politely to get out of the car. His voice, Doc's, becomes gentle. Like the voice of Mr. Rogers, but not an imitation of someone on TV. It is a voice that fits Doc like a glove. Doc is clean-cut, looks more like a dentist than a cop. He thought of his image in terms of basketball: this was the early 1990s, and if there were guys on the force using street style and street language—like the Lakers in their knee-length shorts—Doc, as he thought of it, played for the Utah Jazz, a team whose point scorers were white men in fitted shorts. Men who, like Doc, also resembled dentists, and spoke intelligently about strategy and technique, unlike the retards who got on camera for postgame wrap and said they won by taking their time and picking their shots. Taking my time, picking my shots. That's all most of the players ever said, like it was something they memorized. But really, it was a good formula. It was how Doc did things, too.

Doc says, "Sounds like you've got car trouble." Then he calmly asks the suspect how the burglary went.

"The what?" The guy is confused. Black dude. In Doc's line of work, black people give him the most trouble. Or rather, he gives them the most trouble.

Doc puts the guy spread-eagle against his clunker and takes his stolen loot off the front seat, which is in a pillowcase like Doc remembered using to trick-or-treat when he was a boy, to get the most candy, fuck everybody else. The pillowcase is full of weapons, watches, jewelry, the usual. The guy has a gun on him, so Doc takes that as well. It's a Glock. Doc is pleasantly surprised this guy in a trashed car that won't start has a decent weapon that Doc might keep instead of sell.

Doc's police radio statics out a message: backup is on its way to Beverly and Vendome. Backup? He has *not* called for backup. But according to dispatch it is on its way. Maybe it's a ghost patrol. That's a scam people were running. The commissioner wants so many cars out in the division. Well, screw the commissioner: officers all over town were fooling dispatch into thinking they were out on calls while they sat around eating and gambling, or going to the gym, or banging box in an hourly joint down on Western, the Snooty Fox, a popular spot for guys on the force. It was clean, Doc wants you to know, not your typical Venus flytrap for rock smoking and five-dollar head. The Snooty Fox was classy, with suites and a good ice machine, and they had mirrors on the ceiling so you could watch yourself. (Doc considers it an oddity that a mirror would be for looking at anything but yourself. He would have these conversations with the guys down at Rampart, and Doc always said the same thing. "If I want to see what some whore looks like from behind I turn her over. I don't need a mirror for that. What I can't see without the mirror is *me*.")

Doc decides whatever squad car the backup is, they are probably down at the Snooty Fox getting their dicks wet.

The suspect faces him, hands up.

"Take it easy," Doc says. "Look, neither one of us can squirm out of this, so let's work with each other. I can make this easier. You're going down to central booking. Tomorrow you'll have an arraignment, and the court will appoint you a decent lawyer."

Or they wouldn't, Doc knew.

"At most you'll serve a two-year sentence."

The suspect starts to sniffle.

"Hey, I understand. You were just trying to pull a quick job."

The suspect stares at Doc, not unsuspiciously, because he's scared, and he probably hates cops. "This is messed up," he says.

Doc hears sirens wailing toward the Virgil/Temple/Silver Lake/Beverly junction. Backup really is on its way. If the light is red, he has time while the squad car slows in order to navigate through that multi-lane intersection against oncoming traffic.

Doc takes out a cigarette. "This kind of thing isn't fun for me, either."

He offers one to the suspect, who eyes him warily and shakes his head, blinking back tears.

"You can put your hands down," Doc says, exhaling smoke. "I have your weapon, I know you're not a threat. Just don't do anything stupid. But relax. You're making me nervous."

The suspect looks at him. He keeps his hands raised.

"Relax, seriously. I'm going to let these other guys book you, the car that's on its way. You know why? I hate sending people to jail. Now come on. I'm ordering you to put them down. I can tell you're a good kid. I bet this was your first burglary, which is why you fucked it up so badly. Put your hands down and take a breather. In a moment these guys will cuff you, and the cuffs won't feel good."

The suspect's eyes shine with fear. He begins to bring his arms down a little.

He wipes his wet face with the arm of his shirt.

Remember the era when everyone wore those rugby shirts with thick vertical brashly colored stripes and an offset collar? That's what the suspect had on.

Doc hated those shirts.

The suspect puts his hands all the way down.

"That-a-boy," Doc says. "Try not to worry. I know the officer on intake. I'll ask him to go easy on you. You might even bond out tonight."

The suspect brings his arms not just down, but toward his pockets.

At the moment when the suspect's hands go into the pockets, Doc fires at his face. Twice, aiming upward.

Backup arrives a few seconds later. Enough long seconds to stash the pillowcase Doc has inherited.

Two officers from Central Division pull up.

"Jesus. What happened here?"

The suspect is slumped against the grille of his car. Behind him, a radius of blood speckles the car's hood.

"I tell him hands up," Doc says, "and he goes straight for his pockets. I wasn't taking any chances."

He didn't know why he'd done it. The child rapist could burn in hell, but why did he kill that kid on Beverly?

If the kid had said to Doc, Why are you doing this? Doc might have stopped himself, because he did not know. The kid could not ask that, because Doc hadn't given him time to.

He and his old partner José, it's true they tortured a victim, a manager at a gentleman's club under the 605 freeway, and when they were done they dumped the body near the 710 freeway. But the guy had raped José's girlfriend, so what were they supposed to do? The press made a big deal of the torture, but Doc is no sicko, nor serial killer. He did it to make it look as if someone of that type did the killing.

It wasn't all like that. Doc was a popular detective, someone you might have envied if you spotted him out riding with a handful of other off-duty officers along the cliffs above Malibu on a mild windless day. There was a group of them that went up the Pacific Coast Highway. Doc was usually on his '78 Sportster, not some full-dress late-model fagmobile, as you often see parked outside Neptune's Net on the PCH, the rider handling it like with butler's gloves because the thing is leased. Doc hates faggots who lease Harleys and for the record owned two, paid cash for both, the Sportster and a Softail, the Softail equally stripped down but with cowhide saddlebags for trips up to his place in Three Rivers, where he owned outright a plot of land with a stream running through it, another enviable feature of Doc's old life. Beautiful high country, fantastic trout fishing, clean air. A rustic log cabin where he injected meth and fucked women he brought up from South LA.

Three Rivers takes him to something intriguing: he sees hips and thighs splayed out. It's what happens to a woman's body when the clothing comes off, hips spreading against the spongy push-back of the lumpy mattress in his country place. He sees the cheap wood paneling. A hairy snatch, wet, relaxed-looking. He parts the lips with his fingers, uses the other hand to ready himself. This is working. He can't see a face but he doesn't need or want one. He sees the spread thighs and hears the squeak of that old bed frame as he shifts into

199

position. Feels the heat of a still room on a summer day and this is working.

All the sex he ever had. All that remained were these moments you looped.

Hips, pushing, wood paneling, bed squeak. Hands on his backside (he's a man, okay? It's backside, not ass). He grabs hers. Grabs a handful of it. The way her hips spread out beneath him on that country mattress, that was what helped him get this going. He goes deep. The bed is squeaking like crazy; he's at the finish and that noisy bed frame sounds like it's being split apart with an axe.

But this one, which he sinks into, catching his breath, no. This bed is concrete. He lies back in the still heat of the cell, tries to sustain this feeling of the still heat of a summer day up in sequoia country.

Warm enough his Harley requires no choke, just starter to idle in a liquid transition.

On an afternoon like that he'd go to the biker bar in Three Rivers, leave the woman, whichever one, at the cabin, with confiscated drugs and satellite TV. He sits at the bar and drinks cold draft beer.

People snub Budweiser for these dumb brands no one's heard of, but Budweiser is the king of beers for a reason: it's good.

His roommate is in the common area, plucking the strings of his big yellow guitar. Sounds like Led Zeppelin, but what white-guy bluesy finger work on an acoustic guitar doesn't? The cellmate is a decent musician for a creep who fucked his own daughter.

Everyone else is on the yard. Doc does not go on the yard. If you need it spelled out for you, the prison yard is no place for a cop, even the Sensitive Needs yard—unless it's powder puff softball day, which Doc will risk himself in order to watch.

Doc is feeding his pet lizard when his cellmate returns. He recently discovered that static cling sheets—orderable from Walkenhorst catalog supply—will function as mesh to cover the top of the lizard's cardboard terrarium. The terrarium is made from a Nike shoe box. Doc only wears white sneakers, hospital clean, works on them several times a day with Cell Block 64 and goes through many pairs, thanks to what various people on the force pay him to keep quiet. He's feeding the lizard little pieces of leaf from the cutting he is growing in a jar. He enjoys a bit of plant and animal life in the cell as long as it is tidy and clean and doesn't introduce any weird stenches. He watches the lizard watch his big hand hold out the leaf, and then it—

Something has reduced him to a question mark.

He's down, but coming to. The cellmate, wow. Has wacked him in the back of the head. With Doc doesn't know what. Something major.

He can't get air. Doc is being choked now by a homemade garrote.

Is there any other kind of garrote?

The mind wanders, even at critical moments. They always say "homemade garrote." Doc reaches for it—it's strong, it's made of—

He cannot breathe!

Dental floss? Guitar string?

He is sputtering and grunting with an animal's desire for life. Doc tries to—

He can't—

18

I felt free of Kurt Kennedy in Los Angeles, though several times I had to double-take men who shared his generally repulsive physical qualities, thick bunched calves, ruddy skin, bald and dented cranium, and once I mistakenly thought I heard the gravelly voice. But Los Angeles was a new planet, with Creamsicle sunsets, sandals in January, giant birds of paradise, supermarkets with gleaming rows of tropical produce. I began to relax, to feel free of the suffocating familiarity of San Francisco.

In truth I moved me and Jackson to Los Angeles not only to get away from Kurt Kennedy, but so that I could be with Jimmy Darling after he got the teaching job in Valencia. The property he sublet belonged to an eccentric old painter who was away in Japan. Most of the structures on the ranch had burned in a forest fire, so the old painter lived in an Airstream trailer. He'd built a wood trellis over it that had vines on it, to keep the place cool. Jackson loved it there, because it was almost like camping. Off a ways from the trailer was a milk-green Andy Gump port-a-potty, its door permanently wired open. I went up there to lie in a hammock in the shade with Jimmy, eat purple prickly pear that grew along the property borders, and let Jackson feed apples and weeds to the retired Arabian mares that grazed in a big soggy pasture. We would spend the night but always left first thing in the morning and made the long drive back to my own borrowed place, my so-called reality. I didn't want to live with Jimmy. He was not the sort of person you move in with, make a life with. He did his thing and I did mine, and every few days we got together and entertained each other but kept it light. We walked around the property. He and Jackson whittled together. Scratched the neck of a potbellied goat that was the old painter's companion. When it rained up there, the abandoned swimming pool of the burned-down property next door was overtaken by frogs, whose chorus of croaks delighted Jackson. After I put Jackson to sleep on a mat on the trailer floor, Jimmy Darling and I would drink tequila at a picnic table under a tarp, and then have gratifying and drunken sex in the one bed in the trailer, both bed and trailer too small for two by intent and design.

The painter who lived on the horse ranch was escaping the clutches of various women, Jimmy said. The port-a-potty was a message that women should not get too comfortable. The bed was a twin. Jackson and I only went there on weekends. Jackson was in kindergarten so it wasn't practical to go during the week. The arrangement was fine with me, but sometimes, as I drove toward downtown LA with Jackson in the backseat, I felt I was going down into a solitude that was too airy and roomy. Jimmy, on the other hand, probably just went out into the old painter's studio and started building and making, because he was a builder and maker and had little tendency toward destructive introspection. I would drive past the ugly power plant in Burbank and see the steam billowing from its reactor mouths and be faced with what I did not like to admit, which was that Jimmy Darling was free of worry, and he had a place in the world. He was a somebody. Take the inverse of that, and it was how I felt about myself.

This feeling didn't seem like it derived from something I could fix or improve. It was simply who I was compared to who Jimmy was, which put my life in negative relief. But it would not have comforted me to date someone who was worse off than I was.

Right after I moved to LA, I ran into a guy from San Francisco, a guitar player who dated a girl I knew and had been in a band that everyone thought was cool. He told me fifteen horror stories about his relapses into heroin and his roommate overdosing and his brother overdosing, too, and something about someone named Noodles, a girl who had tried to pin the roommate's death on him, claiming he was at fault for supplying the drugs, and how finally now he was putting his life together, how glad he was to be out of San Francisco, we should hang out, et cetera. He had tattoos I didn't remember from when I'd known him, monster faces up his arms. They seemed like gargoyles meant to ward off bad energy, except he was radiating it, and I wanted to get away from him as quickly as possible.

The apartment I'd sublet was near Echo Park Lake, on a curving street of collapsing Victorians just above downtown. It belonged to a girl I knew from San Francisco, a stripper who was away in Alaska, working up there at the gentlemen's clubs. Lots of girls would go to Alaska to make money, but they never came home with much. They made a lot at the clubs, but life was so dull and confining that everyone drank all the time, and the drinks were expensive like everything there was expensive. Girls returned with an experience of Alaska and no money saved. This girl had a nice apartment because at home in LA she made great money at the clubs in the San Fernando Valley. They had a reputation and, as I discovered, it held up. Discovered, that is, after a rocky start, at clubs in Hollywood that were just havens for tourists, couples who were there to gawk and had no intention of paying for a lap dance. There is nothing worse than when people your own age come along and jeer. It's always better to deal exclusively with customers who know the rules and play by them. The ones who are looking for the game, pretending there are girls in rhinestones and canary-yellow stilettos who truly get off on drowning the faces of middle-aged men with their breasts. The customers we want are those who believe that the girls choose the rhinestones and stilettos because they are the type to wear them, and not because they are merely pretending that type exists. Once I found the right places to work, I was cleaning up. But in terms of exact figures, keep in mind that every service worker paid in tips, whether they are a bartender or waiter or stripper, exaggerates what they make. It seems to be human nature. People don't outright lie. They take their very best day ever, their most outstandingly lucrative shift, historically, and they tell you it is what they average. Everyone does this. So I can tell you how much I made on a Friday night in the Valley, as if it were a typical shift, but I'm quoting my best Friday of all time, which was not typical. The lunch shifts, what I was given when I started, were not great money. Men came for the all-you-can-eat Chinese buffet, and not for company. I sat in the back of the theater, bored, trying not to smell the sweet and sour pork, as I listened to David Lee Roth say, All you got to do is jump. "He designed his own clothes for the video," another stripper told me about six times. It seemed to be the only fact she had on hand, or knew.

Jackson's school was a block away from the sublet, so I could walk him there in the morning. And if I was working, my new neighbors, a large family with four children who all attended that same school, would pick him up and watch him for me. Quickly he was transforming from Jackson into Güero, which was what they called him. The grandmother was from Mexico and ironed every article of the entire family's clothing, including socks and underwear. They were loving people who probably didn't quite understand what I was about, but children involved no judgment or need to understand.

I did not see any doom in the road. I was at least away from Kurt Kennedy, and Jackson seemed happy.

I witnessed doom, though. It was around me. But at the time, I thought the bad luck of other people reaffirmed that I was doing okay.

Take the plumber. This girl I was subletting from had a plumber who was always coming around. He was from Guatemala and really friendly. Too friendly. He had a lot of plans for me. Do you like it when your plumber has a lot of plans for you socially? He made it seem like he and the girl whose place it was had been good buddies and so he expected the same from me. I was trying to start a new life, and this plumber kept calling me to talk about how one Saturday he was going to take me to Home Depot so I could pick out my own sink console, which the landlord was supposed to pay to install, and I said I don't care, just bring one over, I'm a subletter, Victor (that was the plumber's name), what does it matter. But Victor said, as if out of consideration for me and for what I really wanted (whenever people do that, beware), no, no, we'll go together. I'll take you, it's no problem, really.

It was a problem to me because I didn't want to spend my Saturday with Victor. He showed up on the agreed day wearing a shiny patterned shirt and soaked in cologne. So much cologne he seemed to be tapped into the original fount, the place from which it all flows. I dropped Jackson off with the Martinez family, and the grandmother, whom Jackson was starting to call Abuela, looked at Victor and nodded like she understood everything.

Victor and I went to get the sink and the hours doing that were lost for me, because I didn't want to be in his van. I didn't want to be subjected to his happiness, which seemed to be based on nothing, a thin layer of good cheer stretched over emptiness.

I missed Jackson, I missed Jimmy. I wanted a life I did not have. But I also was not ready to admit that. I wanted to get rid of Victor so I could drink beer on my porch as the ice cream truck broadcast its warped and moronic tinkle, and Jackson and the neighbor kids all lined up for type 2 diabetes. It was good to be a stranger in Los Angeles. It was bad to be a stranger in Los Angeles with the company of another stranger in a loud shirt. If everything were so great for this Victor, why was he wasting his Saturday blindly ignoring the blunt and unwelcoming cues from a woman who had no interest in him? I felt desperate, but not in the way Victor was desperate.

After unloading the sink at my apartment, he tried to get me to go drink flaming margaritas with him at a Mexican place on Sunset. I said those give me a headache. They use butane to make them burn, I told him, although that's probably not true. And he says we can have white wine, figuring I was that classy white wine type. Because I'm a nice person, I lied and said I had to work, although I was not working that whole weekend; I was planning to spend a lot of time thinking, sitting on the edge of this gone-to-Alaska girl's bed with my chin in my palm, hearing the ice cream truck, sitting with a blank mind, which might fill later with thoughts on how to live like an adult. I was busy with that. It was important to me. No one bothering me, watching me, harassing me, calling me, following me, sneaking up on me. I'd had that for months with Creep Kennedy, and now I was free and did not want this Victor shading in.

When he heard the lie that I had to work, Victor wanted to take me salsa dancing after I got off. I said no, and after several rounds of his pushiness, I finally got rid of him.

A week later, Victor called me and said, "Romy, are you okay?"

I'm fine, I said. What business was it of his whether I was okay or not?

"I had this terrible dream about you."

Whenever anyone dreams about you, the dream tells you about them, not about you. It's their own private fantasy life and they give it away by announcing who they dreamed about. But Victor was superstitious and was convinced that he should be worried about me on account of his dream.

Victor died in a car crash shortly after that phone call, in the van we'd taken to Home Depot to get the sink.

He'd had the bad dream about the wrong person.

Shortly after Victor died, a neighbor, a young guy named Conrad, overdosed. I knew Conrad was a junkie. He sometimes helped Victor as an assistant, but it was charity on Victor's part. Every day, Conrad's sister came to our street and stood before the wrecked pile across from my place, where Conrad and his spooky mother lived. Every morning the sister called her brother's name for the whole neighborhood to hear.

Conrad's mother, Clemence, had knocked on my door when I first moved in, to tell me not to order any pizzas. I looked at her and she said, "You know those black vinyl containers the delivery boys carry? The pizza warmers? They bring in evil. You see those warmers, and evil is on the way in."

After her pizza box warning, she started talking about J. Edgar Hoover and Jimi Hendrix, and all the other "well-known individuals" who had passed through the neighborhood and to whom her family was connected. She was vague and ominous about her super-heavy connections, these well-known individuals. Okay, lady. I excused myself and went inside. I rarely saw her and I didn't see Conrad much either, but every day I heard Conrad's sister call his name. Every day she stood on the sidewalk and yelled it. Then one day she did not, because Conrad had apparently died the night before. No more Conrad. Still it did not occur to me that the street was cursed, although I did feel a start, a kind of shiver, when I saw a delivery boy get out of his car with a huge black pizza warmer in his hands.

Not long after both Conrad and Victor died, I was at home, busy doing nothing until it was three p.m. and time to pick up Jackson, when I heard the neighbor next door screaming something over and over. It took me a moment to realize the word he was screaming was my name. I went out to see what he wanted. He was standing on the sidewalk with a towel wrapped around his hand, and the towel was raining blood all over the sidewalk.

"You have to take me to the hospital," he said.

When I first arrived, these neighbors had tried to be friendly to me but I kept my distance. They were hard to look at. Shaved eyebrows, sallow skin, dyed black hair, black painted fingernails, a vintage black hearse. Victor did some plumbing work over there and said they kept a baby coffin in the kitchen for their canned foods. They had just bought their building, a fourplex, and were systematically evicting the tenants in order to raise the rent. They were goth slumlords. Two of their tenants had cleared out, but the family in the third unit was not moving. These tenants had nowhere to go. The husband was a diabetic and had just undergone a foot amputation. He was on crutches and insisted on driving himself to the hospital, and his leg got infected and had to be amputated higher up, at the knee. The wife worked cleaning houses, and had asthma and no sense of smell from the toxic products her employers forced her to use. They were poor people without documents, from Mexico, with three children. I knew all this because a few days before the goth neighbor was screaming my name with his hand in a bloody towel, the woman he was trying to evict asked if she could speak to me. I let her in. She sat on my couch and cried and told me about her family and their situation. She said the landlord was

210

trying to evict her and her husband for being alcoholics. "We are Seventh-Day Adventists," the woman said. "We do not drink." I felt so bad for this woman that I looked up a tenants' rights organization and helped her set up an appointment to speak to an advocate. She left and thanked me and I didn't feel any better. Her husband was missing a leg. She had to live underneath these landlords who, she said, made unchristian sounds in the night.

The goth landlord was screaming my name because he'd seen my car on the street. He needed help and knew I was home. He had sheared off two fingers and a thumb with his own table saw. He had the severed parts in a garbage bag. I drove him to Kaiser Hospital in Hollywood, the Burger King of health care, running my horn through intersections along Sunset Boulevard, as the guy bled on the seats in my car, which was a drag because that was a nice car—my Impala. I was stuck with him in the emergency room until his girlfriend could get there from her job. They had him shirtless and tubed with IV pain medication. I was forced to look at his tattoo, a chest-sized upside-down cross.

"Got this to spite my brother," he said, his words thick from pain medication. "He's a minister."

You sure showed him, I did not say.

Victor dead, Conrad dead, the goth neighbor with half a hand. His tenants facing misery, amputation, deportation, the streets.

Bad luck was all around me, although my neighbor and his table saw, that was more like karma. But maybe the worst omen was the veteran, all in black like a grackle. A shadow that crossed my path in the form of a man.

I had taken my car to the shop to have the radiator rodded. The auto shop I went to was off Glendale, and it was an easy bus ride home. The bus I wanted was the 92. I was waiting when this man strolled up, VIETNAM tattooed vertically up his neck. Black felt hat, black clothes, black shoes with no socks, little tinted sunglasses, stylish in an unwholesome way. "I was a POW," he said to me, showing me his home-inked hand: POW.

There are two planes of time: the time of waiting for the bus, and the time when the bus finally pops into view. I was in the wrong plane of time, and stuck with a crazy. Soft heat and exhaust blasted my bare legs as cars accelerated up the hill.

"They cut the head off my penis," the POW said.

"Don't tell me about that."

"I apologize," he said. "Hey, could you spare anything?"

I handed him a dollar, because there was still no sign of the bus and I wanted him to move away. He took the dollar, opened his wallet, but before putting the bill in, he turned the wallet around, so that I would not see what other bills he had in there. It's always this way. Crazy people only lose their cunning last, if they ever lose it.

The bus arrived. I sat in the back. The ghost of my childhood lives in the back of buses. It says, What's up, juts its chin. The POW sat in the handicapped seats up front, struck up a conversation, bothered someone else. He got off at the Arco farther down Glendale, where heroin is bought and sold. I was watching him out the window. I craned my neck to see if he was scoring dope. But what gave me the goddamned right to take note of what he did and where he went? You can't own someone for a dollar.

Thanks to Jimmy the Beard and his idea of a practical joke, Kurt Kennedy drove his motorcycle all the way to Los Angeles. Parked it between two cars. He waited on my porch behind a thick screen of bougainvillea, so that he was invisible from the street.

That morning, a Sunday, it was ninety degrees when I got up. Jackson and I went to the beach with Jimmy Darling. I'd never been to the Venice boardwalk, and perhaps taking me there was Jimmy Darling's own idea of a practical joke.

We strolled along, past the sword swallowers and tattoo parlors and piercing salons. The tables with pineapple incense, blueberry incense, and melon oil. Mango and strawberry hookahs. Crunk and old-school hip-hop blared as hippies danced recklessly, swinging their waist-length beards and beads. Homeless senior citizens slept in pools of urine. Shirtless Rollerbladers, fake-baked and sweaty, weaved among the crowds and the indiscreet piles of vomit. People shoved. Children cried.

This is awful, I said.

Jimmy Darling put his arm around me and said that he liked to think of it as the *very best* California had to offer. We walked over to the skateboard park because Jackson wanted to watch the teenagers riding around in its concrete pools. When we got there an argument was erupting between two skateboarders. One cracked the other over the head with his board. People came out of nowhere, and suddenly there was a crowd of shirtless men, fighting.

Jimmy picked up Jackson and ran. I followed them. We found our car and got in it and sat. I was upset. That crack, board to skull. Jimmy calmed me down. We took Jackson into a bar away from the beach, ate hamburgers and watched a Dodgers game. After the game, as we said goodbye, it felt like I had someone I could rely on. We kissed through the window of Jimmy's truck until I pulled away and said goodbye.

I drove home. Jackson fell asleep in the backseat. It was probably nine p.m. when I parked on my street. I know it was nine p.m. because every minute was later accounted for.

I mounted my stairs, carrying my slumped little boy over my shoulder.

On my porch, in my porch chair, sat Kurt Kennedy. Kennedy, with his dented and bald head, the square freckles, the neckroll, the hoarse voice, the persistence, here he was.

To have moved away, and felt free of him for the first time in months. And to come home and find him waiting for me.

I had the bad luck, too.

19

Candy Peña made baby blankets with the yarn Gordon Hauser had brought her. The blankets were collected by a unit officer and placed in the office of receiving and release. Whenever Gordon passed the office he saw them there, in a giant leaf bag, the colors of the yarn that he had chosen peeking out, garish and sad. One day he asked the officer in R and R about their status. The officer was a scalded blonde with a tight ponytail, brusque, ex-military. She snorted. "These? Nobody wants 'em. I keep forgetting to tell the porters to take them out to the trash."

That same officer supervised family visits, when inmates got thirty-six hours in the prison's version of an apartment, with blood relatives.

Blood relatives. It sounded so violent. Or was Gordon losing perspective, everything warped by what was around him.

Was it difficult to watch them say goodbye? Gordon had asked the R and R officer, before he knew better. He had witnessed, passing family visiting, small children clinging to their mothers and crying hysterically. Someone had painted a lavender hop-scotch pattern on the walkway outside the family units.

"You grow a thick skin," the officer said, her mouth pulled into a frown, as if to demonstrate: this is thick skin. "Especially when you know it's the mother's own fault."

It would have been better if the baby blankets had gone to

the trash. Instead, one of the unit cops had redistributed them to the women on death row who had made them. When Gordon was next back there, Candy Peña had patched together her two baby blankets into a large vest, a sort of poncho, in soft, gauzy blue and yellow. She held it up. "I hope it fits?"

Knit was the past tense of knit. And no one wanted what Candy Peña knit, not even Gordon, who put the vest in a paper bag deep in the trunk of his car and tried to forget about it.

He let whiskey pad his brain at Baressi's one night and was overcome by nostalgia for Simone, the woman he'd dated in Berkeley. Recently she had called and left a message, wondering if he'd plugged in his refrigerator. That had been her joke when they'd dated, meant to imply he was a work in progress, not ready yet, but eventually headed for, life with a plugged-in refrigerator. It was a way of equating his lack of domestic instincts with his rejection of her, which made him guiltier than she knew, because it wasn't quite right. It was Simone he'd had reservations about, not parting ways with bachelorhood. He had not called back, and why not? Now that he was drunkish and lonely he could not think of the reason. The young bartender, with her big smile, her fake breasts pressing against the buttons of her shirt, kept asking the assembled but separate drinkers, all male, if they needed anything. "Y'all have everything y'all need?" She asked it like this was Appalachia and not the Central Valley.

On the TV above her was handheld footage of a city taken over by a Shiite militia, men and boys in white face masks ripping past the camera on motor scooters, piles of debris burning casually in the background. Someone asked the bartender to put on minor league baseball. Gordon would read about the militia when he got home. The war was private. It was between each man and his computer. Gordon might have opted for a more ascetic life and skipped getting DSL, but the previous tenant already had it installed. The landlord said he was one of the lucky ones. Many addresses on the mountain could not get service.

I'll send Simone a postcard, he thought. Be oblique. Not disclose that he hoped to make her cry out like that puma on his mountain, in the scene he imagined. Simone, having come down to his cabin in the woods, his books in little stacks along the dirty floor, his bottle of whiskey on the kitchen counter. A woman there to witness his solitary life, his acquired taste for valley beauty—to the untrained eye, not beautiful. The valley was a brutal, flat, machined landscape, with a strange lemonade light, thick with drifting topsoil and other pollutants from farm equipment and oil refineries. It was a man-made hell on earth but then again a real valley, with mountain ranges on either side. It was the size of industrial agriculture, scaled for that. It was difficult to imagine what it had looked like before it was farmed. It was hard even to imagine what it had looked like farmed in the old-fashioned way, by people. Machines shook the almond trees in synchronous violence. Their fruit fell to the ground with every mechanical jolt. Other machines swept the unhulled almonds into furrows, and yet other automated contraptions sucked the almonds up chutes and into hoppers. That all happened very quickly once a year, the September harvest. Most of the time the huge parcels of almond orchard were empty and quiet.

He paid his tab and walked to the gas station next door. The gas station was the main booze outlet in town and there was a line, men and boys squinting under the harsh lights as they waited to buy their malt liquor and Mad Dog. Gordon retrieved a small Perrier from the refrigerator cases, for the trip up the mountain. The carbonation helped him stay alert while driving. The kid in line behind him gazed at Gordon's drink as he set it on the counter. "What is that?" he asked. The green, pear-shaped glass bottle looked suddenly comely and exotic. Gordon understood the kid had mistaken it for something alcoholic. "It's uh, this French water."

"French *water*." The kid tsked. "I thought it was some new kind of drank."

They had no postcards at the gas station. Try the Dollar Tree, the cashier suggested. He found no postcards of Stanville. Apparently it wasn't a place you commemorated and if he wanted to be in touch with Simone he could just send her an e-mail like a normal person.

That Christmas, his week off, he drove up to Berkeley to sleep on Alex's couch.

"How's your one-room life?" Alex asked.

Gordon did not contact Simone. He and Alex made the nostalgia circuit: the used bookstores, the Irish cafeteria in the flats, the coffeehouses on Telegraph that were filled with good-looking women who worked hard at appearing effortless and natural. The barbecue place on Shattuck and the blues club next door, which could have had a sign, when they were in college, Smokiest Tavern on Earth, but no one smoked in bars now; it was illegal. Alex and Gordon talked about the war. They both checked the same websites obsessively, Informed Comment for analysis and iCasualties for metrics. Found the same things funny and the same things heinous. It was all heinous, but some of it was funny. The way Bush talked about "Mr. Maliki," whom the CIA had installed as president. "I'm trying to *help* the man!" Bush said with real but clueless desperation, at a failed press conference.

Trying to *help* the man! Alex kept repeating.

Just after Christmas, the new Iraqi government hanged Saddam Hussein. Gordon and Alex watched it on the internet.

"He was pretty dignified," Alex said. "He was being heckled as he died and yet I feel he got the last word."

Gordon went over the bridge to San Francisco alone, ate at a Vietnamese restaurant downtown that his student Romy Hall had told him about. Not that she was recommending it to him. She listed it among places she missed. The cook, she'd said, has this funny habit. After he uses them, he bangs his cooking tongs twice, and tugs on his shirt. His smock has a big grease splotch where he does that. And his father sits chain-smoking and chopping meat, upstairs, where the bathrooms are. The cook was there, on Gordon's visit. He banged the tongs twice and pulled on his shirt. The father was upstairs, chain-smoking and chopping a huge pile of meat.

On New Year's, he and Alex went to a party in Oakland, a typical situation of people jammed in a kitchen and asking pointless questions like, What do you do? And, Where are you from? The women paid extra attention to Gordon, not knowing already what the problem was with him, as they had already established with the other single men at that party, according to Alex. Some of them were former grad students who'd branched off from the English or Rhetoric or Comp Lit departments into psychoanalysis. Not just undergoing it but putting out a shingle. Alex said that he'd been labeled a male hysteric, which mostly meant the woman who blithely diagnosed him wanted to sleep with him but found him too wily and little-brotherish for an actual relationship.

When Gordon hesitantly mentioned what he did for work, after being asked several times, the women in the kitchen were on him like a plague of locusts.

"Really? A prison. That must be hard."

"Prison guards. I wouldn't be able to look at those people."

"They don't even wear their own clothes. Like cops, but even worse. What a fucked-up life."

Much discussion among the women about the scum of the earth who worked as guards. He did not have the courage, or maybe it was the will, to ask if these women had ever known a prison guard. And why would he defend prison guards? He hated them himself. But if a person got outside their own bubble they would see that prison guards were poor people without reasonable options. One had just blown his head off in a guard tower at Salinas Valley. He could have told them this, engaged in corrective arguments with these women at the party. But wasn't it obvious? Didn't even wear their own clothes. The interaction brought back anxieties from grad school, the way his peers could casually criticize others they didn't know anything about.

As the first and only member of his family to pursue so-called higher education, maybe Gordon was prone to hypersensitivity. He had encountered people in graduate school who were eager to declare working-class pedigree, and they maybe had one parent with less education, or the family had been "poor," but college-educated. Either way, if someone was insisting loudly on their own authentic origin, this was generally taken by Gordon as evidence they weren't actually working-class. If they were from a background like Gordon's, they would know to hide it, the way Gordon did, because the fact of his pioneering status was itself proof of just how tenuous his escape was.

Some people he knew showed up at the party, friends from the department who had gotten post-docs and talked about their upcoming job interviews, the details of their academic book contracts, as if these were interesting subjects. The women were doing that grad school thing of air-quoting to install distance between themselves and the words they chose, these bookish women with an awkwardness he used to find cute. Gordon did not want to discuss his life with these people. He drank, as a temporary salve for his alienation.

He and Alex woke up with hangovers.

With Alex, at least, Gordon could express something of what it was like at Stanville. He had been describing his students, giving Alex the impression that Romy Hall was just one more student he helped, or tried to help, equal with the others, which made him inwardly aware that it wasn't the case.

Alex started questioning him about his involvement with prisoners. Alex talked about Norman Mailer and Jack Henry Abbott. Alex said he wondered whether Mailer was responsible for what happened after he got Jack Henry Abbott, his little pet project, out of prison.

He wasn't a pet project, Gordon said.

"Yeah yeah," Alex said. "He wasn't. He was a person. But did Norman Mailer understand that?"

His first day back at work, the warden put the prison on lockdown because of fog. It wasn't even real fog. It was haze from crop dusters that sprayed the almond fields surrounding the prison. Lockdown meant everyone confined to their cells. No work exchange, no classes, no movement. He would be paid to do nothing like everyone at the facility, but he felt a sense of regret. He would not see her, would not tell her he'd gone to her Vietnamese place on Sixth Street.

He went home and let impulse drive his actions. Called the number she had given him. Jackson Hall was the name of the kid, written on a pink piece of paper. I am just inquiring. She doesn't even have to know I made this call. The person who answered told him to dial another number. At the new number he was put on hold for a very long time, and then passed to someone's voice mail. After several days, someone called him back and left a message. Gordon was at work. He called the number the next morning, reached a voice mail and left another message. This went on for weeks, because Gordon wasn't home much, since he worked down in the valley and lived up on the mountain.

What he eventually learned, when he spoke with a human being at San Francisco's Family and Children Services, was exactly proof of why he should not have gotten involved.

20

A few years ago some fuckers built a vacation house just across Stemple Pass Road. Motorcycle and snowmobile fiends. They would buzz up and down the road past my cabin most weekends, summer and winter. Last summer they were worse than usual, sometimes made it a three-day-weekend. It was getting absolutely intolerable. My heart was going bad. Any emotional stress, anger above all, makes it beat irregularly. It got so that the constant cycle noise was choking me with anger, heart going wild. Risky to commit crimes so close to home, but I figured if I didn't get these guys the anger would literally kill me. So one night in fall I sneaked over there, though they were home, and stole their chainsaw. Buried it in the swamp.

Couple of weeks later I chopped my way into their house, smashed up interior pretty thoroughly. It was a real luxury place. They also had a mobile home there. I broke into that, too. Found a silver-painted motorcycle inside. Smashed it up with my axe. They had four snowmobiles sitting outside. I thoroughly smashed engines of these.

A week or so later cops came up here and asked had I seen anyone fooling around any buildings. Also asked if I had any problems with motorcycles. The truth crossed their minds. But probably they didn't seriously suspect me. Otherwise their questions would not have been so perfunctory.

I'm pleased I was so collected in answering cops' questions.

21

This is how a guy never, ever wants to wake up: handcuffed, and in a hospital bed. But that was how Doc found himself. Cuffed to the bed. A doctor walked in. Not a prison medical technician's assistant, but a real doctor. He was even wearing a white coat. The doctor leaned over him.

"You're awake," he said. "Can you hear me okay?"

Doc nodded.

"Do you know how you got here?"

Doc shook his head. He had no goddamned idea.

"Okay, that's okay. Let's start with basics. Do you know what year it is?"

"It's—"

Doc did not know what year it was. But it dawned on him that he knew how to answer this stupid question.

"It's the year after last year."

The doctor frowned. "Do you know where you are?"

Doc looked around. Saw nothing but a metal cart with pills in paper cups. An armed guard sitting on a chair. The room had no windows, and there was nothing on the walls. He looked down at his body. Saw a garment that was half a garment. His hand was plastered with tape holding a needle in. Tubes ran from his hand up to a metal stand with a bag hanging from it, half full of clear liquid. A person who must have been a nurse came in and eyed the bag. Squeezed it in a way that seemed reckless, and walked out of the room. Doc's cuffed wrists were chained to the bed's metal rails. His ankles, too, were manacled to the bedrails. He had no clue where he was. All he knew was that his skull felt like it had been split in half by a concrete spillway. Icy water splashed through the spillway, pushing his brains apart.

"Any sense of where you are?" the doctor asked again.

"Yes. I am directly above the center of the earth."

Hey, at least it was an answer.

The doctor smirked. "All right, funny guy. And can you tell me your name?"

"I can," Doc said. "I know my name. I know it!"

"Congratu-fuckin-lations," the guard called out from his chair.

"It's Richard L. Richards. See this?" Doc glanced at his own forearm, where he had a big dollar sign tattooed and underneath it, FUCK YOU I'M RICH. It was a joke. He was Rich, Rich Richards, even if people called him Doc. He'd discovered it on the wall of a tattoo parlor in Hollywood, among the designs customers could choose. Doc didn't have amnesia. He knew who he was. Fuck you, I'm Rich. He just got his bell rung somehow and could not remember the some or how.

He had a shackle around his waist. A stun shackle, actually. If he tried to pull away, it would zap him good and fierce.

"What did I do?" he asked the doctor. "Did I kill somebody?"

The armed guard at the door laughed long and loud. "Did I *kill* somebody," he imitated in a mock-high voice.

"You sustained a traumatic brain injury," the doctor explained. "You almost died. You've been in an induced coma for eight weeks now, while we waited for the swelling to go down."

"Has this asshole been sitting there guarding me the whole time?"

"Time and a half, actually," the asshole said.

The doctor explained to Doc that he was in a hospital in Lodi. "Fuck, I hate Lodi."

But had he ever been to Lodi? He wasn't sure.

Traumatic brain injury, they kept repeating at him. The doctor gave him a pamphlet, "Educating Your Loved Ones About Your TBI." It was what they gave out at that hospital, which did not treat convicts unless it was forced to. Doc didn't have any loved ones, but he read it anyway. He would be sleeping a lot, his imaginary loved ones were meant to understand. He might seem to have undergone a personality transformation, and present now as more mild, or more angry, less or more prone to violent outburst, gifted in a savant-like way, or blunted and dulled in intelligence and executive functioning. Loved ones, for those who had them, should be patient about these changes, and about the recovering person's confusions and sensitivities, his vertigo, his atypical ideas and erratic moods.

Doc did have a lot of strange thoughts over the days he lay in that bed, waiting for the nurse to come in and squeeze and change the IV bag. Mostly they were thoughts about country music stars, who roamed his mind like ponies on a circle track. These stars, men and women both, were fancy, dressed to perform for thousands onstage and many thousands more in television land. They were folks who seemed like old friends of the family, but he didn't know what family, or whose. There was a reunion feeling crowding into his mind, many people gathering on the stage for an all-star number. Dolly Parton with her dimples. Roy Acuff. Ray Pillow. Ray Price the Cherokee Cowboy. Skeeter Davis. Ferlin Husky. Everyone in on "Wildwood Flower."

Cut to a commercial for Martha White Flour, sung by Flatt and Scruggs.

The doctor said that brain injuries could do that. Make you see a memory clearly, or hear music, or in this case both.

Doc's sadistic foster dad, Vic, had been fond of the Grand Ole Opry and watched the TV show. Porter Wagoner was his foster father's favorite. Porter Wagoner wore denim jackets with cutaway tails to showcase his fry-pan-sized rodeo buckle. His face was tall and oval-shaped like the canvas opening of a covered wagon. His slack creases could have sliced ham, slacks that were too form-fitting to need any belt, much less a rodeo buckle, and the idea that a dandy like Porter Wagoner had been a winner or even a contestant in any legitimate rodeo was not realistic, but it was part of the culture.

Time pedaled past, Doc's thoughts free-floating, giving the days and nights a seamless sameness, dazed wakefulness, a fresh IV bag, an exchange of lighthearted hostility with the guard by the door, and knockout sleeps.

One day they put him in prison clothes and shuttled him back to New Folsom, but not his former block. Doc had to go to the skilled nursing facility, because he slept twenty hours a day and had balance issues, fell over when he tried to walk.

He knew what year it was. He knew where he was. He could not remember why he hated Lodi, but maybe it wasn't important. Fuck you, I'm Rich. The information was back, more or less, but he felt changed. Altered. Not just on account of the country music piping in through one ear, or via some other entry point, piping in and filling him with sounds and images from the past. The most extreme difference was his temperament. It was like someone had gone in there, into his head—not the biological goo packed into the skull, but the *real him*, the memories and feelings, the images stored up. As if someone had gone in there and mucked around, changed things, while he was in the coma. He felt different. He felt good. Even if he suffered from debilitating headaches and did not always have words when he went to say them. He had this feeling that everything was going to be okay. Which was strange, because nothing would be. He was serving a sentence of life without parole. And he was a cop, and now that well-guarded secret was out. Everyone knew, which was why his cellie had tried to kill him. Doc was greenlighted. His future would only be shitty. He would be transferred to a prison that was all protective custody. Once there, if his cover got blown, if people found out about his background, there would be no place left to transfer. It was likely Doc was going to die a violent death. And yet, he took things one hour at a time and didn't panic. He felt a sense of peace, and it was new, a new feeling for him. Probably his edge had been blunted, just like the pamphlet for his imaginary loved ones had warned.

"I feel good. I feel pretty fucking good," he said to the blank walls of his little cell.

"What did they dose you with, honey?" a voice from the next cell called out. "I want some. All they give me is Ultram."

"I don't get any drugs," Doc said. "I just feel good. It's 'cause I got my brains bashed in. What happened to you?"

"I was jumped, and the cops watched. No one helped me."

His neighbor had a high voice. Doc liked the sound of it. He had overheard the nurses. His neighbor was a powder puff, a "she." Her name was Serenity and Doc wanted to know all about her.

"Are you white or black?" he called through the wall.

"I'm all colors, honey."

But he saw, through the slim window in his cell door, when they took Serenity to the showers, that she was black. She was thin and delicate-boned and had the face of an angel. A fucking angel. He saw it. Chick was good-looking. But the poor thing.

Her arm was in a sling, and her leg was in a cast. They rolled her down the hall in a wheelchair. The way she smiled when she turned back to her nursing attendant amazed Doc. She had a woman's smile, and something about her smile, it made the world worth smiling over.

He tried to get a glimpse of her every time he heard the commotion of her cell being opened.

"Hey, All Colors," he said one morning. "I think you're beautiful."

"You're not my type, love."

"How do you know?"

" 'Cuz I seen you. Your head looks like a softball, with all that stitching."

Doc laughed. "I seen you, too. They really messed you up, didn't they?"

They had beat her unconscious. She cried as she told him about it.

Later, when Doc thought back on what Serenity told him, he knew he wasn't completely changed now. He knew he was still the old Doc, because he could stoke his own anger by thinking about what had happened to Serenity. He wanted to obliterate the two people who'd hurt her. Put bullets in their skulls. Put their bodies in his trunk, and eject them into the dumping ground of desert between LA and Vegas.

He was growing fond of the voice next door. The girl next door. He used to insult the powder puffs, and why? These were ladies, in a men's joint. He had enjoyed their boobies but he didn't treat them like humans. Serenity was pretty close to a genuine lady; she had no pecker. There was nothing "down there." She made fun of him for saying it that way, but in the presence of a woman he didn't want to talk crude. She'd had a sex change but it was prison cell surgery, performed on herself in a moment of bravery and desperation. She almost died from blood loss. She got better. They put her in general population. She was attacked, raped and beaten, by two men in her unit. The prison wanted to keep her permanently in ad seg.

"They said they can't guarantee my safety. Even if they put me in a snitch prison I might not be safe."

She was petitioning to get reclassified as a female and sent to a women's prison. There was another inmate in the state system who had done this, her lawyer told her. It was Serenity's dream.

"I hope your dream comes true for you," Doc called to her through the wall.

Soon, Doc himself was going to snitch prison, but he did not tell Serenity this, or really anything personal. What was there to say? I was a crooked cop who murdered people? His eggs might have been scrambled, he might be weak and softer than before, but he wasn't stupid.

Over those months in the skilled nursing facility, when he wasn't yelling back and forth with Serenity, he listened to the country music that was more or less playing all the time. There was a finger on a button in his brain pressing play. He heard Grandpa Jones. Booger Beasley. The Possum Hunters. The Fruit Jar Drinkers. The Tarpaper Sharecroppers. Stringbean and his String Band. Stringbean was a singer who wore pants belted at the thigh, way down low, attached to his shirt so the whole ensemble would stay up. It was funny, back then. In the 1960s. At least his foster father, Vic, thought it was funny and wanted Doc to laugh alongside. Or Vic wanted Doc to go fetch him an ashtray. Stringbean was tall but his pants were tiny, because belted down low, at his thighs, and much shorter than a tall man's actual legs. Stringbean was not making fun of the way young black males had their pants so low down. It was way before all of that. If you told Stringbean that his pants were gangster style, and also prison style, belted at the thigh, well, you just wouldn't. There would be no way to explain it. The comedy show on the Grand Ole Opry was for white people. Country music was for white people, even when it was sung by Charley Pride. Stringbean's low-slung pants were a freakish, accidental echo. Hillbilly bands sang jingles for hillbilly flour, which was a brand. Hillbilly. Little Texas Daisy Rhodes sang the ad with the Golden West Cowboys. She had bad skin and dark eyes and a grainy lurid appeal. Not pretty, but pretty sexy.

Hank Williams was malnourished and his spine was crooked. Minnie Pearl had been cleaning rooms as a maid when Judge Hay gave her the big break, at the old-maid age of twenty-eight. Hank Snow had been a cabin boy. Marty Robbins was raised in a tent, caught wild horses for a living. Porter Wagoner had a third-grade education. Dolly Parton had a dozen siblings and no indoor plumbing. Country music was a homey affair. And not the homey of people who wore low pants like Stringbean, but not as a joke, not the homey they meant, which was another word for brother or friend.

Texas Ruby Owens burned up in a trailer fire. A trailer fire was a hazard for many sorts of people, Doc's people. But also the types of people Doc arrested. Doc had shown up on the scene of a trailer fire in Westlake in the early 1980s. It was a slovenly place vandalized by its own inhabitants, Mexicans who mixed their beer with clam and tomato juice, lit superstition candles, and passed out. Forgot about the candles and one fell over. "Par-tee shack," Doc had said after the firemen had doused the flames and the trailer was just a charred shell, hissing and steaming. Doc had thought it was funny these people had burned themselves homeless. Fuck, I was such an asshole.

He told Serenity he had been a bad person. He'd hooked up with another bad person, and they killed a guy together. He told the whole story to Serenity, of Betty and her husband, and her husband's hit man. Serenity said if the dude was a hit man, maybe they'd done a good thing. Maybe Doc wasn't all bad. Serenity was a flirt, she sugarcoated, probably part of why he liked her so much.

"I killed a kid for no reason," he said, switching to the worst fact, the scene outside the pawn shop on Beverly. "Blew his brains out."

"I killed someone, too," Serenity said, to Doc's surprise and irritation. This was his big confessional moment and it turned out they were both assholes. And suddenly Doc wanted to have a pissing contest, insist he was worse. But then he remembered Serenity was a lady and not to compete. He tried to focus on what she was saying.

"My cousin Shawn had this stupid idea to steal some shit from a house," she said. "No one was supposed to be there. They were just some people with jobs and they were supposed to be at work, but they were home. Shawn went off the plan and tied them up but the man got loose and escaped. All we had was the woman and she was screaming her head off. Shawn ordered me to shoot her. I did what he said. I'd give anything to bring that lady back."

Serenity got her reclassification. The state considered her female. After that everything went fast. They had to whisk her out of the prison, because they suddenly had a woman deep in the nursing ward of a men's facility.

Doc felt all her excitement and nerves through the wall. He congratulated her and wished her luck.

"I'm scared," she told him. "What if the women don't accept me?"

Doc told her what Judge Hay had said to Minnie Pearl when she was just starting out, green as the hills of Tennessee, and nervous to go on out there on the big-time stage at the Grand Ole Opry, in front of so many people.

"You got to just go out there and love 'em, honey," Judge Hay had said to Minnie Pearl, and Doc repeated to Serenity.

"Just go out there and love them, and they'll love you right back."

Six weeks later, Doc's counselor told him he was well enough for a medical yard on a Sensitive Needs block at a snitch prison in the high desert.

"I cannot fucking wait," Doc said, with not the slightest trace of sarcasm.

22

I got a visitor one day. You don't know beforehand who it is. They call your name and send you to visiting. I had been at Stanville three and a half years, and no one had ever come to see me. I didn't even get mail. I had written to a few friends from San Francisco. None of them wrote back. People fall away quickly when you disappear into prison.

I couldn't imagine who had made the trip.

When I got through strip-out I saw that it was Johnson's lawyer.

"I don't have news for you," he said, in response to my look of hopeful surprise.

"I came to see how you are. The thing about retirement is you don't retire from thinking. From here I'm going up to Corcoran to visit a guy who got five life sentences, and another who is life without. You look healthy."

"I'm not," I said. "I'm just tan." I had been spending so much time on the unshaded yard that my arms and legs were the cake-brown color of unglazed donuts.

Teardrop was also in the visiting room. She was sitting with an old man. The guy was sweating profusely. He looked about ninety-five. I didn't know people that old could sweat. Teardrop was six feet tall, strong, semi-masculine, angry, and beautiful, her hair pulled back tight, face like a weapon. This old man was stooped, and bald, and kept clutching his chest. It was obvious he was a runner she'd hustled through the mail. At a different table was Button Sanchez, also with an old man. He'd bought her an entire smorgasbord from the vending machines: microwave hamburger and french fries, ice cream sandwich, and two kinds of energy drink. She was smiling at him as he fondled her breasts with his eyes.

Teardrop and Button, and other women around me, all working their Keaths: it was not that different from the Mars Room, except here they were preening and selling their asses for prepackaged junk food. Or in Teardrop's case, a bag of heroin.

I needed runners like the rest of them. I, too, now had a page on a pen pal site. But what could be gotten this way had no real value. It did not lead to peace of mind, to help for Jackson. It led to nothing but animal existence with mail order cologne, two choices, Tabu or Sand & Sable.

"Is there any way to contact my son?"

"That's outside my area. If I could help you with that, I would, but I can't."

"I have to get out of this place."

I watched the old man slip Teardrop a package, and Teardrop shove it, deftly, into her prison pants.

"You've got to help me."

The lawyer opened his briefcase and took out a stack of papers.

"I'm getting rid of records and thought you might want your file. It's the material from your case, depositions, notes, witness interviews, discovery."

Seeing that stack of paper, the record of what happened, of what happened to me, I was overcome. I yelled at him to keep from crying. I said I'd been doing research and was pretty sure he'd given ineffective counsel.

"Oh dear," he said, "that would be such a waste of your energies."

"Why? Because it'll make you look bad?"

"Because it doesn't work. Even in these unbelievable cases, where the lawyer is totally out to lunch, they still side with him. One guy fell asleep during cross-examination of his client. Another was a felon himself, handling a murder case as community service, but had no experience as a trial lawyer. Think those guys were 'ineffective'? Not according to the Supreme Court. You got a very tough deal. There's no question, and I feel for you."

"If only I could have afforded a lawyer."

He shook his head. "Romy, the people who hire private lawyers, but can't afford a good one, I mean an expensive one, oh boy is that painful. You should see the private attorneys people end up with. Guys who do DUIs, suddenly handling a capital case. It should be illegal. You were much better off with the public defender's office."

It was hard to imagine I could be any worse off and I said so. Tears ran down my neck. I wanted to unload on this man. And yet he was the only person who had ever come to see me.

Teardrop's visitor collapsed on the table. The cops from the cop shop rushed over. The old man seemed to be having a heart attack. An alarm sounded. Medical technicians came rushing into the room.

"Visiting is over," the intercoms boomed. "Visiting is over. Return to your units."

Hauser had made it pretty obvious he liked me. Everyone in class knew. It became a joke, Conan humming "Here Comes the Bride" as I walked into the classroom trailer, sweaty and coated in woodshop dust.

Sammy went into overdrive about Hauser's crush on me, speculating that maybe he'd adopt Jackson, when I told her I had given Hauser a number to call. Sammy was a walking historian of every person who had faced every adversity in prison and could produce examples of all the cases where staff, or even guards, had stepped in and raised the children of imprisoned women. She went on about it and meant well but it didn't comfort me. I didn't think she was reading things right, that any of her examples were relevant. I didn't know how to explain it to her: this is a normal and nice college-educated boy who probably separates bottles and cans from the rest of his trash. He's not going to adopt my kid. He'll marry a nice girl like him who also recycles and they will have children together, their own.

But in truth I had begun to live for his GED class, even if I didn't admit it. I was determined to work on him for Jackson's sake, but I also worked on him for a more minor and less delusional reason. He knew places I knew. When I talked to him, I became a person from a place. I could roam neighborhoods, visit my apartment in the Tenderloin, with the Murphy bed, my happy yellow Formica table, and above it, the movie poster of Steve McQueen in *Bullitt*. If you're from SF, you love *Bullitt* and are proud because it was filmed there. Plus, Steve McQueen had been a delinquent kid who became a star but stayed cool, did his own stunt driving. I teased Jimmy Darling that compared to Steve McQueen he was hardly a man. Jimmy was not offended by that, because, as he told me, he was not aspiring to become one.

Just up the block and around the corner from my Tenderloin apartment was a dive bar called the Blue Lamp where I sometimes went after work with a few girls from the Mars Room. The bartender, an adorable old lady who wore turtlenecks with a sparkly brooch pinned to the neck, was always happy to see me and my friends. She bought us drinks, and we tipped her generously in return. Around midnight the French cook would appear—not a chef but a cook—an alcoholic in a stained prep smock printed with the name of a downtown hotel. The cook was from Brittany and smoked foreign cigarettes that gave off a terrible stench. He told the same joke over and over and it wasn't even a proper joke: he looked at us girls from the Mars Room and shouted, "I am lesbian!" punching his own chest for emphasis.

As the bar closed one night, there was a catfight out front. Hookers who worked that area, brawling down on the ground. People from the apartment building up above dumped buckets of water on the fighting women, like people do to cats, to get them to shut up. The women kept on, soaked, with ruined hair, wilted and torn outfits that were half off them from fighting. Everyone but me was laughing at the fighting women, wet, and struggling, rolling around on the pavement, trying to hurt each other. I was haunted by that scene, although I really don't know why.

We were all waiting for afternoon count—you have to sit on your bed until it's completed—when Laura Lipp announced to our room that she had a surprise for us, not a good one. She lay back in her bunk and gave us her Juggalo grin, elated to be the bearer of bad news.

"Spit it out, psycho," said Teardrop.

"I know you all love nicknames, but I don't answer to Psycho." Teardrop grabbed Laura's hair and yanked. "Say it and shut up." Laura cried in pain, her hair in Teardrop's fist.

"There's a man in this prison! There's a man here and they want to put him on C yard!"

What outraged people most, as the campaign grew, was that this prisoner, Serenity Smith, had killed a woman, before he operated on himself and became one. A hysteria brewed that a dangerous man was being placed among us, and that we would be left to fend for ourselves. We might have to share a room with him. Undress in front of him. Shower next to him. And he was evil, evil, evil.

Because Laura spilled the beans, they delayed mainlining Serenity Smith, hoping the situation would calm down.

Factions formed. Conan, who had to endure the daily humiliation of "Miss" and "Ma'am," who had to get a series of psychological evaluations and fill out endless paperwork and wait years for approval in order to simply wear boxer shorts instead of granny drawers, was on the side of acceptance. He and some of the other stud broads on C yard, our version of men, had a community and they decided, as a group, that it was important to support Ms. Smith, as Conan respectfully referred to her. To welcome her. Because cops were assholes about anyone who didn't conform to narrow gender norms, and we, they, hated cops, and needed to stick together. I wasn't excited to possibly room with a woman who had been a man who had cut his own dick and nuts off. But as the tension brewed, and I heard about the plans to jump this person, clobber her, I saw the face of a woman I had known at the Blue Lamp, on Geary. She sat at the bar dressed like a secretary, in a glossy auburn wig. She was petite and exceedingly feminine. Pretty, but strange. She had a scratchy voice like someone with permanent laryngitis. I guess she was biologically a man but no less female, and fragile, for that. She sat alone at the bar, sipping at the needle-thin straw of her gin and tonic. She pursed her pink painted lips and waited to be approached by men. I remember her leaving with one, and returning, later, with a black eye covered in makeup. Is that woman from the Blue Lamp with her pink lips and her auburn wig, her ritual lonely post at the bar, is she still alive? Maybe not. Just because Serenity Smith had previously been a man didn't mean she wasn't vulnerable.

They kept Ms. Smith in protective custody. When they moved her, it was like they were moving someone on death row, double escort, with sharpshooters trained on her from the gun towers. Women screamed obscenities. She was gassed with jars of urine.

The anti-Smith struggle was a hate campaign, complete with biblical passages and claims about morality and Christian values. Laura Lipp used the copy machine in the clerk's office to make flyers. She wrote letters to the governor, the warden, congresspeople, whoever else. Her mother was campaigning outside. Laura flipped her shiny sheet of hair and claimed outrage that a killer would be housed among us.

I had started helping Button with her homework for Hauser's class. I took more pleasure in it than I would have guessed. It was a big-sister thing. Sammy was my big sister and I was Button's, and Conan was something like the dad. We had a family. It was not that comforting, but it was something, even if Button was a pain in the ass. Always angry, and ready to fight. But when Teardrop ate Button's pet rabbit, I saw a different side to Button.

Teardrop had boiled the rabbit in a pot with her stinger while the rest of us were programming. When we came back for afternoon count, the room was infused with the heavy smell of cooked meat.

"What kind of spread is that?" Conan asked.

Brunswick stew, Teardrop said.

Afterward, Conan kept saying, "Didn't even have no seasoning, I mean *nothing*," as if that was the infraction, eating Button's pet rabbit unseasoned. "Anyway, a proper Brunswick stew is squirrel, not rabbit."

Button crawled into her bunk with her rabbit's little shirt that she had sewn. She stayed that way for a day.

"Are you sick?" a unit cop shouted at her.

Button, face in her pillow, did not answer.

"If you are not sick, and not going to your assigned program, I'm writing you up, Sanchez."

The way Button clutched the little shirt reminded me of how Jackson held his stuffed ducky when he slept. He had been sleeping with the ducky since he was a baby. He would grip it tight, all night long. The last time I saw the ducky was the night I was arrested. Jackson, crying, police all around him. Holding his ducky and screeching, Mommy! Mommy!

"You can get another rabbit," I told Button. "You're good with them."

Eventually she did, and trained it, put the same clothes on it, gave it the same name.

Only once had Button talked to me about her own baby. She told me what happened. From prison they took her to a hospital, where they stored her in a room with an armed guard. The guy even followed her to the bathroom, where she tried, in cuffs, a waist chain, and ankle shackles, to clean herself, wash the blood and afterbirth from the insides of her legs, put on the postpartum underwear and giant maxi-pad they tossed her way.

"They had somebody on me the whole motherfucking time."

I pictured a cop standing over the newborn, already half criminalized, the cop watching it to be sure of no sudden movements.

Button had been badly torn up by the birth, and could barely walk from the stitches a doctor had given her. "A woodpecker," she said, "with a do-rag that had American flags all over it. Not one flag, but many flags, all different sizes. All I could see was that pattern on his head as he sewed me up. These fucking flags. I said, How many stitches am I getting? He goes, Try not to think of it like that."

A nurse gave Button a squeezy bottle with stuff to squirt on her stitches so she would heal right. Button was shackled to the bed, but the nice nurse held the baby girl up to her. Button had forty-eight hours to find someone to claim her. Button wasn't sure she knew anyone who had a working car and could get to Stanville to take a baby. She watched the baby breathe, in its hospital crib. Stared at the baby's perfect little face as she slept, the closed violet eyelids, the little mouth. In her exhaustion, Button slept, too. Woke up and her baby was gone. The guards said to get dressed. She put on her prison clothes. They said she could not take the squeezy bottle for her stitches. She was shoved in a van cage, where she bled all over the hard plastic seat and was in so much pain from her torn-up crotch that she had to sit on one buttock for the entire ride back to prison.

Jackson had asked me where his ducky came from. "Your dad gave it to you," I said. He looked at his ducky with love and wonder. Kissed it.

His dad never gave him anything. That kid Ajax from the Mars Room had stolen it for me in an airport gift shop, on his way back from visiting his family in Wisconsin. I'll give it to my son, I'd said. He looked confused, like he'd forgotten I even had one, but I kept Ajax at a distance and he and Jackson had never met.

I told Hauser I read *Jesus' Son*, and asked him why he chose that book. I was paranoid he thought I was a no-good ex-junkie like the characters in the stories.

He said he gave it to me because it was excellent. That it was one of his favorite books.

There was one story where two guys strip copper wire out of a house, and the main guy sees the other guy's wife floating in the sky and thinks he's entered the other guy's dream and it all made sense to me, I told Hauser. I said I knew people who did that, stole copper. Some of them were like the guys in the book, drug fiends looking for quick money, but there were others who did it like it was a profession.

Hauser kept getting me books, and after I read them, I passed them to Sammy, who read them, too. Sammy and I had both skipped seventh grade. We didn't either of us turn out honors students, so it's a strange coincidence. I'd gone to schools with Mexican girls, and we shared attitudes and a certain look: black chinos, Chinese shoes, the Maybelline eyeliner you heat with a lit match, and so I could reminisce with Sammy to pass time. On weekends I'd sometimes go to her housing unit and look at her photo collection. I'd get to see the visuals of all the stories she'd told me when we were locked up in ad seg together. Pictures of her when she was young, and of other people, friends of hers from over the years. Her at CIW, a women's prison down south, which Sammy called CI *Wonderful*. "It was before mass incarceration," she said, as if mass incarceration were some kind of natural disaster. Or a cataclysm, like 9/11, with a before and after. Before mass incarceration.

They'd had a swimming pool at CI Wonderful. There were bathing suits, state-issue, but you had to wear your underwear inside them because they were shared. I reveled in these details of prison the old way, before now. I'm sure it was lousy but according to Sammy some people had goldfish in tanks. They didn't have huge towers with gunners and miles of electric fence. It wasn't concrete living. The rooms had wood shelves, and wood cabinets. They had green grass. Their canteen was stocked with makeup you could buy, and everyone's favorite was a lipstick called purple flame. There was a golf course next to the prison grounds, she said, and someone's boyfriend had dragged a batting machine onto the golf course and batted balls stuffed with heroin and jewelry into the prison's main yard. When I felt low, Sammy would tell me stories about CI Wonderful. It was paradise before the fall.

Sammy's whole collection of pictures was prison photos. One was of a sad, beautiful girl named Sleepy who was life without parole. It was Sleepy's only photo of herself, Sammy said. Sleepy gave it to her when Sammy was released to Keath. This girl Sleepy had no one. She gave the picture of herself to Sammy because she wanted to be sure someone free remembered her, thought of her from time to time. I never met Sleepy. She was transferred north before I arrived. But I knew why Sleepy gave that photo to Sammy, what she wanted from her. There was something about Sammy that came from, and stayed in, the world—the old one, the free one. Poor Sleepy had probably thought that if she could live in Sammy's heart, she could live. It made me so depressed I wanted to tear up the photo when Sammy wasn't looking.

There was nothing to celebrate but sometimes we had parties. It was Conan's passion to plan them in our room. He had been getting everyone to set aside psych meds. What you do is buy peanut butter from canteen, or, if, like me, you have no money

245

for canteen, you share Conan's peanut butter. Put a dab of it on the roof of your mouth before you go to pill call. When you open your mouth like a horse to show them you properly swallowed your meds, you're cleared, but the pill is in the peanut butter, unswallowed. Those with dentures hide the pill under them. Some people just cheek it really well. People from all over unit 510 had contributed. Conan unveiled the stash of pills after evening count. He mashed them with the bottom of a shampoo bottle and made "punch," which is pills dissolved in a container of iced tea. It's a short island iced tea. Sammy snuck over to our unit and came to the room during unlock, when the big hand on the clock was in the imbecile's red wedge.

"I'm feeling streaky," Conan said, and mixed the punch.

I wasn't myself feeling exactly happy as I gulped my share. Sammy refused her cup. She was staying clean, she said. I knew I could stay clean and still drink punch. We aren't all the same. It was a Sunday night. Conan put on the radio to Art Laboe's request and dedication show, which was everyone's weekly favorite.

"This one is from Tiny, up at Pelican Bay, for Lulu, aka Bonita Blue Eyes. Tiny wants to tell Lulu he loves you more than anything, and his heart will always be yours. He's there for you through and through, and he is never going anywhere."

"That's 'cause the motherfucker doing life," Conan said.

An oldies song came on. The trills and dollops of the singer's voice pelted me with unwanted sensations of longing. I drank another cup of punch.

At the next unlock, people crowded into the room. Laura Lipp put her pillow over her head and tried to ignore us. Conan played booty music and Button danced for us.

Later I danced for us, too, but I didn't have a clear memory of it. Just Conan telling me, after, "Sometimes you see something and got to have it."

Conan was strong, and muscular—he had that name for a reason—and he made me laugh. I stopped laughing when I ended up in his bunk that night, and the soft army of his tongue went to work. *Jesus Christ*, I kept whispering. Instead of his usual comic retort, he went deeper. We were still at it when I heard an incredible bang. The noise shocked the hell out of Conan, who reared up and gashed his head on the upper bunk. It was Officer Garcia, who was on night watch in our unit, banging on the window with his billy club.

The mood was ruined, so Conan and I cut out the unexpected bunk session. I wrapped his wound, which was bleeding, and we drank more punch. Everyone crowded into the bathroom, which the cops can't see into from the observation glass.

Maybe because she was young and small, Button was the most sideways. She started talking about God. She said it was God who was in the guard tower on the yard. Which tower, someone asked, Tower One or Tower Two? She said, "He's got the high field on us. He sees us."

Conan said, "That's not God. That's Sergeant Rintler, one more Elmer Fudd up there, taking naps, jerking off. Duck-hunting motherfuckers."

Conan adopted a cowboy twang. "Ma'am, step back, ma'am. Don't make me write you up, ma'am."

Button started to cry. "But they control the whole sky. This is the world now. If He's not in the towers, where is God? Where is He?"

Laura Lipp walked into the bathroom. We stopped talking and stared. She looked like the Exorcist. She'd snuck punch from us. She was loaded.

"I'm from Apple Valley," she said.

"We know," everyone shouted. Sammy stood to push Laura out of the bathroom.

"But *I* never knew. I didn't listen. Didn't hear. I never

understood what that means. The valley of apples. It's about temptation. Right? Sin. See? Poisoned fruit. Oh, it feels so good," she said, "to have a place to put your anger, to punish someone like you've been hurt. That is the truth and every woman like me knows it. The one who hits her child with a hanger or a belt or who shook a baby, it's all the same. You do it because it feels good. They won't say. They won't tell you how it is. They don't have the courage. I'm telling you. The devil goes in us and we do it to feel good. I wish they had stopped me but no one did. God, He stopped the hand of Abraham. He *intervened*. But where was He when I needed him? He wasn't there. No one helped me. No one." She stumbled like a blind person, kneeled on the floor on her hands and knees, and sobbed.

I took the liberty of sleeping in Conan's bunk that night. Things had gotten so weird that I needed the company of someone not-insane.

I dreamed I had just won on *The Price Is Right*. There was a crushing sound of applause, cheers, and whistles when my name was called. It was a deafening waterfall of clapping and screaming. I was trotting toward the stage in this pounding noise, the cheers of the studio audience, when I woke.

Conan was already up, dabbing wet toilet paper where he'd bled from his head wound. I adjusted his bandages.

"My head is killing me," he said. "I couldn't sleep because I kept being woken by this zrrrrp, zrrrrrp, like someone was trying to restart a car that was already idling."

"I dreamed I won on *The Price Is Right*."

"It's . . . a new car! The thing about that show is the woman doesn't come with the car. You don't get her. Just the car."

We all suffered pill hangovers at work that day. "I feel like Blacula," Conan said. "That final scene where the sun hits him, and he's just greasy layers of smoke rising up from the clothes he had on."

At lunchbreak in the woodshop, Conan gave me the "I'm not actually into snow bunnies" talk. I loved Conan, but not like that. It was play incest in my play family and we were just friends.

Officer Garcia passed by the shop. Conan yelled, "Yo!" He pointed at his own bandaged head and glared at Garcia.

I ran into Hauser while waiting to go through work exchange.

I have some news for you, he said.

He had been able to find out who Jackson's case manager was. I started thanking him profusely and he said thanks were not appropriate.

But you went out of your way, I said.

"Your parental rights were terminated. I'm not sure if you were aware?"

"Terminated meaning what?"

"I was told they do this so a child can be fast-tracked for adoption. So that children can join new families. I wasn't even supposed to be told this. The woman was doing me a favor by looking up the case. All she could say is that on account of the length of your sentence your rights were terminated and the child is in the system."

"I'm in the system. Jackson is a little boy. He doesn't belong in a system."

"What I was told is that he is a ward of the state. I think that means he's in foster care."

"Where, do you know? Can I write to him?"

"I don't think you understand," he said. "And I didn't either, until it was explained to me. But finding out where your kid is, inside the child welfare bureaucracy, it's like trying to find out information about a complete stranger. Except the stranger, in this case, leaves no accessible records, on account of all the layers of privacy rules for minors."

"But I'm his mother. They can't tell me I'm not his mother. He needs a mother. Why are they doing this?"

I was aware of the tone of my voice, the look on my face, a sense that I was coming at this guy, the messenger, as if the news he brought me were his fault, but I could not stop myself from filling the air with my emergency.

We were on lockdown that night, so I could not talk to Sammy. I was stuck in my room. I went to Conan. Back to Conan. That I had to cry helplessly and not be the protector for my child put me back into the drifting unreality I had felt that first night in county jail. I had done something that could not be reversed. But Jackson, he did nothing. He was innocent. And now he was lost, spit into the world with no love, no one.

When I was able to calm down, Conan told me a story.

"My little brother and I stayed with my grandmother when we were little. She lived up in Sunland. There were horse farms there. She had a yard. It was almost the country. We loved her, and we loved living with her. My mom came one day to take me and my brother away from our grandmother. She said we were moving in with her. We barely knew our mom. She didn't raise us. My grandmother and my mom got into a fight. My mother beat our grandmother, right in front of us. Beat her up in her own kitchen. There was nothing we could do. We cried. We were scared. I was seven and my brother was five.

"We had to go live with my mom and her boyfriend in Bell Gardens. Her boyfriend was an A–one bastard. He picked on my brother. Why, I don't know. Maybe because he was a boy. When I turned eleven he started picking on me, but in a different way.

Motherfucker raped me. And not just once. It became, like, a regular thing. So me and my brother, when I was twelve and he was ten, we left. We had this idea to go to our grandma in Sunland. We had not seen her in years because she and our mom did not talk. I remembered the house. I knew exactly where it was, off the main boulevard up there. We caught a bus. It took a long time to get there, because we kept getting on the wrong buses. Finally we were close. We walked to her place and my brother was so excited, he kept talking about our grandma, trying to remember things she cooked, her funny and old-fashioned way of talking. How she slept in a chair. We never saw her go to bed. It was like she was on a vigil, to watch us, and she never let herself take time off. Woman slept in a chair, waiting for us to need something.

"We got to her house, I was sure it was the place, but our grandmother didn't live there anymore. The people in the house told us they moved in after she died. She'd died and we didn't know. So there we were in Sunland, with no money, and no grandmother, nowhere to go. We slept in a park that night. The next day we started hitching. We ended up in Santa Barbara, and slept on the beach and dumpster dove for food. We snuck on Amtrak there, hid in the bathroom when the conductor came through, but then people were knocking so we risked it, took seats. My brother started to get sick. He was shitting his pants and vomiting on the train. He was ill and couldn't control himself, and we didn't have tickets. The conductor comes and says, you can't stay on the train. So the train stops at the next station, and we were kicked off. My brother was a mess. He was burning up, lying on this train platform wherever we were, some town, and we were scared the police would get involved. They'd call our mother, and we would have to go back to her and that asshole she lived with.

"A man offered to help us. He promised not to call the cops. He took us to the Salvation Army. The people there, they put my little brother in a bed, with sheets and everything. They took care of him. They said he had dysentery and that he could have died. They let him rest and helped him get better. They gave us clean clothes. They fed me spaghetti and meatballs.

"There are some good people out there," Conan said, "some really good people."

23

When Doc was a teenager, President Richard Nixon performed on the Grand Ole Opry. Doc and his foster father, Vic, had watched it together on television. It was spring of 1974 and Nixon had already been disgraced, which burned up mean old Vic, who was loyal to the end.

President Nixon came out onstage at the big new theater in Nashville and greeted the people of Opryland, USA.

When the crowd died down, President Nixon said that country music was the heart of the American spirit. It was traditional music that praised simple values, love of family, love of God, and love of nation. Country music was patriotic and Christian, Nixon said.

"It started here, and it's ours," President Nixon told the Opryland audience. Those in TVland were listening, too, American boys with crew cuts and big ears, like Doc, who was seventeen, knob–limbed, horny, and depressed.

"It isn't something that we learned from some other people or nation, it's not something we borrowed or inherited from somebody else. Country music is as native as anything American you could ever find. It reflects values that are essential to our character, at a time when America needs character. Country music comes from the heart of America, and it *is* the heart of America. God bless the Grand Ole Opry," Nixon said, "and God . . . bless . . . America!"

The Opryland crowd went wild.

Nixon sat down at the piano and pounded out "God Bless America" in an ugly style, his hands like mechanical levers slamming up and down. As he finished, Roy Acuff appeared, a yo-yo unspooling from his palm.

The big-eared boys in the theater audience, and those lying on rag rugs at home, all perked up to see Roy Acuff handle a yo-yo with such grace.

A jug band from Mississippi began to play. The singer, a barrel-chested baritone, launched into a song about a pulpwood hauler who demolished a roadside beer joint with a chain saw.

Why did he do it? The song explained why. The pulpwood hauler did it because the bartender called him a redneck and refused to serve him a cold beer. So he destroyed the place.

Next, to entertain President Nixon, who loved wholesome country music, came Tammy Wynette, who sang "D-I-V-O-R-C-E."

Roy Acuff did "Wreck on the Highway."

Charlie Louvin sang "Satan Is Real."

Wilma Lee and Stoney Cooper performed "Tramp on the Street."

Porter Wagoner chose a crowd pleaser with "Rubber Room."

Loretta Lynn belted out "Don't Come Home A-Drinkin'."

"Let's have a moment of silence to remember our beloved brother, banjo picker David 'Stringbean' Akeman," Grandpa Jones told the audience. "Stringbean should have been here tonight. He was my best friend. My neighbor. My hunting buddy. And most importantly, a fellow member of the family here at the Opry. Four months ago, as many of you know, he was murdered, along with his wonderful wife, Estelle, by two lowlifes from down Dickerson Road. Let's remember this simple man, with his long shirt, his short pants, and his love of old-fashioned mountain music."

Nixon's face turned to cold plastic as the room fell silent. He looked like a professional mourner, someone they'd brought in to set the dour and ceremonial temperament.

The mood lightened when Cousin Minnie Pearl came out and told the crowd that after the Secret Service body-searched her for this special occasion, she got in line to let them do it again. She told jokes about inbreeding and incest, and sang a song about being so jealous, she got a bulldog to watch her lover while he slept.

Del Reeves sang a number about a truck driver dreaming of what he'd like to do with a highway billboard's almost naked girl.

Porter Wagoner performed "The First Mrs. Jones." Mr. Jones, the man in the song, has killed his first wife and is warning the second Mrs. Jones that she'll go the same way as the first if she leaves him.

There was a song about a moonshiner who outruns the police.

Another in which a man murders and buries his wife, but he can still hear her nagging all night long.

The Opryland audience erupted in riotous laughter.

Nixon sat stage left, jowly, regal and stiff, president of this great, great country, his overly long arms gripping the sides of his chair like a tractor's stabilizer bars.

24

In his essay celebrating the wonder of wild apples, Thoreau concedes they only taste good out-of-doors. Even a saunterer, Thoreau says, would not tolerate a saunterer's apple at a kitchen table. Their bitter flavor was best rationalized in the context of a beautiful autumn walk. Gordon Hauser walked whenever he could, up logging paths, through grazing meadows that were federal land and went on for miles. He found animal skulls, shotgun shells, an old landfill of antique bottles, some of them not even broken. On a cow trail above his cabin he came upon a paper wasp's nest. It looked like a half-crushed helmet lying on the path. Gordon carried it inside and placed it on his table, this grand and mysterious, half-deflated, torn-open thing.

He often stayed out until dark, to watch the slow transition to night. He liked to regard the entire process from start to finish. As the last light disappeared, he heard screech owls. Great horned owls. Sometimes barn owls. On a May evening, Gordon found an owl on the ground, flapping its feathers and shuddering. Its head was as large as a tomcat's, and furry. It made a clicking noise, and tried to back away from Gordon with its huge thorny feet. The eyes were human, with round pupils like a person's. Eyelids like a person's, too. It blinked and stared. He assumed the owl was injured, and that if he didn't do something, it would be eaten by a predator. He went home and made calls. Gordon and his phone calls. That was the extent of his personal life now. Contacting bureaucracies. A county ranger told him it was probably a young owl dropped from the nest, normal for this time of year. They shake off baby feathers and take flight, she said. Gordon went back and it was gone. Once he thought he saw it, between trees at dusk. Could have been any owl, but it was harmless to want to think it was the fledgling.

After walking he'd fix dinner, a can of soup, the staple of his one-room life, and then he'd go online, where he had developed a bad habit, an addiction whose hooks had gone in painlessly and quick. He had started running their names, as the women would call that act. To run someone's name was to have a contact on the outside google the person, or ask around.

The prisoner who asked to have a name run was not looking to review the full file of sad details, to rove over the inopportune mug shot available to all, especially in Florida and California, where they were uploaded by county clerks, making it seem as if a disproportionate share of screw-ups came from those states. The images were all the same: sour light and custodial formatting offset by the wild eyes and mussed hair of people yanked from life, arrested, numbered, ingested, and exposed.

The details of trauma and poverty that surrounded the crimes themselves—which were sometimes available if a case had media attention, or if the trial transcript or case summary was online— were not what the women inside needed or asked after, when they had a name run. What the women wanted to confirm was did their cellmate, unit mate, work partner, prayer group associate, friend, fuck friend, or enemy, did that person hurt a child, or turn state's evidence. Those were the two types that needed to be verified, baby killers and snitches.

Gordon's search was more open-ended. He didn't know what he was searching for. He hoped some equilibrium could be established from the process of obtaining facts. He also sensed that this thing about facts and equilibrium was a lie he told himself to go after squalid details that were none of his business.

By their own social codes, you were not supposed to ask what people had been convicted of. It was common sense not to ask. But the opprobrium on asking was so deep it seemed to also bar speculating, even privately. You weren't supposed to wonder about the facts that had determined people's lives. He had in his mind something Nietzsche said about truth. That each man is entitled to as much of it as he can bear. Maybe Gordon was not seeking truth, but seeking to learn his own limits for tolerating it. He did not type some names. He resisted typing Romy Hall, diverted the temptation to other inquiries.

The first one he looked up was Sanchez, Flora Martina Sanchez, whom the others called Button. Her case was all over the internet. Sanchez and two other teenagers had assaulted a Chinese college student near the USC campus. He was pre-med, and the one allotted child his family was state-sanctioned to have. According to the confession Sanchez provided, the student had tried to "karate chop" her. All three kids mentioned in their confessions that the victim cried in a foreign language as they hit him with a baseball bat. The bat was green aluminum, Worth brand. It had on it fingerprints of the two boys and Sanchez. Sanchez had waived her Miranda rights. They all waived them, gave confessions, went to trial, got life without parole.

They didn't know what they were doing. Gordon was sure of this as he read.

When they tried to rob the student, they did not know what they were doing. When they killed the student, they knew even less. When they were picked up, each separately, the morning after, and brought in for questioning, and spoke freely, but each in self-interest, to homicide detectives, with no parents present, and no lawyers, they did not know what they were doing.

They had chosen the victim, one of the boys said, because they assumed he was rich, since Asian. They had only wanted his backpack. They weren't trying to kill him. The student managed to walk home. His roommate heard him snuffling from beyond her closed bedroom door. She figured he'd caught a cold. She didn't know the reason he was snuffling was because he was aspirating blood.

Gordon believed in a kind of Hippocratic oath, not just as a teacher but as a person, to do no harm. Maybe this snooping was harm. He did it anyway.

All these details in the newspaper articles built a portrait, a set of impressions. Gordon had met Button on the other side, a lost little girl who looked twelve years old. Once, when Sanchez smiled as Gordon praised her in class, he saw her young essence. It was so wanting, and bright, he'd had to look away.

The word violence was depleted and generic from overuse and yet it still had power, still meant something, but multiple things. There were stark acts of it: beating a person to death. And there were more abstract forms, depriving people of jobs, safe housing, adequate schools. There were large-scale acts of it, the deaths of tens of thousands of Iraqi civilians in a single year, for a specious war of lies and bungling, a war that might have no end, but according to prosecutors, the real monsters were teenagers like Button Sanchez.

In the primitive part of the mind, violence was body-to-body, punching and clubbing and cutting. Those people went to prison. Were not offered any kind of mercy. Signed up for Gordon Hauser's class. Did or did not do the reading.

After indulging in the difficult facts, he all at once grasped why these kids, Button and her friends, had killed the poor student and ruined their own lives.

The student was not a person to them. That was the reason. They would not have harmed someone they knew was a full person. He was alien to them, his fluency in Mandarin something the kids never considered.

The student had snuffled loudly. His roommate had told the courtroom, through tears, and through a Mandarin interpreter, that she thought he had a cold.

There was one photo that Gordon looked at again and again, of little Sanchez and her codefendants in trial. They slumped with tough kid postures and they all wore glasses. He was her teacher and never once saw Sanchez put on glasses. Their public defenders probably insisted they order them and it was among the few health services you could get in county jail, a pair of prescription eyeglasses, or maybe the lawyers went to Walgreens and bought them one-strength-fits-all readers. The photo of them in their glasses, bored and distracted at their own murder trial, made Gordon hate Sanchez. The glasses were meant to alter the jury's perception. To bend the truth. But he was disgusted with himself for this sudden hate, and maybe guilt and innocence were not even a real axis. Things went wrong in people's lives.

Reading about her case, Gordon felt he was trying to cross an eight-lane freeway on foot. He had his argument worked out, about why she was a victim, when he found an article that quoted a Youth Authority counselor who testified that he'd overheard Sanchez talking about the crime. "We didn't even get anything off the nip," Sanchez had said.

Those were the worst nights. In the light of day his mood improved. As he drove the roads that wound down to Stanville, the hillside grasses green-tipped and mohair-soft, heart-shaped clots of mistletoe clustered in the branches of the oak trees like giant beehives, he knew that he could not judge. I cannot judge, because I do not know.

Gordon was familiar, from his time at college and graduate school, with rich kids. If you grew up rich, you played a musical instrument, violin or piano. You were on the debate team. Preferred a certain brand of jeans cuffed just so, maybe you puffed a ciggie or smoked bowls with your friends in your dad's Lexus, then were late to your SAT tutorial. But so many kids did it differently, and were done to differently. If you were from Richmond, or East Oakland, or, like Sanchez, South LA, you might be trained from birth practically to represent your block, your gang, to rep hard, to have pride, to *be* hard. Maybe you had a lot of siblings to watch and possibly you knew almost nobody who had finished school, or worked a stable job. People from your family were in prison, whole swaths of your community, and it was part of life to eventually go there. So, you were born fucked. But, like the rich kids, you too wanted to have fun on Saturday night.

All children are looking for a positive self-image. All children want that. It is obtained in different ways.

No Tank Tops, the sign had said at Youth Guidance. Because it was presumed the parents didn't know better than to show up to court looking like hell. The sign might have said Your Poverty Reeks.

Gordon's knowledge of murder had been, for most of his life, confined to literature. Raskolnikov killed the old pawnbroker. It was a feverish decision of Raskolnikov's to destroy his own life and shift into dreamtime, a dream that would not break, as a fever might. He was a miserably poor graduate student, like Gordon had been. It was almost funny, how everything in

Dostoevsky's novels came down to rubles. A word that sounded like something heavy and made of brass. Rubles. Put them in a sock, like you'd put a padlock, and swing.

At the end of *The Brothers K*, Alyosha asks the children to always remember the good feeling they share, in praising and celebrating the life of their beloved dead friend, the lost child.

Remember this always, Alyosha says, and he means, as an antidote. Retain the innocence of the most wholesome feeling you ever had in your life. Part of you stays innocent forever. That part of you is worth more than the rest.

Sanchez was in prison and would die there. She had told Gordon she'd never had a visitor. Few of the women he knew got visits. When he asked, they made excuses. There was embarrassment that no one came to see them. It did not occur to them that it wasn't a reflection on them, wasn't their fault that traveling to the prison required a reliable car, time off work, money for gas and meals and a hotel, and for the high-priced vending machines in the visiting room.

He kept looking, searched others.

He knew, at a certain point, that he was doing it to forestall looking up the person about whom he was most curious, and most hesitant to betray.

It would be easy because her name was not common.

It was hard for him to let go of his guilt for having been the one to tell her about her son. He didn't like the way it made him feel. As if he had power over this woman now, on account of her needs. In class, the thoughts ceased, because in person she was not needy. She was the student he could rely on to answer a question in a generative manner, so that he could tell himself the students were with him, and not lost, not against him.

She laughed at his jokes and spoke in a way that confirmed his arguments about the worth of what he was doing, because she obviously benefited from having literature to read and discuss. But that was all a grand lie, even if true. He was attracted to her, and she was forbidden. He thought about her frequently, since his fantasies were not patrolled by the corrections department.

"Did you ever see the green flash," she asked him after class, "down at Ocean Beach?"

He had not, he told her. She explained that it was an optical effect at sunset, when rays from the top of the sinking sun turned green. She had never seen it either, she said.

"Are you sure it isn't a story cooked up by the Irish drunks who live out there?"

She laughed. They were standing outside the school trailer. It was a June evening when the sun sets late. The light was gold from valley haze and low, slanting into her eyes, filling the irises.

Looking at someone who is looking at you was a drug as strong as any other.

"Move it, Hall!" an officer yelled. It was time for evening count. "Move your ass, now! I said go!"

He researched the green flash of a setting sun. It existed. There were websites with lengthy explanations of the physics of light. He did not type the three words of her name. Instead, he kept on with the others. Betty LaFrance, who asked the guards to reserve a parking space for her hairdresser. Betty, whose letter he'd sent, and when Gordon asked how her boyfriend was, she said, "I had him strangled." He was sure she was lying but when she said it the hairs on his arms stood up. He found her page on a prison pen pal site.

"Single and ready to mingle, an old-fashioned gal who likes

champagne, yachts, gambling, fast cars, VERY expensive thrills. Can you afford me? Write to find out."

There was a list of standard questions Betty LaFrance was obliged to answer on the site, for its users.

Do you mind relocating? (No).

Are you serving a life sentence? (No).

But at the bottom, under *On death row?* she'd had to check (Yes).

Of Candy Peña, Gordon learned that her mother had worked concessions at Disneyland in Anaheim. Candy Peña had worked at a McDonald's. Her manager testified for the defense that she had never given him any problems. The mother of Candy's murder victim, the little girl, that mother had cheered in the courtroom when the death penalty verdict was announced. "YEAH!" she'd yelled.

And then Gordon found another quote, later, from the victim's mother, who said she felt for Candy Peña's mother, knowing herself what it was like to lose a child.

London: at first he found nothing. They called London Conan, or Bobby. He typed in "Bobby London," and found a Yelp page for a restaurant in Los Angeles. The top three reviews of it all started the same way: Fuck you, Bobby London!

He remembered that the first name was Roberta. Bingo. "Woman who masqueraded as man convicted and sentenced to men's prison for armed burglary." Another headline: "State Goofs." London was not masquerading but one of the most natural people Gordon had ever met. London was London.

It seemed London had already served for the burglary, had gotten two strikes for it, and was on a third, for fraud. London was doing life for having written a bad check.

This gallery of people.

Every name he could think of, to avoid typing Romy Leslie Hall.

Geronima Campos, who had painted Gordon's portrait: Geronima had apparently dropped her husband's torso off a bridge somewhere in the Inland Empire. They found it and later the head, which had a bullet in it from a gun registered to Geronima. Geronima had no alibi. Her husband's blood was in her bathtub, in her car, and on the clothes she'd worn the day of his disappearance.

Geronima was involved with a peer counseling group and taught human rights law to any prisoner who wanted to learn it. Geronima was a prison elder. She had associate degrees by mail order and a flawless disciplinary record. Geronima had gone up for parole eight times and been denied every time, despite her file of service and support from people on the outside who organized to help her. There was an internet campaign page, to advocate for Geronima's next parole. Those who signed the petition included their reason for doing so.

Geronima has done her time.

She is no longer a threat to society.

Free Geronima.

She is a survivor of spousal abuse.

Geronima is an indigenous elder lesbian who is being unjustly held at Stanville Correctional Facility.

Being a lesbian is not illegal.

She is needed in her community.

She has served her time.

She is not a threat.

Free Geronima.

She had indeed served her time. She had done the time the court had given her. And Gordon knew Geronima. She was an old woman who liked to paint. Everything was true. It was time for Geronima to go home. She had served the sentence they gave her.

Every time Geronima went before the parole board, which

Gordon pictured as a series of Phyllis Schlaflys all in a row, frowning, with stiff hair, in industrial pantyhose and little rippling American flag pins like Republican candidates wore for political debates, she told the board she was innocent. Her supporters said she'd done her time and was no longer a threat. She faced the parole board and said, I'm innocent. It made no sense. But Gordon understood why she said it.

Whatever space Geronima would have needed to find a way to face what she had done was not provided in prison. Prison was a place where you had to be strong to get through each day. If you thought about some awful act you'd committed, every day, in graphic detail, enough to prove to a parole board that you had insight, the proverbial insight they wanted, needed, to let you go home, you might lose your mind. To stay sane, that was the thing. To stay sane you formed a version of yourself you could believe in.

And if she did show insight, tell them what was on her mind the day she killed her husband, why and how she did it and what she felt after, excitement, guilt, denial, fear, revulsion, if she showed the board how honest and precise she could be in her knowledge of her crime and why she committed it, if she spoke openly about the impact it had on her victim and on others, on society, if she trotted out the whole horror of it, she would, at the same time, freshly reactivate for the parole board all the reasons why they had wanted to lock her up. You could not convince them. There was no way to win.

Just let her go home. Free Geronima.

But the contradiction, that Geronima faced the parole board and said, "I'm innocent," while her advocates outside said, "She's done her time. She is no longer a threat": that bothered Gordon.

Still. Geronima, and Sanchez, and Candy, all of them were people who suffered and along the way of their suffering they made others suffer, and Gordon could not see that making them suffer lifelong would accrue to justice. It added new harm to old, and no dead person ever came back to life that he had heard about.

Alex had been calling, e-mailing, but Gordon had nothing to say to him because all he thought about was women in prison and it wasn't fun conversation. He was in some kind of exile.

He felt hopeless as he sat in Baressi's and envied the others at the bar, men in construction and farming, who made it seem as if the Central Valley was not about prison, and for them it wasn't.

"Aw, come on, there's plenty of hope," Alex might have rejoined, playing Kafka, "no end of hope, but none for you, Gordon."

There was a new singer on the piano. She was good, or maybe just Stanville-good. Gordon got a bit drunk without meaning to, walked over and put a twenty-dollar bill in the big brandy snifter, the international standard piano-tip container.

"Would you like anything special?" Her voice was happy and light.

He could not think of a single song to request. He'd tipped her because he could. "Sing your favorite? What you sing alone, when no one can hear."

" 'Summertime,' then," she said without a pause.

Walking back to his seat, he wondered if asking her to sing for a stranger what she sang in private was creep territory. Some people violate others regularly as the natural course of the day, of life. He knew this. He was not those people. Still, he wondered.

As she sang, he understood that whether or not it was her private song, she gave him nothing. She was performing. She was a performer by profession. She sang "Summertime," and Gordon was swept away by the passionate range of her mediocre voice.

"I'm sorry about your fiancé," he said one night as Romy Hall lingered after class. He was stacking photocopies in an unnecessarily fastidious way to draw out their few minutes together, before a guard oversaw the students' transfer through work exchange.

"What happened?" It was easy, he found, to affect the concerned tone of an advisor, when really he was fishing for information, to know if there were competitors.

"He wasn't my fiancé. And he's not dead. He moved on."

She said there were women on her unit who got married to men they met through the mail. "Jimmy wasn't a loser like that," she said. "He had a life. I'm sure he's out there living it."

She made fun of the crafting craze in prison, but said it was good to work with her hands. She was doing jewelry, she told him, in explanation for what she asked Gordon to bring her. He didn't entirely believe her, but in a sense he did, because he didn't let himself speculate. He was all done speculating. He would be leaving Stanville soon. He was going back to school, to get a master's in social work. It was probably an improvident time to quit a job, with the economy tanking, but the rhythms of the world did not always coordinate with the rhythm of the person.

How's the life of nature and captivity? Alex asked by e-mail.

This morning I saw a peregrine falcon eating babies from a sparrow's nest, he replied. *A lot of commotion. High drama in the Sierra Nevada.*

Oh, I bet those are delicious, Alex wrote back. *There's a little songbird eaten whole, bones and everything, by French aristocrats. Illegal, and, by custom, enjoyed with a cloth over the face and head, like an executioner's hood. Maybe what we lack is tradition and elegance in our relentless destruction of nature. So when are you coming back?*

The day after he gave her what she wanted, Gordon drove into town. He parked on Stanville's main street, which featured storefronts with soaped windows. There was a small Catholic church on the end of the block. An old building with thick adobe walls. The doors were open. It looked cool inside.

Our Lady of the Valley smelled like the lining of an old woman's purse. Our Lady's Pocketbook, which had been collecting powdery makeup residue and mold spores for decades. Gordon had no religion, though the idea of mercy, offered by churches, a Christian god, but never the state, had been in his thoughts. He sat down at the end of a row of pews. On the other side of the aisle was a confession booth. The sinner's side had a screen for talking to the priest. The screen was a metal plate randomly hole-punched. It looked like a road sign riddled with bullets.

Wind was moving through the church, from a single propped door in the back. Papers somewhere lifted and flapped, suggesting presence, but then again not. Suggesting wind stirring papers, and no one present, except Gordon. He stared into the vents, from his seat on the pew.

There were real, epistemological limits to knowledge. Also, to judgment.

I can only know myself, if I can know anyone. I can only judge me.

It was Thoreau who'd said that first.

I never dreamed of any enormity greater than I have committed. I never knew, and never shall know, a worse man than myself.

Why was Thoreau Thoreau, while Ted Kaczynski was Ted?

One stayed formal in Gordon's mind, the other, strictly first-name basis. Ted.

It was more familiar to be angry and bad. Maybe that was why.

Norman Mailer had not smuggled wire cutters into a prison to give to Jack Henry Abbott. Norman Mailer wrote letters, used influence. Mailer bragged that Abbott's release was his doing, bragged until suddenly it was a liability to have his name involved, and then denied his role, and then could not resist bragging again, said he'd do it all over for art, for the sake of art. It was 1981 and they put poor Abbott in a halfway house on Manhattan's Lower East Side. He was surrounded by junkies and sleaze and took to carrying a weapon for protection. He knew nothing of living in society and mistook one thing for another, thought he was being threatened in the old way, the jailhouse way. Took out his knife and stuck it deep in his attacker's heart. You don't have much time to fight in prison, and so your moves are gambits, prearranged. Guy died immediately, there on First Avenue. Jack Henry Abbott went back to prison and so much for dinners with celebrities and writers and good-looking women with names like Norris. Who the fuck names their wife Norris? He means their daughter. Gordon knows you don't name a wife.

Gordon's cabin was mostly packed. Two cartons of books, some cook pots, a Melitta thing you place over a cup, clothes in garbage bags. He put a log in his stove, watched the gold-blue liquid updraft, to be sure it caught, and then he typed her name. He had made rules, and this was one, to look only now.

Romy Leslie Hall.

Nothing. No entries found.

Romy L Hall. Hall prison Stanville. San Francisco life sentence Hall.

He looked and looked, as the wood burned down, shifted softly, embers making their mealy tick.

Jimmy San Francisco teach Art Institute. Nothing. He spent hours looking through the faculty lists. There was a James Darling in the film department. Googled James Darling. Film festivals. Artist's statement. But he wasn't even sure this was the guy.

He listened to a dog bark, somewhere down the mountain.

People in that area made nature domestic, and also hostile, with their guard dogs, their beware-of dogs. German shepherds. Dobermans.

The dog barked and barked, down the mountain, echoing up it. An excavating three a.m. bark, digging and digging at nothing.

25

The next summer I set a booby trap intended to kill someone, but I won't say what kind or where, because if this page is ever found, the trap might be harmlessly removed. I also strung a neck-height wire for motorcyclists across the divide trail above Rooster Bill Creek, after roaring motors spoiled a hike for me. Later I found that someone had wrapped the wire safely around a tree. Unfortunately I doubt anyone was hurt by it.

Up South Fork Humbug, I shot a cow in the head with my .30-30 and then got the hell out of there. I mean a rancher's cow, not an elk cow. I also went down at dawn and smashed my neighbor's mailbox with my axe in such a way that it looked as if some vehicle might have hit it.

The following November I traveled from Montana back to the Chicago area, mainly for one reason: So that I could more safely attempt to murder a scientist, businessman, or the like. I would also like to kill a communist.

I emphasize that my motivation is personal revenge on those who deprive or threaten to deprive my own autonomy. I don't pretend to have any kind of philosophical or moralistic justification.

26

Sammy's date was coming up. We'd been in prison together almost four years. It was October and every day the sky was the same blue dome, us, under it, also in blue. Some would get release dates and go. Sammy would go, and good for her. The forever feeling on main yard, of thousands of women in blue, would stay, and I would stay.

The mountains beyond the yard were forever, too, but they were not the automated concrete prison forever. I dreamed of ancient worlds up there, a lost civilization of people who would give me a chance. It was a childish dream that came from a book we read in Hauser's class. The mountains, brownish purple on a winter afternoon. People in a hut where a fire crackles. They take in the stranger and teach her to live. In some of my day-dreams, Jackson was already there with those friendly strangers, waiting for me. He was among the people who would give me my chance. He was dirty and strong, a feral boy who had made his way bravely. He was there in the hut, waiting with the others for my arrival, my rehabilitation, to use the language of this place. They don't help you with it. You have to do it yourself.

"When I get out of this place maybe I can try to do something for you," Sammy said.

I knew she meant what she said, but Sammy was in and out of prison and barely able to help herself. She was a loyal person with problems of her own.

I'd written probably forty letters to the case manager. The case manager sent only one letter back, a short note saying that my rights had been terminated and suggesting I get a family court lawyer if I was attempting to appeal the termination, but that I should understand terminations were almost never overturned.

Serenity Smith had been in protective custody almost a year now. Some had given up the fight, figuring they would never mainline her. Laura Lipp kept it up. It was her passion. There were people who felt that Laura Lipp was not a good leader for the group, since she had murdered her own child, an infant, to get revenge on a man. Two young women, newbies looking to make names for themselves, beat up Laura and cut off all her hair.

Laura kept a low profile after that. The movement grew against Ms. Smith, newly validated by its loss of Laura as leader. The Norse was involved. The Norse informed on women who held hands, which was illegal at Stanville. So was hugging, or any kind of sustained physical contact between inmates. "This is all out," the Norse said. "I ain't living with deviants. They want to throw a man in the pen with us and expect us to take it." The Norse talked about Stanville as if she were its redneck protector of family values, a proud defender of the institution's standards, and not just one more pathetic and angry prisoner. Teardrop, too, got involved, probably because for Teardrop aggression and beating on people were a good outlet. Teardrop and Conan, historically road dogs, got into it over the issue. "How can you not want to protect a sister?" Conan asked, meaning a black sister. Teardrop said the last thing she needed was ghetto motherfuckers up in her grill. They fist-fought in the port-a-potties on main yard and Conan won. Teardrop was moved out of our room.

"Has anyone gotten past an electric fence?" I asked Sammy. We were walking our track, out of listening range from the watch office microphones.

"Two guys at Susanville."

"But how."

"They used something wood to wedge up the bottom of the fence and went underneath. A broom handle, I think. Dude at Salinas Valley climbed. He grounded himself somehow. Almost got over and they shot him down."

Conan jogged toward us. "I was running, and over near the bathrooms I saw this white figure, a man, with his arms open. He was in white clothes, the pants kind of belled at the bottom. I thought it was Elvis, you know, from the wild years, when he got fat and had those stupid sunglasses. But when I got closer, it was the trash bins."

Conan's vision was going bad from his diabetes. He had an appointment to see a medical technician's assistant, which was our version of doctor, in eight months' time.

"Hey what did Elvis drive?" Conan asked me.

I hadn't laughed about him mistaking the trash bins for Elvis. He always turned to cars when he knew I'd gone bleak.

"A Stutz," I said, but with no life in the words or in me. "He drove a Stutz Blackhawk."

Jimmy Darling had gone to Graceland with a camera and said there was nothing to film there. Nothing to see. Except for the graffiti on the wall surrounding it.

Isn't it all made to look glitzy and impressive? I asked.

Yeah, he said, it is.

What about the car?

The car, he said, was like the Virgin Mary on toast. Try to photograph it, and the miracle vanishes. He'd paid extra to see the airplanes. Elvis's private jets. Inside one was a double bed. Stretched across it, over the covers, a super-wide airplane seat belt. Looking at the belted bed, and the one executive's chair, near the window, Jimmy Darling felt the spirit of Elvis in the plane, up late, inside the night, hurtling across the sky, lonely as hell, no one with him in his darkest hour. Jimmy Darling was visited, in the airplane, by the wind of Elvis's empty soul.

Hauser, too, knew the mechanical museum at Ocean Beach. "See Susie Dance the Can-Can," he said, as proof. The Camera Obscura, where a large dish showed the froth of the waves. Kelly's Cove, which in my group wasn't about surfing, just drinking, and boys. A huge sign that announced Playland, but no Playland around. Only the sun-bleached sign next to a fake cliff, man-made, which people said was there to trick the Japanese during the war.

There's a pizza place up Irving, Hauser said. They spin the dough in the windows.

I saw everything. The stretching floury disks that collapsed on the hands of the dough makers in their chef's hats, fists working the disks around, dough growing in girth, orbit, then back up in the air. I saw the huge wreath of flowers that hung from the closed entrance one morning, announcing the death of the old man, the pizza patriarch. I'd never seen a wreath that large. I was eight or nine. Not yet into trouble. I linked flowers with death. That huge wreath connected them for me.

I saw the shining lid of the ocean from Irving Street, the way it rose, on a clear day, like something that breathed, that was alive, down at the end of the avenues.

My son likes churches, I told Hauser. When I brought Jackson into Grace Cathedral he had a natural instinct to quiet in the home of someone's god, not his, as we weren't religious. He gazed around and then said to me, in a whispering happy voice, like he'd landed on something, an idea, "Mommy, when I grow up, I think I might want to be a king."

He was never once a brat, I told Hauser, but as I said it I tried to dampen the instinct to talk up Jackson too much. People should know that some kids are not just nice people, but superior to most adults. But I didn't want Hauser to pull back, suspect I was foisting an adoptee on him. Even as that was my plan. It was the only option I could imagine actually working. People in prison were full of dumb fantasies about how their futures might go. My own were all I had. "You've got something with him," Sammy said. "Most of them don't get involved with prisoners. Too jaded. We'll just be getting over on them. But he is *open*."

Hauser had a lost quality. He wasn't someone who seemed to have much happening outside work. Not that he discussed his life with us. He did not. At Stanville, he was an oddball to the rest of the staff. The guards made fun of him, mostly as a way to make fun of us. Go teach those dumb bitches to read, Mr. Hauser. Teach those cows two plus two. They thought what he spent his life doing was pointless, not a worthy endeavor like watching us on security monitors or masturbating in a guard tower.

Hauser wasn't an idiot. He was no Keath. But sometimes he acted like one. When I asked him to bring wire cutters to the library, I was pretty sure he'd do it. I had no plans to use them. I did it to test him.

Candy Peña bragged that Hauser was her boyfriend, that he got her "a whole grip" of knitting supplies. Anything she wanted, Candy told whoever came back to ad seg and was on her vent. If she wasn't on death row Candy would know you don't brag about something like that. You keep it to yourself and you cultivate it.

Jackson's twelfth birthday was on a Tuesday, the 18th of December. I woke up that day and looked at the picture of a seven-year-old, which was all I had, from the last time I'd seen my son, more than four years earlier, when my mother brought him to the county jail. I'd met with them through scratched Plexiglas. He'd already grown so much. He was five when I was arrested. I didn't know what he looked like now.

I hid the photo in my bra. All through class time that afternoon I thought about what I was going to say to Hauser, what words I would use to pressure him to help me with Jackson. I didn't follow the class discussion, never once raised my hand. I was focused on the moment I would give him the photo.

I knew things weren't going right when he looked up from his desk, as the others filed out. He was not happy to see me: that was the clue.

"Today is my son's birthday."

I put the picture down, to show him what a beautiful kid Jackson was. No one ever said Jackson wasn't beautiful.

He barely looked at the photo.

"This is him," I soldiered on. "You can have it."

It was Jackson's class picture from second grade. He was kneeling on a fake log with a fake autumn background. Smiling and shiny like his face was a polished apple.

Hauser did not pick up the photo. "I can't accept it."

"I'm giving it to you. I want you to have it."

"I know you do, but it's not right. Save it for yourself."

Didn't he at least want to see what Jackson looked like? I

asked, trying to control my tone, because anger would get me nowhere. I was ready to lay things out, to ask for his help. I started to, and he interrupted.

"I'm really sorry about your son, but I can't be involved."

It was the Christmas holidays, a joy-free time for us at Stanville.

In January, when classes were scheduled to resume, we were told continuing education was suspended. Hauser had quit his job, or been fired. Whatever happens to staff they don't tell us. Rumors fly but no one cared much about Hauser except Candy Peña. Candy hollered up the vent to Teardrop, when Teardrop did a stretch in ad seg, that Hauser had been walked off because of his overfamiliarity with Candy.

I'd hit a dead end. It was me alone with my pictures of Jackson, the newest of them almost five years out of date. I had the wire cutters Hauser had given me, back when he was behaving like he was supposed to. I had a large dowel I'd made in woodshop. I hid them both on the yard, beyond Tower One. I dug with my hands. I'd seen the Native American women do that, to hide their tobacco on main yard. It had rained, which was when people buried things. Patiently clawing, using their fingernails, their hands, as tools, to dig. I stayed behind Tower One a long time, as long as it took to bury the dowel and the wire cutters. No one reprimanded me, or saw. Perhaps Sammy was right, that it was a blind spot. It was just dreaming. If that dream came true, it was a dream of death. I'd get fried on the fence like the rabbits that got too close.

A coyote died on the fence, hung there for everyone to see.

Coyotes had lived in the alley behind the place I'd sublet in Los Angeles. They trotted along the sidewalk past our house in the middle of the day. At night Jackson and I could hear their cascade of yips. Jackson would act scared and clamp on to me but in a pretend way, because it was fun to be scared of wild animals that were outside if you were inside with your mom. I remembered Jackson telling me coyotes have a longer snout than a wolf, that this was the main difference, the shape of the face.

We were on lockdown while the guards turned off the fence in order to pull off the dead coyote. The time of Angel Marie Janicki was over. No one was getting out.

Sammy's release was soon. She planned to parole to a halfway house, a strict reentry program where she could be trained for employment. She was seldom up for the yard now. Stayed in her room, out of the mix. When someone had a release date coming, enemies would try to draw that person into trouble, to ruin her chances.

A television crew came inside the prison to film Button and a handful of other people who had been convicted as juveniles. Button spent all her time preparing for the filming, as if it was a beauty contest. "You need to look sad," I told her. "Young. Innocent." But it was her big moment and she wanted to look fabulous. She tailored clothes in return for a hair treatment in the cosmetology training salon. She stole makeup from a woman in the room next to ours, a loner who was afraid of her. She slapped the woman doing her hair for curling her bangs incorrectly. She'd become a punk and we wanted her out of our room.

The crew filmed all day during visiting hours, Saturday and

Sunday. On Sunday I was on the yard with the other lowlifes who had no visits, which was the majority of us. Some visited with church people, strangers who volunteered contact from the goodness of their hearts. The women I knew who met with them did it to have visitors, and to be able to graze the vending machines. I sat on the yard and made fun of the phonies who pretended to be indigenous so they could do sweat lodge ritual with the real indigenous women. There was no mistaking who was from a tribe, since they controlled the tobacco trade and shopped canteen with their tribal funds.

That Sunday night, Button would not shut up about the documentary film. Everyone was going to know her story.

"I should not even be in this place," she said.

"What makes you so special?" I'd had enough of her.

"I was fourteen when my crime got committed. The brain is not fully developed at that age."

Probably it was true, about a kid's brain. Everything here is about choices, decisions, as if people are making them when they commit a crime. A fourteen-year-old is not making choices. She's in the prison of the present tense. When I was that young, I could not imagine anything beyond that day, the next. But Button still pissed me off, separating herself from the rest of us like that.

There was a prisoner named Lindy Belsen who had been convicted as a juvenile and had her sentence commuted by the governor. She was famous at Stanville. A team of volunteer lawyers had gathered around her. They built up her case as a story of human trafficking. She'd shot her pimp in a motel room. He'd groomed her for prostitution from the age of twelve. It was a sad story, and maybe she deserved to go free, but the way her lawyers positioned her as an undisputed innocent was difficult for the rest of us. Lindy Belsen was an ideal face for free-world activists who wanted a model prisoner to fight for.

She was pretty, and spoke like an educated person. But most important, she could be depicted, convincingly, as a victim, not a perpetrator. A lot of people in the prison resented Lindy Belsen, because what did her story, the story her lawyers told, say about the rest of us? Few were happy for her when she left.

They mainlined Serenity Smith to general population. They put her on B yard, but close custody. In a regular unit, but confined, with seven other close custody prisoners, unable to come and go from their room. Eventually they would lift her confinement, move her to a regular room. Conan and his transgender counseling group were committed to protecting Serenity. They had meetings about it. They were on her side. Other people were making weapons to fight them. Conan and his group planned to surround Serenity, a butch security force, to keep her safe from Teardrop and all the other dangerous people who wanted to hurt her.

Sammy said a prison riot was an awful thing. There had been one at CIW, north against south. It was a meat grinder, she said.

To prevent organized violence on the yard, the cops wouldn't say when they were lifting Serenity's close custody.

It wasn't my issue. Life went back to normal. After Hauser left, our continuing education options were healing groups that met in the gym: Self-Esteem. Anger Management. Transitional Living (only for women with release dates), and Relationships 101. There were budget cuts and other changes. Woodshop was no longer available for level fours, like me. I started working in the cafeteria, where cops put their hands on me as I slopped Mortimer portions. The kitchen supervisor wore a big button that said DON'T EVEN TRY IT. Don't even think of attempting to manipulate me with your sob stories and needs. That was how a lot of the staff was. Those who were open didn't want to help us. They wanted to make cash for smuggling contraband.

I got a letter from Eva's father. I'd written about ten letters to his address to try to locate Eva and this was the first news back, after five years in prison.

"Eva died last year. I had been collecting your letters and was planning on giving them to her but could not locate her. I thought you should know that you can stop attempting to reach her."

Sometimes I imagined that Hauser would write me. He'd ask to be put on my visiting list. Now that he wasn't working at Stanville, the fraternization rules wouldn't apply. He'd be out there in the free world and ready to start something up. Even though I wasn't remotely attracted to him, we'd get married and have conjugal visits with Jackson. Hauser was earnest and gentle. He would have made a good father. I had no way to get in touch with him to tell him so, and the joke had been on me, even as I thought I was using and manipulating him.

One night, I had two dreams about water. In the first one, I was with Hauser. At least I think it was Hauser. It was a placeholder man who connected to me, obligated to me somehow. There was a rainstorm and we watched as the LA River rose. It went over the concrete banks. Hauser dove in to swim, but without having noticed the swift speed of the water. It carried him downstream. I wondered if he could swim strongly enough to grab a tree branch or root, hold on to something and pull himself out. I went to a store. I told the clerk that my friend had gone into the water. She said, "The river is rushing ninety-one miles an hour." I felt that Hauser was dead or hurtling toward death. I woke up.

When I fell back asleep I had a different dream. I was driving an old car. The clutch was rough and the brakes jerky and the gas slightly delayed, the steering clumsy, but I was familiar with the car and knew how to handle it to make it respond. Something was happening up ahead. I stopped and got out. There was a man threatening to kill himself. There was a young woman trying to talk him down. Then the three of us were walking together along a sea wall or embankment. It was Ocean Beach. Huge waves swelled and fell, as if the water were at an incline, not level. It was steep water. The man started going out onto the embankment. The young woman was suddenly me. The man looked at me, who was not me, but the responding person to him in the dream, he looked at this me and began to go out into the water. I said, No, don't. As I said it, I realized that he was luring me into the water, by suggesting he would end his life he was luring me to end mine. I woke up and worried that Jackson was thirsty and that there wasn't a cup of water next to his bed, but then I realized I was in my lower bunk in room fourteen of unit 510 of C yard.

Sammy was released. She said she was nervous and didn't want to go. I felt her excitement, underneath what she claimed. The reentry program was on skid row and she was worried. "Hang around the barbershop long enough," she said, "and you'll end up with a haircut."

She gave me her piggy-printed eye mask and some other stuff. Promised she'd write me. We hugged goodbye.

People say your time hits you in waves. Mine was hitting me. I could see no way to accept this as life, to live it to the end.

I was depressed and sleeping a lot. One Sunday, I missed breakfast and the first unlock. At lunch I went out to the yard to find Conan.

Laura Lipp and her yard crew were sweeping dirt. It was a sunny day and the yard was packed. There were probably two thousand women out there.

I pushed through the turnstile and when it squeaked open it was like everyone had owls' heads, on swivel. I didn't know what was wrong but the tension was thick.

I walked past the basketball courts, looking for Conan. There was a game happening, girls on the sidelines picnicking with canteen spreads.

"Here she comes!" someone screamed.

I thought the screamer meant me and I panicked. People came running toward the main entrance from all over the yard. The players on the court stopped their game. The ball rolled into the basket but no one was under to claim it. It bounced on its lonesome across an empty court. Everyone was running toward the turnstiles.

Serenity Smith passed through. She had come on the yard alone. Walking tall, and proud, a beautiful black woman with long and graceful arms.

Laura Lipp and her gardening gang moved toward her with shovels and rakes in their hands. I heard a shriek. It was the Norse, running toward Serenity. Conan, Reebok, and their crew ran to attack the Norse and the gardeners. People were coming from all directions.

The first person on Serenity was the Norse. The Norse grabbed her and tried to pull her down. Serenity fought back. Conan pushed the Norse down and started monkey stomping her. Every bit of anger that had ever been in Conan came out of the sole of his boot, which connected over and over to the head and face of the Norse. The Norse's head started to leak.

Serenity was running to escape Laura Lipp and her horde. Laura Lipp hit Serenity across the back with the flat side of her shovel, knocking her down. Laura fell on Serenity and was scratching her face. That is how some women fight. They can't help it, it's instinct. Serenity got up, pushed Laura against a spider table, and started punching her. Alarms sounded, the deafening zonk–zonk–zonk that means GO PRONE.

The other gardeners were tugging on Serenity as Serenity punched Laura. Garbage cans were hurled at them. The alarms kept sounding. Everyone fought.

Teardrop got hold of a shovel and was beating Serenity with it like you might beat a rug to get the dust out of it. Slow, heavy thuds, one after the other. Serenity screamed. The alarms zonk-zonked. I had the thought that maybe the cops were letting this happen. Letting Serenity be hurt or even killed.

No one went prone. The yard was in chaos. Orange clouds of pepper spray were directed at the piles of fighters, who kept on struggling. The cops retreated to the watch office, for their own safety. There was a sound I'd never heard, like an air siren. They had a situation. It was out of their hands. Alarms and sirens wailed.

I backed behind Tower One. There was a guard up there, but he had his weapon trained on the rioters. He was shooting wooden projectiles at them.

I dug and claw-tore at the earth behind Tower One until I found what I was looking for.

The way razor wire tugs on fabric: it holds you like hands pulling you back. Saying, Don't go. Stay. Stick around. Don't leave. If I stayed in this place, it would be slow death until I found a way to do it quick.

I sliced myself up good making a hole big enough to get through the inner fence.

I got through to the second fence, the electric one. The alarms were wailing and I was ready to risk death. I touched the fence with the dowel I'd made in shop.

No shock.

I nudged the bottom of the fence, wedged it upward, and slid, in the dirt, underneath, breath held, prepared to fry.

But then I was on the other side, on the dirt road where the perimeter truck travels. I had reached the edge of the universe.

One more fence to cut through. I could still hear the alarm, the repeated command to heed commands, the pop of projectiles.

I clipped quickly, worked a hole, pushed it open with the piece of wood, to avoid cutting myself worse than I already was.

I was in an almond grove. I heard the alarm in the distance. I ran under the trees, crossed a road, and kept running.

27

When Gordon Hauser was twelve years old, there had been a community-wide crisis, an excitement, when a convict named Bo Crawford escaped from the old county jail in downtown Martinez. An occupying force descended around San Pablo Bay. There were stakeouts, armored military vehicles, sharpshooters, teams of dogs, road closures, and thrilling reports that Bo Crawford had left traces or been sighted in Pinole, in Benicia, in Vallejo, Pittsburg, Antioch. For ten whole days, the county was on lockdown, until they finally caught Bo Crawford, hiding in an abandoned shack along the Carquinez Strait just beyond Port Costa.

To be on the run was no vacation. You had to look over your shoulder every second. People said it was worse than prison, but, as Gordon had imagined things, it was too late for Bo Crawford to put himself back. He was forced to survive in the cracks, the margins, hiding in a world with no good places to hide. Where everyone bought guns, including Gordon's own father, and waited to spot the escaped man on their property.

Two children saw Bo Crawford near the parking lot of the C&H refinery in Crockett.

A waitress at Flippy's in Rodeo said he came in one morning at dawn, ordered bacon and eggs. When she ducked into the kitchen to call the cops, he fled.

He entertained the whole county, people in every community, and the loners, too, with no community, everyone hoping for and fearing his arrival. He was famous and would make them famous. They could be the ones to have been touched by his escape. He was a wanted man. A dangerous man.

What was he wanted for? Escaping. Also, armed robbery.

A woman who worked in the jail's laundry facility, Vena Hubbard, had fraternized with Bo Crawford, developed feelings for him. She began dreaming of a new life. It all came out later, in newspaper exposés that attempted to narrate the breakdown of security at the jail. There had been talk of Mexico between Vena and Bo and, before heading there, a quick stop off at Vena's place to kill her husband, Mack. They would drive to the border in her car, a Honda Civic. They had maps and her savings, as well as a shotgun that belonged to Mack, which they would take with them after killing him. (Would a shotgun even fit in a Honda Civic? Gordon had wondered.)

Bo had native intelligence and impeccable self-control. He did two hundred push-ups a day. He meditated. He sawed, little by little, a hole in the rear wall of a storage closet of the laundry facility, while his work crew partner ate the fried chicken and macaroni salad that Vena brought into the jail to feed the men on her laundry crew. Later, there was intense focus on Vena's role in illegally bringing food into the laundry, a sign of her weak character and submission to prisoner cunning. "I only let 'em have what I couldn't finish and was gonna throw out," she testified at an inquest. She had brought in, according to inmates who worked in her laundry facility, meals to feed twenty men, which included party-sized submarine sandwiches and entire flats of Costco lasagna. Fat-Ass was how Bo referred to his work crew partner, whose real name was J.D. Joss, and who was in on the plan, but was not the same high caliber of escapee as Bo. While it was Bo whom Vena truly loved, J.D. carried on with her in a more explicit manner, which gave Bo the time and space he needed to investigate the hatch he'd breached in the laundry closet. J.D. had sewn, using the laundry facility's machine, a secret flap in his jail pants, so that Vena could play with his cock under the supervisor's desk where she sat, with J.D. next to her. Meanwhile, Bo was tracing an escape route through a pipe that led under the jail and, eventually, to a storm drain in the street.

On the assigned day, Vena's one day off, she was to meet Bo and J.D. on a designated corner, with the Honda Civic, the maps, the shotgun, and the money. J.D. and Bo left the laundry facility through the opening in the storage closet, while the fill-in supervisor ate his lunch. They made it through the storm drain and walked to the corner in Martinez where Vena was meant to pick them up. A car drove past, not the Civic. J.D. jumped into the bushes of someone's yard. Bo, as he later told police, yelled at J.D. to Act Fucking Normal. Like a free person, and not like some idiot jailbird on the loose.

No Civic came to rescue them, and so they were quickly both jailbirds on the loose, who could only hide, who had no maps, no weapons, no plan, nothing.

When the hour had come for her to pick them up, and then scoot back over to her place to kill Mack, Vena and Mack Hubbard were watching a TV movie on the couch. It kept being time to leave and the movie kept playing. Mack, for the first time in months, was paying attention to Vena. He put his arm around her on the couch and his arm seemed to say, "I know you had a plan for Mexico, and murder, but this isn't so bad, is it?" The time to meet Bo and J.D. melted away. Probably they had not really gone through with the escape. That was her hope. But what if they came for her?

She lay awake all night, started at every sound. Mack snored like an idiot, with no understanding that his life was in danger. But he was a simple man, and that was why she'd fallen for him, and then it was why she despised him, and now it was why she liked him again. She hugged the mound of his back and prayed for her own salvation, for her and Mack, for every small thing in life she had not known to appreciate.

J.D. Joss and Bo Crawford separated. J.D. broke into an abandoned house, ate spoiled food, drank spoiled water, soiled his pants, and left clues. He was caught almost immediately, drunk, covered with insect bites, with a backpack that held a half-eaten package of Oreo cookies and a hammer.

Bo eluded capture for ten days. He created a legend in the small factory towns around San Pablo Bay, like the one where Gordon Hauser grew up. Authorities later closed the jail in downtown Martinez. Built a new one. Modern, state-of-the-art. There would be no more escapes.

During the tense ten-day stakeout, a woman called a local radio station. She lived on the outskirts of Crockett and had seen Bo Crawford emerge from the trees, down near the railroad bed. She faced him unafraid, she said, tried to catch his eye, to *let him know.* Gordon remembered that so well. Her voice over the radio.

I wanted to *let him know.*

What did the woman want him to know? Gordon wondered, when he thought about this many years later, after hearing the news about Stanville, about Romy Hall.

What did she let him know, down by that railroad track? And what did *she* know?

That Bo Crawford existed. That he was a man on the run. She saw him, and she wanted him to see her. She was willing to take the risk. He was dangerous and possibly armed and she stood unhidden and adamant. She looked right at him. If he looked back at her, he would know that she knew that he had no right on this earth to freedom.

They will get you.

That was what she wanted to tell him with her look.

28

Part of the intimacy with nature that you acquire is the sharpening of the senses. Not that your hearing and eyesight become more acute, but you notice things more. In city life you tend to be turned inward. Your environment is crowded with irrelevant sights and sounds, and you get conditioned to block most of them out of your conscious mind. In the woods you get so that your awareness is turned outward, toward your environment. You are much more conscious of what goes on around you. You know what the sounds are, that come to your ears: this is a birdcall, that is the buzzing of a horse fly, this is a startled deer running off, this is the thump of a pine cone that has been cut down by a squirrel. If you hear a sound that you can't identify, it immediately catches your attention, even if it is so faint as to be barely audible. You notice inconspicuous things on the ground, such as edible plants or animal tracks. If a human being has passed through and has left even just a small part of a footprint, you'll probably notice it.

IV

VI

29

Kurt Kennedy woke up with two empty rosé bottles and a headache. The stewardess, he gets that you don't call them that anymore, but the other term has never taken up residence in his mind, anyway the bitch took his drink away while he slept. Not the rosé, which had been in the knapsack between his knees, but his rum and Coke, which he'd ordered, and wasn't finished drinking when she removed it from his tray, and that was the thing about an international flight. The booze was free and you drank it and no one bothered you about how much. They weren't supposed to cut you off. He put on the help light over his seat. He was going to insist on another drink because he wasn't done with the one she took away. The stewardess arrived and told him she took his drink because he was sleeping. He said that it exactly helped him sleep and was why he needed it back.

She bent down close.

"You and I know it's a silly rule, but you can't bring your own wine bottles on the plane."

Trying to butter him up with her "you and I." I've got plans when I step off this bird and you aren't coming with me, old lady.

She was probably forty. Actually, she was a good-looking broad and he'd take a forty-year-old. Kurt himself was fifty-four. A woman his own age, the thought of it made him want to puke. But a lot of things were suddenly making him want to puke. He might puke for no reason. He didn't feel very good. He'd been out all night in Cancún and had about ten nightclub stamps inked over the back of his hand. The last half of the night he could not remember. He had an image of getting into someone's jeep, a man older and even drunker than he was, and the guy could not get out of his parking spot, just kept ramming the car in front, and then the car behind, then repeating, until Kennedy yelled at him to stop and got out of the guy's jeep, but what happened then? He doesn't know. He woke up at his Novotel and had pissed himself in his clothes.

At least he would not miss his flight. And he had time to shower, because, as every man knows, that's supposed to wash off the misery and get him shipshape for traveling. He retched into the methane-fuming drain. People don't know how to make anything. Can't even vent a sewer pipe.

He got the wine at duty-free because he could, and because he wanted something of his own to drink on the plane. Made him claustrophobic to have to sit and wait for them to bring you something. Just watching the cart not come down the aisle made his mouth drier than Death Valley, and his medication already made his mouth dry. He wasn't going to wait, he was going to bring his own beverages on the airplane for the long flight from Cancún to San Francisco. Got the two bottles and a coffee cup. Opened one of the bottles at the gate and starting pouring, tipping the knapsack like it was a drink, a T-shirt wedged between the two bottles to keep them from clinking.

He would not call it loaded, how he felt when he got on the plane. He was only starting to relax. He'd been on edge the whole time in Cancún. It was supposed to be a vacation but minute by minute he kept checking in with himself to find out if he was having fun, and he didn't know and this made him anxious, so he took another Klonopin and lay down or got up or went to the bar or walked around on the sand, but it burned his feet and he had to face down the fact that he was not a beachy-type person and just wanted to get home and go to the Mars Room and see Vanessa, put her body on his lap. It was the only way in the world he knew to get peace. Every person deserves peace. He meant, whether anyone deserves anything is beside the point. He needed certain things to feel okay. Vanessa was among those things. He needed dark and heavy curtains, because he had a sleeping problem. He needed Klonopin, because he had a nerve problem. He needed Oxycontin because he had a pain problem. He needed liquor because he had a drinking problem. Money because he had a living problem, and show him someone who doesn't need money. He needed this girl because he had a girl problem. Problem was maybe the wrong word. He had a focus. Her name was Vanessa; that was her stage name but for him it was her name–name because it was the one he got to know her by. Vanessa filled in around all the hazier thoughts in his mind with something that was specific, and real. When he was near her, he felt good. Every person deserves to feel good. Especially him, since he was himself.

"Sure you can bring wine on the plane," he told the old stewardess, crease lines forming around her mouth as she took in his reply. He gestured to the overhead bins, full of other passengers' bottles of duty-free wine.

"Unfortunately you can't drink it while you're on the plane."

Too late, he thought at her. He had drained both bottles, one at the gate, and the other just after takeoff.

He pressured her to bring him another drink. Pointed out that there was another hour to go and he had a dry thing with his mouth.

She was suddenly conciliatory, too much so. She's scamming me, he knew, and indeed, she brought him a straight Coke, with no airplane bottle, claiming the drink had rum in it.

There was a couple next to him turned inward to each other like they didn't really want to talk but he tried anyway. Sometimes shooting the breeze with people kills time. He told them about his boat and he didn't actually have a boat but he'd been talking for so long like he did have a boat that he basically, at this point, owned a boat. But they weren't interested. So he turned to the kid across the aisle, started telling him about his boat. Sometimes he thought of people as kid, called grown men kid, but this kid was a kid-kid, Kurt realized.

How old are you? he asked.

"Thirteen."

"*Nice.*" Kurt said it with a way-to-go, all right, kind of tone. Kids liked to be encouraged. He was rewarding this kid for being thirteen. Thirteen was puberty, old enough to get off. He'd like to show the kid a picture of Vanessa. Let him in on the marvel of women who know how to act like women. Not like this stewardess and probably most of the women on this airplane, women everywhere these days, who hardly acted like women at all. If he had a picture of her he would show the kid. There was a porn actress who looked a bit like her, but he didn't have a photo of the actress, either.

A woman came up the aisle and leaned over the kid. Kid got up from his seat. A man came up the aisle and sat where the kid had been. They were a family and they were switching. Nice knowing you, Kurt said, and the kid said, You too.

No one would talk to him, or rather, listen, so he got his book out, *Chickenhawk*, a Vietnam thing he'd been trying to read for three years. It interested him because he had begun long ago telling people he was in combat, but he never was. He was stationed in Germany. The book was about a helicopter pilot and Kurt wasn't even halfway through. Because it was taking him so long to read, and was a secondhand copy with cheap paper, he kept it in a Ziploc bag. He read a few pages on the airplane as he sipped his rum and Coke with no rum thanks to the cunt stewardess, but reading was difficult for him. The problem with reading was how relentless it was. You managed to concentrate long enough to read a whole paragraph and then there was another one, and they just kept coming. He did it mainly as an act, for the other people on the plane, except no one was watching him or noticing. He put *Chickenhawk* back in the Ziploc. He could not get his screen to work so he closed his eyes and planned for when he'd be home and could go see Vanessa.

Fog was barreling down the street as he got out of his cab that night in front of his apartment. Sometimes the city was cold like no place on earth. He was wearing shorts like the tourists who lined up for the cable car on Powell. Morons never got the news about the weather in San Francisco. He knew it was cold. He'd had to wear shorts on the plane because his only pair of long pants smelled of piss.

Next day he got up and went to the Mars Room. It was a Saturday and Vanessa always worked Saturdays.

She wasn't there.

He had been gone one week in Cancún and while he was away, she apparently quit the Mars Room, according to the cashier in the lobby. Kurt didn't know the cashier and figured the guy didn't understand who he was, a regular who spent a lot of money in the club. He looked up—the cashier's booth was on a platform like a chip dispensary at a casino—and told the cashier to get the manager. The platform dwarfed all who approached, and yet the cashier could have himself been a dwarf, the platform was that high, although it was unlikely. The manager came out and shook Kurt's hand. Kurt was a regular and the manager wasn't going to blow him off completely. But he said what the cashier said: we don't have a Vanessa on the schedule. *A* Vanessa. As if there might be various Vanessas and none were working Saturdays, or even at all.

He went to Clown Alley for a burger, because he had nothing else to do. Clown Alley was in North Beach, around the corner from a place Kennedy used to frequent, when he didn't know better. Didn't know about the Mars Room, and about Vanessa.

The place near Clown Alley was a stage with private booths. The women pranced around and play-touched themselves, while the men, in private booths along the edges of the stage, watched the women play-touch while they touch-touched themselves in their private booths. You could pick if you wanted two-way glass or one-way glass, so that the women who play-touched could see you, or not see you, touch-touch. If you wanted eye contact or were some kind of Henry the Flasher you could get what you needed but it cost, like everything in life does. He liked that place okay because he didn't know better. After he started going to the Mars Room, on Market Street, he never went back to the place with the booths, but he still ate at Clown Alley because they cooked a good burger and he could park his motorcycle, a BMW K100, in front of the glass windows and be on watch in case some shit-for-brains knocked it over, one of those people, and there were a lot of them, who careened around the sidewalk like a zombie.

He returned to the Mars Room that Saturday night, hoping she was working, but Vanessa was not on the schedule.

Could she have changed her stage name? Some girls changed frequently. One week they were Cherry, or Secret, and the next week they were Danger, or Versace or Lexus or something stupid like that. Vanessa was a traditional and believable woman's name and it suited her and she had not changed it, he didn't think, because he paid the entrance fee and went in, spent an hour scanning the room, and didn't find her, not that night or the next day or night, or on any of the ones following those.

The first time Kurt ever saw her, he had been keeping company with a hothead named Angelique. He and Angelique were dancing in the tunnel-thing at the back of the Mars Room. They called it dancing but the whole time you're just trying to rub up on them. There was another couple in the tunnel thing, a businessman and Vanessa. Her body was pressed against the businessman. She danced with the guy like she really meant it. She was glued to this man in a suit, in her bra and underwear. Angelique said loudly that Vanessa was breaking a rule and was she high, what drug was she on, because you can't fuck in the tunnel. It was fine to massage men's laps with your buttocks but if you did that frontally, other girls would get on your case.

"Yeah, I'm high," Vanessa said, swaying into the businessman. "It's a drug called happiness. You should try it sometime." She continued to grind against the businessman, the man himself taking no notice of the argument between the two women and instead moving against pretty Vanessa like a man might dance with his wife on their golden anniversary, or in a TV commercial spotlighting an occasion like that, to sell Viagra.

Kurt thought it was funny. Later Vanessa passed him on the aisle and he told her so. She said I don't like to talk but if you want a lap dance I'm twenty a song. So he gave her an Andrew Jackson, as the girls called them, and that's how it started. The usual way it started with any girl at the Mars Room, except this chick was not just using him for the money. Something was happening between them.

They all did a stage show or were supposed to and when it was Vanessa's turn, he sat closer to the stage than usual. When Angelique saw him alone and tried to offer company he told her to get lost.

Vanessa had a song that was clearly hers to perform to. She moved inside the song like it was about her. The singer had a weird voice. Kurt didn't know if it was a man or a woman and that seemed pretty odd but it fit with this chick even if she herself was one hundred percent girl. "Come on down to my place, baby, we'll talk about love." Vanessa wore mirrored sunglasses that gave a comic edge to her performance. She put her legs up and they were the most gorgeous legs he'd ever seen. Some of the girls there had pale and flabby legs, shapeless tubes that reminded him of glass syringes. Vanessa's legs were leg-legs, long and tapered. It was a joke—comedy—that this world-class chick was onstage at the Mars Room. He was in on it, you better believe it. She was high on life the way everyone ought to try sometime but hadn't or couldn't because they were not free the way she was, this sexy chick with her amazing legs. Cute ass. Her tits were cute, too. Grab-able. Handful-sized. And then she showed the whole thing, bending upside down from behind. That was his favorite, the way it all looked suspended from behind, when they bend over. She was doing it just for him. She knew. This chick really knew. That was the thing about Vanessa. She wasn't an idiot barking up the wrong tree. It was all the right tree. She understood how to turn him on and she was doing it.

She sat with him when her stage show was over.

"Know what I like about you?" It was a setup, for him to answer his own question. "Everything."

He liked to be the one to do the talking. He felt good with her. He felt comfortable. He loved to touch her. His hands were everywhere.

He gave her twenty after twenty, went out and got more money, and gave her that, got more, and gave her that, too, because he really, really, really liked this girl.

He started going more frequently to the Mars Room. He was on workman's comp and had a lot of free time. And he was under a spell. He spent everything on this girl. All she had to do was turn and look at him, seated in his lap, and he'd hand over the bills.

Before he'd gotten his job as a process server, which paid well but almost killed him, he had worked security for the Warfield Theatre, which was a block down Market from the Mars Room. Boy, did he have stories. Eight nights of the Jerry Garcia band. Ten nights of Jerry Garcia. Pathetic hippies would camp out on the broad sidewalk, make their own disgusting street village, with drumming and people freaking out on drugs, and security had to keep clearing out their encampment and maintain order. He was still friendly enough with some of the security guys at the Warfield, and when he started going to the Mars Room, he parked in front of the theater and asked them to watch his bike.

There were women in San Francisco who rode motorcycles. This bothered him. Because women, how did they understand the physics of it. If you don't get physics you can't be in control of speed. Wouldn't catch Vanessa riding any motorcycle. She wore little high-heeled shoes and short dresses when she was leaving the Mars Room. He could put her on the back, though. Teach her how to hold on tight, lean with him as he leaned. So many broads didn't even know how to be a passenger, leaned the wrong way when he cornered. Hold on like you're part of this, he tried to explain, but they didn't get it.

He was supposed to be at home recovering from his accident, but he got bored at home. He'd crashed outside the projects on Potrero Hill and mangled his leg, slid all the way across the intersection with his knee trapped underneath the very large and heavy gas tank of his K100. Had four operations and walked now with a limp. They called it an accident but to Kurt it was attempted murder. Kids in the projects had dumped motor oil in the middle of the street so he would wipe out. He had tried to serve legal documents, simply doing his job, to an address in the projects repeatedly without luck. On his sixth visit, he knew, as soon as he hit the intersection and went into a slide, what they'd done to him. But there was no way to find the actual kids and prove it.

He was stuck at home, waiting for his knee to heal. He was told it might not. His apartment on Woodside became a waiting room with no end to the waiting. He would shuffle around, sit on his couch, flip through a magazine, change the TV channel, stare into the fridge, watch cars move down the street, do his ten exercises, watch cars try to parallel park, hardly anyone knew how to properly parallel park, he'd sit on the bed, read the same sentence over and over in his book, *Chickenhawk*, realize he was doing that, put the book in its Ziploc, change TV channels, and finally, get up, ride over to the Mars Room, and limp in to see if Vanessa was working.

He knew a lot of girls there now but the only one he liked was Vanessa. He told her he was a homicide investigator. It wasn't a total lie. He wanted to investigate the kids who tried to kill him by putting a lake of motor oil in the intersection near the projects. He had learned not to tell people he was a process server because when he explained how you serve papers, the tactics you are forced to use, it didn't sound noble. People treated him like he was some kind of scumbag repo man.

He talked to Vanessa about all the tensions in his life without giving details. He talked and talked.

He touched her bare skin with his hands and said things, expressed feelings, and got attached. He got attached to her.

30

I ran a row of almond trees. I went two over, and a row down, and two more over, and again down, down, down. My only option was to run. Run, and find a place to hide until night.

Because of the mountains, I knew east. The lines in the orchard are straight, and when I got to the edge of one and met a road, I saw that the roads were also straight, which was how I remembered them from the bus into prison. I crossed and kept running, crossed and kept running. If they were already after me, they might have trouble locating me exactly, on account of my zigzagging. I zagged but kept eastward, toward the big mountains.

I came upon a drainage ditch. It had an open pipe that I could fit into, where I could hide until it got dark.

In the ditch I saw that I was bleeding. I hadn't felt it, not even the wetness on my pants. The cold water seemed to stop the bleeding. There was a long gash in my thigh, from the razor wire.

After listening for some time to the sound of the water, I was able to hear through it. To distinguish other sounds: Insects. A crow. The drafty whoosh of a car passing on the nearest road. I drank with my hands, from the water in the irrigation ditch.

At nightfall, I got out of the pipe. I walked quickly in my wet and tattered prison clothes. I could not see the mountains, but I knew which direction they were. Everything was straight here. I was inside a giant grid; empty of people, but made by people. The whole world, at least this one, the Central Valley, from the mountains to the western horizon, was a gigantic prison. Orchards and power lines instead of razor wire and gun towers. Unmanned, and man-made.

The grid helped me know where I was going. I could avoid getting lost, while staying off the roads, and instead travel the lanes of the orchards.

I walked all night, slower and faster.

Before dawn I came upon a house with old junked cars parked around it. The kitchen leaked a cold mercury light. A smell of guavas wafted from the yard. There was a laundry line with clothes on it. Clothes, I should take those clothes, but with that light in the kitchen it was dangerous. I heard a sound from inside and took off walking. I passed several more run-down shacks on that road, all dark, no clothes advertising themselves to be taken. After a long stretch of no houses, there was another, and it had clothes drying on plastic chairs next to the porch. I risked it, sneaked to the chairs and took pants and a shirt.

At daybreak, I was on the edge of a small town. It had a park with a trash can where I stashed my state clothes. I had on the others, a man's stiff, rough jeans and T-shirt. I practiced walking, not running, acting legal, not illegal, like a person who had a right to walk along a road.

There were no more orchards here, no more gridded roads. The road curved past trees and outcroppings of rocks and open grassland. I found a secluded clump of bushes and slept under them. I slept on and off, until it was dusk. I was weak but forced myself to walk as night fell. I'd had no water since the drainage ditch, and no food.

I heard an animal cry out. My heart had been pounding since I left the prison yard, pounding out my alertness to fear, to cops, to any sign they were gaining on me. Now, I was afraid of the dark, too. Of this animal, which shrieked again. Its cry was almost human, but in the almost human manner of an animal in the wild.

I had walked for a long time when I saw lights. It was a crossroads with a gas station, and a road that wound upward toward the mountains. It was the middle of the night. The gas station was open.

A pickup truck pulled in. The driver got out to pump. A man alone. I sensed this was right. That he was the person to ask. I walked over.

"What's up," he said. Chubby guy in an acid–wash Marlboro jacket.

"I need a ride."

"A ride. Maybe. Maybe. You married?"

"I'm not married."

"You got a dude hiding around here, you guys gonna jump me or what?"

I said I was alone.

"Where you headed?"

"Up." I nodded toward the mountains.

"How far?"

"To the top."

"Sugar Pine Lodge, you work up there or something?"

"Yeah."

"All right. Let me just refill this. *You can have a ride.*" He said it in a singsong voice, as if random women at remote gas stations were always begging favors, and he was once again consenting.

He grabbed a soda container from the seat of his truck. It was gallon-sized and said Thirst Destroyer.

He turned the heat up to eighty-eight degrees and sipped from his huge stupid drink and chattered about how he was going to get into vending machines. The gash had opened back up and I was bleeding on the seat of his truck. I was dizzy with thirst. But if I made that clear to him, how badly I needed him to share his drink, he might know.

I watched him drink from the straw, thick as a gas can nozzle, and tried not to faint.

"All you got to do is make the investment and restock them, collect the money." From there he would take his profits and buy a franchise. "Takes forty-five K to buy a Dunkin' Donuts. A Taco Bell is more. What you do is start with the vending machines, then you get a Dunkin' Donuts, pull the equity from that, and *then* you buy a Taco Bell."

We swooped left and right up and around hairpin turns. He drank from his soda. Belched.

"I got a lot of plans. I want to get into real estate. You know what they say?"

He was waiting for me to answer.

"No."

"If you can flip an ounce, you can flip a house. That's pretty cool, right? Just 'cause no one's hiring, doesn't mean you can't find a hustle. You got to know what opportunity looks like. Have you seen those posters, We Buy Ugly Houses Dot Com? Those guys are raking in bank, turning a bad situation to their advantage, right? Here's another one: a man who thinks outside the box, *stays* outside the box. That's deep.

"And: tell me who your friends are, and I'll tell you who you are. I don't fraternize with losers. I'm on the program. Hey, I got to take a leak."

He slowed to a stop on the shoulder, put the car in park. He did not step out. The motor was running. He stared at me.

"You like to party?"

"No."

"You might party with me, though."

"I don't think so."

"You asked me for a ride and all."

"Because I needed one."

"Well then, we can make it win-win."

"You take me up to the mountains, and we'll see what happens."

"All right then. That's cool. Okay." He got out, walked to the road's edge, and unzipped his fly. He had finished about half his gallon-sized Thirst Destroyer.

I slid into the driver's seat while he pissed into the underbrush. I put his truck in gear and drove.

31

One night Kurt Kennedy followed Vanessa as she left the Mars Room. He wasn't any kind of creep. He was just so attached to this girl that he needed to be sure she was getting home safe. He watched as she got in a Luxor cab, and he followed that Luxor cab, on his motorcycle, to a residential hotel on Taylor Street. It was on the upper edge of the Tenderloin, at Nob Hill, the Tenderknob, a skeezier building than he would have pictured but it was where she lived. He watched her go in that night. And some other nights. A lot of other nights.

There were times she went to some scumbag's house, an apartment in North Beach, instead of her own. Guy seemed a likely homosexual from Kurt's point of view, and she didn't go over there often enough for things to be serious.

He felt it was his job to watch out for her. It was a responsibility. He parked near her building some mornings, around the corner, on O'Farrell, with a good view of the entrance. Sometimes all day Sundays, since the Mars Room was closed. If she came out, he put his face shield down, circled on his bike, and was able to follow if she got on the Geary Street bus. Or if she got in a Luxor cab. Why did she only ride in Luxor cabs? He was worried the driver was another boyfriend or some guy trying to get in her pants, but he confirmed, through this work he was doing, that they were random, different drivers.

If she walked someplace instead of taking a cab, he circled, and kept up by going slow. Sometimes she emerged from the building with a little boy. Holding his hand. Isn't that sweet. Like a mom, except he was sure she wasn't the boy's mother. It didn't fit. Maybe the kid lived in the building. Once, she was with the kid and another woman and two other kids; Kurt thought it was a good bet all three kids were the other woman's, it explained things. It bothered him that aspects of Vanessa's life were walled off from him, even as he trailed her and knew exactly what she did, where she went, on a given day. As long as he could watch her leave the building, see where she was going, and know when she returned, he had not entirely lost the thread.

Keeping the line there, keeping track, staying focused on her, that was what he did, and wanted.

At first she had no idea. It was cleaner then. Those were the early days. But he encountered a period of time where she didn't show up to the Mars Room, so he naturally wanted to talk to her. Was that so bad? It seemed like a small thing to him. He just wanted to say hello. He could not see her at the Mars Room, so he orbited closer to her home. Found her nearby. She acted like he was doing something illegal by shopping in her shitty little corner market. A store is public. Anyone can go to a store.

After she saw him in the store and got huffy and left, when she was finally back at work and he did his whistle thing in the Mars Room, his pssst, to get her to come sit, she ignored him, went down the aisle of the theater and sat with some other guy. Every day, same thing. No company. His money was suddenly not good enough. He kept showing up, kept trying. Waiting by the stage for her to dance.

Boy did he miss her. He really missed her. He tried to tell her. All he could do was keep trying. He sat with Angelique, gave her sweaty dollar bills, not even fives.

The way he got Vanessa's number was by going through her trash, which was in an open dumpster next to the building. It was on the sidewalk, basically public. He'd seen her put a sack in that dumpster. He took the whole sack home, bungeed it to the bike. Sorted, and felt purposeful and happy. Her discarded utility bills were in there. He knew her name now, too, but he didn't think of her by it. He felt it was a commitment she'd made, to him, or to somebody, a bigger thing, that she'd said, "I'm Vanessa." He was sticking with it. It was an agreement and he wasn't going to let her just back out of it like it was nothing.

The phone number was printed on the top of the telephone bill. He called it. She answered. He hung up. What choice did he have? If he said, "It's Kurt," she'd hang up on him. He knew this because when she saw him outside the Mars Room, or outside her building, or near her building, in her store, anywhere that he found a way to stage a manner of running into her, she ignored him. So when he called, he had only a moment to hear her voice, and then he hung up before she did, or would. He called, she answered, he hung up. He called, she answered, he hung up.

Sometimes, on a tough day, a day of boredom and excruciating knee pain and a feeling like the world he knew, lived in, was scratch paper some god had crumpled and tossed toward a wastebasket, crumpled, tossed, and missed, he was helpless not to call. He called twenty, thirty times, before she disconnected the phone, he guessed, pulled the little plastic thing from the box on the baseboard, and it rang and rang but was not ringing any longer inside her apartment. At which point, he had no choice but to go over there and park and wait for her to come out. He knew from process serving that it took vigilance to track someone down. He had done it plenty of times. People could not fool Kurt. He was a professional, even if he could no longer work.

He was more or less on twenty-four-hour surveillance when this trip he'd planned to Cancún came up. Cheap package thing he'd booked months earlier, before he met Vanessa. He used to like to travel, and it was sad how reluctant he was to go. But he figured it would be good to get a break from thinking about her. He would not get the money back if he postponed his trip. He'd prepaid so he had to go. He didn't really get a break. He thought about her every moment he was in Cancún, trying not to think about her.

Since she wasn't at the Mars Room after his return, he had to go to her building.

At first, he waited out front. But then he went in. There was a booth at the entrance, an old man in it with greasy gray hair that looked yellowish.

"Five dollars," the man said.

What?

"Five bucks to go up," the old man shouted at Kurt, as if that clarified. It was a racket. A building where drug dealers lived, and management wanted a cut. The old man snatched Kurt's five. His hands had long fingernails that looked burnt at the tips, like melted plastic.

People were on the second-floor landing and there was no other word for it: they were milling. Acting shifty, talking in low voices, doors opening and closing. Kurt tried to be casual. Said he was looking for a friend of his.

White girl, huh? You looking for her? Door eight, my man. Door eight.

Two guys on the landing started arguing. A woman emerged

from another room and yelled at one of the men. Kurt knocked on number eight while these people shouted. There was no answer.

Three days, he staked out her building. She did not come or go so far as he knew.

He went to all the usual places. The deli where he'd seen her get sandwiches on break from the Mars Room. The corner market near her flophouse building.

One day he recognized one of the guys from the landing outside, on Taylor, leaning between two cars, selling or buying drugs or whatever he was doing, and the guy said to Kurt, "Your girl moved out."

He went into the building to speak to the greasy old doorman. Explained he was looking for someone, a tenant.

"Tenants move in and out all the time. Practically every day."

This girl lived here for a while, Kurt explained. Brown hair. Pretty girl. Nice legs. Nice everything. Know what I mean?

The old guy shook his head. Just no. No to every question you are planning to ask.

"I'm an investigator," Kurt said obliquely, thinking he'd pretend he was a cop. He'd done it plenty of times, in order to serve papers. It didn't work.

"Get a warrant, asshole, then you can look at the rent roll."

His knee operation had failed and he was going to have to get another. He was in pain all the time and had settled into a new routine of breakfast beer and six-hour naps. When he could, he went over to the Mars Room and hobbled in with the cane he was now forced to use, but she was not there. Angelique told him she had definitely stopped working there, but he suspected Angelique pretended to have information so she could bilk money from Kurt.

And then it was suddenly Easter, for no reason. He went to the Mars Room and won the Easter egg hunt.

The doorman, big bearded guy, said, "You're looking for Vanessa, right? She left a message for you, said to give you her address."

She had moved to Los Angeles. Why did the guy give him her address? He did and didn't believe that Vanessa wanted him to have it. The doorman had a shit-eating grin. Kurt didn't see what was funny. He didn't know if the guy was bullshitting him, or if this was for real, but he had to investigate. He went home, packed a couple things, got on his bike and rode all the way to Los Angeles, stopping only for gas, power bars, and Red Bull to wash down his medication.

By the time he arrived at the address, his cycle fairing was green with insect guts. The knuckles of his gloves, too. He was in terrific pain. His knee felt like a thing made of brittle plaster that someone had been repeatedly bashing with a ball-peen hammer. It made a crunching noise when he walked. He'd had to use that leg to shift gears all the way down the 5. He wasn't supposed to be riding at all. He was not supposed to be up and around, not even walking. When he did walk, he had to use two canes, one in each hand.

He found her house and parked. Made it up the three stairs with a lot of effort, and knocked. No one answered. He could have guessed that no one was home. It was a duplex with a glass door and he could see into the place. It had an unoccupied look. It was late afternoon, and hot. There was a porch. It was in the shade, and it had a chair. He sat down in the chair, took two more pain pills. He would rest, and wait for her. He had time. He was not in a hurry.

He woke to voices. It was dark, he'd slept right into night, and he was confused for a minute, forgot where he was.

There were footsteps on the stairs.

After all this time, here she was. With that kid, who he had decided long ago was not hers, but someone else's.

"Vanessa," he said.

His knee was so swollen that if he tried to stand on it he'd fall over. He needed his canes. They had both slipped to the ground, out of reaching distance.

It was dark on the porch. He could not see her well, but from her voice she sounded mad. She said he had to leave.

"Vanessa, sweetheart. Vanessa, I just want to talk to you." He reached out. He missed her so much. He needed so badly to touch her. To feel the heat of her skin. She reared back, hastily unlocked the door. She put the kid inside and came back out.

All he wanted was to talk to her. He just needed to talk to her. He said that, again.

"Get out," she said. "Get the fuck out of here."

He could not stand up. He had a hammer-bashed sack of dust where there was supposed to be a knee and he was unable to put weight on it.

He reached for his cane, the closer one. She went toward it, like she was going to hand him the cane. She picked up something else, looked like a crowbar. It made a heavy clink on the concrete as she lifted the thing, whatever it was. It was too dark for him to see much.

"I told you to go. To leave me alone."

"Hey!"

She had whacked him with it. She did it again.

Checkers, he saw. A black and white pattern. Patterns. He heard a loud buzzing in his ears. Pain flooded over his head. The concrete floor of the porch slammed up at him. Blows came again from this heavy iron bar.

Stop! He screamed. Stop!

V

32

There were no towns, just dense woods I carved into with the truck's headlights. I was in the high mountains when I reached a crossroads. Locked metal gates blocked both directions. Closed for the winter, the signs said. If I turned around and went back down toward the valley, cops might have the road blocked by now.

I took the lid off his drink and finished it. The ice cubes hurt my throat as I drank them. I left his truck on the road and walked into the woods.

The air was colder up here. Cold and dry, thin in my lungs. The moon was out. A half moon and it shed light enough to see the path I was on. I was surrounded by trees. I heard only the soft crumble of pine needles and branches popping underfoot as I walked.

By dawn, fog had settled in. It clung low, a vapor lurking among tree limbs. I had veered off the path. I stepped over logs, edged sideways along a ridge, dipped down and across a hillside, where I came upon a tree whose trunk was the width of about ten trees. Or twelve. Or twenty. It was the size of a small house, with huge gnarled roots, like lions' paws, that spread out at its base. Thick vertical lines of red bark wrapped up its trunk like strips of velvet. Mist was caught in its branches, which started high above me, halfway up the tree. Most of the tree was limbless bark, and way up there, in what could have been sky, a city of branches. I made my way around the base. On the other side was an opening. This giant tree was hollow inside. There was another giant-sized tree across from it. They had grown here, together.

I could see other huge trees as the fog lifted and thinned, and a brightness showed through, the forest revealing itself in day. Now that I knew the scale, that such a tree was possible, I spotted other giant trees on this hillside. I had walked right past them, and not known. They had been camouflaging themselves by their hugeness. So many times wider than any other tree. Secrets in plain sight.

I stepped into the tree's cavern. It was tall inside, with a roof where the tree closed itself, up above me, out of reach. The inside walls had dripping washes of black sap running downward, shiny and thick. I touched the sap, expecting it to be sticky. It was smooth and cool as glass. There was red sap, too, also glasslike. And yellow sap. Sometimes a redhead is considered a blond. They called him Güero and told me it meant blondie but Jackson's hair is light brown.

The floor inside the cave was covered with tiny pinecones. This huge tree made baby cones. I needed water and food. My leg hurt. Maybe I had a fever. I didn't feel right. They were surely after me. I had left the truck at the split. Walked all night. I lay down and slept.

I woke to a humming. Not far, but close.

I got up and stepped out of the tree. The humming was louder, but near the trunk, like the tree itself was making this noise. The sun was up, its beams painting the upper part of the tree gold-yellow. The sound was bees. I saw them, like dust

332

motes, floating in and out of the sun's rays, which flooded the high branches. They lived up there. Their sound was traveling down the trunk, making everything hum, even the ground.

From inside the trunk, the bee's hum was the tree's hum.

The tree's sound was silent, so the bees spoke for it. Their sound was its sound, the one it had me hear.

I heard another sound, a clip-clip. A family of birds scuttled past on the ground. The little ones poured over a steep embankment like Ping-Pong balls, following the large ones. They ran under a bush and stayed there.

Both trees had charred areas around their trunks, inside and out, wood burned black and dry, fractured into a geometry of crackles. Probably the trees had been hit by lightning. Whole forest burning up around them, and they had lived on because they lived on. Because they could. Maybe they were a thousand years old. Two thousand years old.

To the tree, that might not be so long. Just life. Like life to a human is life-length. There were other scales of life. The tree was so tall I could not see up it, only to the baby arms, the small branches that began high, sky-height, tall enough that this tree stretched to another world, or to the end of this one.

The future lasts forever. Who said that and what did it mean. The tree arrowed upward, to the time when Jackson would be a man, and beyond that, well beyond it. Would have his own child. Die.

I heard a new noise. A drilling sound, quick, short. Are they here? What are they doing? Then again that sound, a drill. It was a woodpecker doing its lonely work. They were not here yet.

You run until you find a safe place and that tree was mine.

The forest at night is true dark. I had to feel my way out of the tree. Outside, I was under a glitter of stars. I heard a rustle, from wind. I heard those little birds settling down under the bush, or doing whatever they do.

I saw the thick path of the Milky Way or what I guessed was it above me. I'd never seen it. Or had I? I knew what it was. There were bright stars among the scatter of dimmer ones. The sky is junked with stars and if you live in a city, you don't know. If you live in a prison you do not see a single star, on account of the lights. Here, I was halfway into the sky. Where people are gone, the world opens. Where people are gone, the night falls upward, black and unmanned.

Light beams crisscrossed the forest.

They were here.

I heard a helicopter overhead. Jerky searchlights swept the ground.

Grandma's closet, the kids used to say. That was what they called a wind shelter where you retreated to light a joint. Under the stadium stairs or in a bus shelter. The piss-stink shelter at Forest Hill. Grandma's closet. Any place could work.

All the talk of regret. They make you form your life around one thing, the thing you did, and you have to grow yourself from what cannot be undone: they want you to make something from nothing. They make you hate them and yourself. They make it seem that they are the world, and you've betrayed it, them, but the world is so much bigger.

The lie of regret and of life gone off the rails. What rails. The life is the rails. It is its own rails and it goes where it goes. It cuts its own path. My path took me here.

I wish Jackson could see these trees. I never took him here. I didn't know this place. That it was. Is. He saw redwoods at

Point Reyes. These are the other kind, bigger, stranger. Do people know these trees are here? He might see trees like this or something else—like this—in being not known, and not expected, either.

There are some good people out there. Some really good people.

The helicopter came low. A voice echoed, like from the PA on main yard.

Hall. You're out of bounds, Hall.

The life is the rails and I was in the mountains I dreamed of from the yard. I was in them, but nothing stays what you see from far away when you get up close.

Yes I think I'm special. That's on account of me being myself. I have no one else to regard except Jackson, who I regard. Believe me. They called him Güero but he wasn't a blond. They called him Güero because they loved him. They didn't love me and they didn't have to. There was no need for it. They loved him, and I loved him.

The damp from fog, like now, it's inside me. I'm safe from it. Doesn't even make me shiver. That kind of cold forms the deepest layer of my memories, from growing up there, treeless streets built on sand and the bad ocean, the broken bottle ocean with its big curve of concrete wall. Fatal Drownings Occur Here, the signs said on each stairwell down. Stairway to bonfire, to spray paint, to fistfight. Grandma's closet at the beach was any car. Or behind a car. Or depending on the wind, in those stairwells. Fatal drownings occur here.

We swam in our clothes. We never once worried about drowning. Death was not in our future. No person lives in the future. The present, the present, the present. Life keeps on being that.

Hall, we have you surrounded.

They were talking to me. Sounded like yard orders.

Telling me to rejoice that Jackson was not here. That life does not go off the rails because it is the rails, goes where it goes.

Barking of dogs. Closer now.

Lights bathed the forest, everything bright as day.

Hands up, they said. Step out slowly with your hands where we can see them.

If Jackson were here, I could not protect him. He is safe from this.

I emerged from the tree and turned into the light, not slow. I ran toward them, toward the light.

He is on his path as I am on mine. The world has gone on for a long, long time.

I gave him life. It is quite a lot to give. It is the opposite of nothing. And the opposite of nothing is not *something*. It is everything.

ACKNOWLEDGMENTS

For her wisdom and expertise on the visible and invisible net of the penal zone of the world—and for the thousands of other things she miraculously knows—I am grateful to Theresa Booboo Martinez.

I thank Mychal Concepción, Hakim, Tracy Jones, Elizabeth Lozano, Christy Clinton Phillips, and Michele Rene Scott for everything I've learned from them. Thanks also to Ayelet Waldman; Molly Kovel; Joanna Neborsky; Maya Andrea Gonzalez; Amanda Scheper; Justice Now of Oakland, California; and Paul and Lori Sutton.

I thank Susan Golomb for so many kinds of incredible support, and Nan Graham for her belief in me and for her crucial and unerring editorial guidance on this novel.

I thank Michal Shavit and Ana Fletcher for editorial input, as well as Don DeLillo, Joshua Ferris, Ruth Wilson Gilmore, Emily Goldman, Mitch Kamin, Remy Kushner, Knight Landesman, Zachary Lazar, Ben Lerner, James Lickwar, Cynthia Mitchell, Marisa Silver, Dana Spiotta, and most of all, Jason Smith, for what feels like an endless supply of intellectual generosity.

I thank Emily for bearing witness in multiple ways.

Thanks to Susan Moldow, Katie Monaghan, Tamar McCollom, Daniel Loedel, and everyone at Scribner.

James Benning's *Two Cabins* project and his film *Stemple Pass* directly inspired my thinking on Henry David Thoreau and Ted Kaczynski. I thank James for his friendship and his help, his willingness to engage in extensive dialogues over the past several years, and for the use of his Ted diaries.

The Guggenheim Foundation, the American Academy of Arts and Letters, and Civitella Ranieri each provided vital support while I wrote this book.

penguin.co.uk/vintage